BLUE DEATH

John O'Neill

iUniverse, Inc.
Bloomington

Blue Death

iUniverse books may be ordered through booksellers or by contacting:

iUniverse
1663 Liberty Drive
Bloomington, IN 47403
www.iuniverse.com
1-800-Authors (1-800-288-4677)

ISBN: 978-1-4759-2645-3 (sc)
ISBN: 978-1-4759-2646-0 (ebk)

Printed in the United States of America

iUniverse rev. date: 06/13/2012

BOOKS BY JOHN O'NEILL

Baby Girl Lauren
Blue Death
White Death (2012)

ONE

Dr. Ryan Kendall took hold of the patient chart from the exam room door and quickly scanned the fresh pages. He always took these few seconds to familiarize himself with the person waiting for him inside the room. Sometimes the task was perfunctory, for he knew many of his patients by name and remembered much of their history. Just as often, though, it was an integral part of the visit, especially with a new patient, as was the case in this room. Much could be learned from the life bits that a new patient had already committed to paper and electronic memory.

Gender and age were absorbed in a second. Neighborhood, occupation, marital status, spousal occupation—all important, all registered in a few more seconds. Medical history, medications, allergies—all noted, sorted, stored. Certain aspects of a person were generally also readily apparent. Serious type or jokester, well or sickly, all of this was more often than not reflected in the writing, the emphasis, and the parenthetical notes that were often squeezed in between the lines. Though the human condition is infinitely complex, most people were fairly easily categorized for the purpose of a new patient medical examination.

The forty-eight-year-old male waiting inside this exam room was no exception. Downtown corporate attorney, resides in the affluent neighborhood of Chevy Chase just minutes away from the Washington, D.C. line, patient information and medical history forms downloaded and filled out in neat script, almost assuredly by his spouse, which he had then edited. A spouse who would have most likely also made the appointment, put it into his electronic calendar, and called his assistant the day before to remind he or she to remind him. Just so that some important meeting didn't suddenly materialize and give him an excuse to bail, as he was probably prone to do at doctors' offices. Yes, twenty-five years past medical school graduation, twenty of them in the day-to-day practice of medicine, Dr. Ryan Kendall thought he pretty much knew what sat inside this room. For although this man named Drew Garrett was seemingly content having the author with the perfect penmanship complete his forms and label his general health as "Excellent," he had been unable to resist his own personal imprint on the paperwork.

His hand on the exam room door, Dr. Kendall smiled as he envisioned the scene. Most likely it had been while Garrett was in the waiting room signing the personal privacy acknowledgement. It would have been his last chance alone with his forms, and with the "Please no Cell Phones" sign staring him in the face, and the quandary of whether his handheld device qualified as a cell phone or a mini-computer, Drew Garrett had surely become restless. Where the information form asked for his spouse's occupation and she had written "Homemaker," he had inserted a slash and written "Comptroller." Where it asked the reason for his visit and she had written "A complete skin screening examination," he had put in parentheses "By order of the Comptroller." And for the piece de resistance, where it asked for the patient's sex, he had squeezed in "Sometimes" next to the "M." This, Kendall surmised, would have even brought a smile to Garrett's face as he capped his pen.

Dr. Kendall opened the door. Drew Garrett was sitting in a chair, his thumbs racing around on a phone that Kendall recognized as the newest model of handheld digital technology. For several seconds, without looking up, Garrett continued typing. Finally he stopped, put the phone in his blazer pocket, and stood.

"Sorry—had to finish that."

"Right. I'm Dr. Kendall. How do you do?"

"Drew Garrett. I'm well, thank you."

Garrett was smiling slightly, as if he expected to be congratulated, or perhaps chastised, for his waiting room humor. Kendall chose to ignore it, instead taking a few seconds to study the man's face. Garrett was handsome in the striking way that even other men appreciated. He looked younger than his forty-eight years, his face weathered from the sun yet still fairly free of any deep furrows. His hair, surely once almost blond, was now a shade of sun-tinged brown and was just starting to recede from his upper forehead. He looked healthy and jaunty, his angular face daring whomever or whatever to go ahead and try their luck. Whatever his area of expertise at Connors and Murphy, the D.C. law firm that employed him, Kendall was sure he was quite successful.

"Please have a seat," said Kendall. "Let's just go over a few things and then we'll take a look. So you're in good health? No medications?"

"Right."

"And you haven't had any skin problems that you're aware of?"

"Not that I know of."

"Have you ever been to a dermatologist?"

"Maybe as a teenager. I don't remember really."

"Alright. Well, let's take a look around and make sure you're okay. You're pretty fair, so this is a good idea. Did you get much sun growing up?"

Garrett looked at his hands. He apparently had never thought of himself as fair.

"I was a lifeguard."

Kendall nodded. "Is your wife concerned about anything in particular, or did she just want you to get checked?"

"Checked," said Garrett, checking the air in front of him with his hand. "Can't be too careful with the annuity."

"Right. You can leave your underpants on and if you could take everything else off that would be great. You can have a seat up on the table and I'll be back in just a minute."

"Take me two sec's," said Garrett, reaching for his tie.

Kendall went to see another patient while Garrett undressed, knowing the man's phone would be out in about thirty seconds. When he returned several minutes later, Garrett was back in his chair scrolling through his e-mails.

"It's cold in here, Doc'."

Kendall walked to the air vent and adjusted the control. Somewhere around age fifty, guys like Garrett tended to mellow somewhat. By then they generally realized that they were perhaps not going to be a Fortune 500 CEO, or the face of Washington, D.C. corporate law. Around fifty or so they came to some modicum of inner peace that decreed that what they had accomplished was okay. All in all they were still uniformly successful, still able to command their parcels of power, which were often sizable. Until then, however, everything peripheral to themselves was simply atmospheric debris orbiting the center of their universe.

"Sorry. We'll get you out of here as fast as we can."

Garrett put away his phone again and sat back on the table.

"I'd like to look at your back first," said Kendall. "Can you lie down on your stomach, head down that way?"

As Kendall would have expected, Garrett was in excellent physical shape for a man of forty-eight. He was probably within a few pounds of the weight at which he had graduated from college and law school, and he obviously exercised regularly, including some element of weight training. The bodily structure and function that he could control he did, and he did it well.

Kendall took a moment to take in his skin. To take in what Garrett, the product of generations of Garretts and evolutionary rearrangement, could not control. He was not pale in the way of the most fair-skinned Irish and Scottish—the redheads who freckled and burned with just a sniff of the sun. He was still fair, though, perhaps capable of a mild tan with multiple sun exposures, but still far more likely to burn. And burn he had, probably more as a child, when lobster-red backs and faces on the boardwalk were not yet a stigmata of child abuse.

The evidence was abundant. From the middle of his back to the top of his neck his skin was almost covered with freckles. Some were tan, some were a darker brown, and a few smaller ones on his upper back were ink black. Commonly mistaken for moles, and generally harmless in and of themselves, these benign accumulations of pigment were the calling card of ultraviolet radiation. Interspersed among the sun spots were a number of moles. Most were clearly normal, but Garrett also had a few that were visually atypical. Kendall took a seat on his stool, put on his magnifying glasses, and slid closer to the table. The most common victim of serious skin cancer or malignant melanoma was a fair-skinned, blue-eyed adult male, and the most common location was the upper back.

"Do you see something?" said Garrett, somehow sensing that Kendall's radar had kicked in.

Kendall's face was now only inches from Garrett's back. "You have a number of moles on your back. I just want to make sure they're okay."

Connors and Murphy, where Garrett had listed himself as a partner, was one of the most prestigious law firms in the city. Though the firm was large and had several areas of legal expertise, their reputation had been built in the courtroom defending nationally known politicians and corporate executives who for one reason or another had come into the spotlight of the law. The senior partners were often in the news; the junior partners and new associates rarely saw the light of day from anywhere other than their desk. Garrett himself was most likely a trial attorney. This was not the place or the patient in which to make a mistake.

"You keep looking at something," said Garrett, craning his head backwards to try and see exactly what it was.

"You have a few areas that are a little irregular. They've probably been like that for a while. Nothing to be concerned about."

Garrett put his head back down on the pillow.

"My wife's worried about my back. She wanted you to check it carefully."

As if he wouldn't, thought Dr. Kendall. As if a fair-skinned, sun-damaged trial attorney with lots of moles wouldn't get his attention.

"I think she read something in a magazine about skin cancer."

"We look at everything from a cancer point of view," said Kendall and moved along. But Garrett, of course, was right. Kendall had seen something, which for the moment he was trying to avoid. It was in fact the very first thing he had seen when he looked at the man's back. After a hundred thousand screening exams, the normal moles and freckles and blood vessels all became background noise. The abnormalities and unusual normal variations often leapt out at first glance, as had this nickel-sized, pinkish elevation sitting near the top of Garrett's right shoulder.

"Let's look at the front of you and then we'll go over everything," said Kendall.

Garrett turned over and Kendall resumed his inspection. Feet clear, thighs clear, same scattering of moles on his abdomen, same sun damage on his chest, neck, and face. Nothing else that caught his eye.

"Okay," said Kendall, taking off his magnifiers and pushing back on his stool. "Big picture of things you're doing okay. You do have a fair amount of sun damage so we need to be careful and check you regularly. You also have a few moles on your back and stomach that you and your wife need to watch and make sure they're not changing. They're okay right now, but you do need to watch them and I'll look at them once or twice a year."

As expected, Garrett's forehead furrowed with the once or twice a year idea, but Kendall went on before the attorney could respond.

"You do have one spot on your right shoulder that I'm not sure about," said Kendall. "It could just be a normal mole, or even a scar. But if I can't look at it and tell you that it's normal, the bottom line is that we should take it off and make sure. I can do that right now if you want. It only takes a minute."

Garrett, lying on his back naked except for his boxers, said nothing for a moment. Kendall, watching his face, thought he could follow the thought process. Sun damage? Irregular moles? Spot on his shoulder? Garrett sat up, looked at his arms, tried to look at his shoulder.

Kendall slid next to him and put a finger on the spot. "Right there. Do you want to see it in the mirror?"

"Yes, please. I'm not sure what you're talking about." Garrett was quieter now, and frowning again.

Kendall got him a hand mirror and stood him up so he could look over his shoulder into a mirror on the wall. "There," he said, putting his finger on the spot again.

Garrett moved closer to the wall and moved the mirror around. Then reaching over his shoulder and putting his own finger on the spot, he said, "You mean that?"

"Right."

"I think I've had that all my life," he said, shrugging. "You're talking about that little bump, right?"

Kendall put his finger on it again. "Right there."

Garrett looked again, shrugged again. "I've had that for years, I think. Caroline's never said anything about it. What about all these guys?" He pointed at several dark spots on his abdomen. "They're okay?"

"They're okay right now. Like I said, you need to watch them to make sure they don't change, but they're okay now. I'd really like to take that other spot off, though. We need to be careful. Even though you might have had it for a long time, it might be changing."

Garrett scanned his abdomen one more time, then lifted the mirror to look at his back again.

"And all those guys on my back are okay?"

"For now, yes."

He handed Kendall the mirror and shrugged. "Your call, Doc'. I think it's been there a long time, but if you want to get it, go ahead." He looked at his watch. "How long will it take?"

"One minute. Why don't you lie down on your stomach again."

Kendall called for a nurse and bent over the spot one more time. Syringe in hand, for a moment he paused. Garrett, he knew, could certainly be correct. He might have had this lesion since childhood, perhaps have even been born with it. It could also just be a normal scar, or some other benign lesion. In a few days Kendall could easily be calling Drew Garrett and affirming all of this. Nevertheless, there was still something about the lesion that bothered him. The color was just a little different, and he thought there was the slightest trace of pigment in it. Plus, it lived on his back alone. People who grew benign lesions generally tended to grow more than one.

Kendall pulled the skin taught around the lesion and readied to anesthetize the area. Over the years he had learned many things about the practice of medicine. One of them was an absolute—despite Garrett's certainty, it wasn't worth missing the unusual melanoma or other forms of skin cancer.

"Little pinch. You're all numb now. You won't feel anything else." Kendall took hold of a razor blade and ten seconds later the eight by seven millimeter dome-shaped piece of skin was floating in a small bottle of formalin. He quickly stopped the bleeding with an electrosurgical coagulator, then left the room to write while his nurse put a small bandage on the area and went over the wound care. Finished with Garrett's chart, he looked around at the other exam rooms. There were two patients waiting for him.

He walked back into Garrett's room and extended his hand. "It was nice to meet you. I'll give you a call as soon as I get the pathology report back on this. When I call you I'll also go over with you how often you should be checked and anything else like that. Let me know if there are any problems."

Garret was sitting on the table, still reeling from the jabs that had just rocked his morning. "Sorry, Doc', I'm just trying to understand this. I mean, what do you think it is? Is it cancer? Should I be worrying about this? What am I supposed to tell my wife?"

"I'm not sure, Mr. Garrett. That's why I wanted to take it off."

"'You're not sure,'" repeated Garrett, his face firming. "Do you mean to say you have no idea what it is?"

Kendall mulled this statement for a moment. Not so much the statement really, for of course he had an idea of what it was, or wasn't. More the line of questioning, the interrogation. It was one of the occupational hazards of practicing medicine in the suburbs of the nation's capitol. He had spent a number of years in more rural areas where questions such as these might have been entertained, but were rarely asked. Patients there just did as they were told. Partly out of an old school respect, but partly also out of an innate understanding that Kendall in fact did not know, and he would call them when he did. That any further discussion was all speculation and could do more harm than good.

"I'm not trying to worry you," said Kendall, "and I wish I could tell you more, but I just can't right now. My sense is it's probably okay, particularly if you've had it as long as you think you have. But, it caught my eye, and I want to be careful."

Garrett looked at him for a moment before reaching for his clothes. "Okay, Doc'. Give me a call," he said.

But it was not okay, Kendall knew. Not in Garrett's world. He could almost hear the man saying it to himself:

Caught his eye? What the hell does that mean? We can put a man on the moon, and this doctor, who's supposed to be one of the best in town, who's twenty-five years out of medical school and twenty years into practice, can't even look at a little goddamn bump on my shoulder and tell me what it is? Do you mean to tell me he can't tell a mole from a scar?

Kendall shook Garrett's hand again and turned for the door. "I'll call you as soon as I can," he said.

Two

The vision and words of Drew Garrett, Esq. stayed with him all morning. So much so that several times between patients Kendall almost called him to attempt a better explanation of some of the nuances of the skin business. Though he was medically hardened by the years, he did understand that what seemed so simple to him was in fact quite complex and indecipherable to many. And to those with a good grasp of many things cerebral, these helpless medical encounters could be intolerable. Having been on the other end of some, he felt for Garrett. With each move to the phone, though, he had stopped short, suspecting that it would be a circular conversation with Garrett most likely ending up more frustrated. Or worse, perhaps suspicious of what might have really motivated Kendall to make the call. Indecision? Doubt? A mistake, even?

To the contrary, Kendall was quite comfortable knowing what he didn't know. This winnowing of data to its barest elements and choices was in the end what was often thought of as the art of medicine. It was the purest form of this game they played—this game of cheating death, of lasting one more lap than your knees or heart or mind were intended to run. It was the universal truth that all thoughtful and experienced physicians eventually came to. And although it was an oxymoron of the first degree, it was nevertheless true: the longer one practiced medicine, the less one really knew.

That's not to say that there is no intellect involved, no critical mass of information that must be immediately retrievable. Surely there are facts and bodies of knowledge that are completely within one's grasp. In the end, though, that was not what the players and their families wanted to know. The answers to the game's most valid questions were just a guess, just a random shot at the realities of cellular misfirings, of genetic unions gone haywire, of immune systems gone rampant and carnivorous.

The evidence, Kendall knew, was everywhere, everyday. Who was to know why just last year a single cell in his neighbor's forty-year-old healthy ovary suddenly decided to go crazy and multiply? Who was to know why it heeded none of her body's valiant immunologic attempts to contain it, even annihilate it? Why it mutated and multiplied and finally broke free to send its clones careening through her vessels and into her liver, and lungs, and brain? And then left three young children motherless. Who was to know?

Who was to know why eight-year-old Billy Daniels, whose story was in the *Washington Post* just last week, took his last trip to the emergency room for his asthma? Why that particular night his lungs shut down so tightly that the five doctors and three nurses surrounding his bed could not make a single one of their drugs or manipulations free him from his own bronchiolar death grip?

Every day the obituaries were laden with these mysteries. And then there were the tragedies, and the headline deaths. Who had an answer for the parents in the emergency room? For the mother who miscarried at eight months? Who was to know?

No, at its heart, the practice of medicine was not a game of knowing. It was a game of exclusion, of knowing what things weren't, of cheating death by closing the door before it got its foot in. It was a matter of sensing danger, no matter its source or name, and cutting off its legs. What Kendall would have tried to explain to Drew Garrett was that for the moment, the exact nature of the bump on his shoulder was irrelevant. Until a competent pathologist analyzed it and put a name to it, all that mattered was that it was off of his body and floating in formalin. All that mattered was that it was now dead and incapable of bodily harm. The rest could be dealt with later.

"That was the last patient, Dr. Kendall," said Sammie, Kendall's head nurse. "Can you go over these biopsies with me so we can go to lunch?"

Sammie was sitting behind a counter with eight small bottles of formalin in front of her. Rachel and Devon were behind her working at the sink and autoclave. At the end of every working morning and afternoon, the tools of the trade had to be scrubbed and sterilized. Then there was the flesh to deal with. Each piece of tissue that had been removed had been placed in a bottle of formaldehyde that was labeled with the patient's name and the site of the biopsy. Each bottle then had to be packaged with a pathology form and sent off to any number of laboratories and pathologists.

"McKenna," said Sammie. "Mid forehead and right arm."

Kendall sifted through the stack of charts in front of him, pulled out Joseph McKenna's, and checked his notes. "Basal cell carcinoma on the forehead, and squamous cell carcinoma on the arm." Then looking at the man's insurance card, he said, "American Labs."

Sammie pulled out an American Laboratories pathology form from a rack in front of her, jotted down the diagnoses and sites, and pushed the form and McKenna's two bottles to the side. "Chu," she said, picking up the next bottle. "Left anterior calf."

"Wart, questionable keratosis. American."

This daily exercise of modern medicine elicited the same rise in Kendall's blood pressure with every go around. Most of the major insurance carriers had volume contracts with laboratories and other diagnostic facilities. With many patients then, he had no choice of laboratories or pathologists. The tissue specimen had to be sent to the contract lab or the patient was responsible for the bill, which otherwise would be covered under their health insurance. Undoubtedly this business model was beneficial to the insurance carriers and their contracted laboratories, but it was anything but that to Kendall and his patients. The volume labs were generally staffed by pathologists who were underpaid, overworked, and often of questionable training and competence. It was truly a maddening dilemma, for the biopsy itself was often the simplest part of the whole process. It was the actual interpretation of the tissue under a microscope that could change a life forever.

Fortunately, a few of the major insurers still provided Kendall with a choice of laboratories. When he could then, he utilized a smaller specialty lab with known and trusted pathologists. The Washington D.C. area also had no shortage of wealth, and some patients would simply pay the extra money for the pathologist of Kendall's choice.

"Garrett," said Sammie. "Right upper back."

Kendall opened the lawyer's chart and deliberated about the diagnosis for a moment. The piece of flesh from Garrett's shoulder, grayish now as it turned lazily in the bottle of formaldehyde, still left him uneasy. If he had to bet he thought it was benign, but the slightly different hue of red and the trace of pigment had stayed with him all morning, as had the man himself. Kendall did not want some unknown pathologist making this diagnosis.

"Let me do that one," he said. "Do you have a Chevy form?"

She looked at the chart from across the counter. "He's got Oxford Life. It has to go to American."

Kendall had already pondered that question: Should he call the man? Explain the lab dilemma? Offer him the choice? Confident that Garrett would be willing to pay for a respectable lab and pathologist, he had already decided that the call was unnecessary.

"It's okay. He won't mind," said Kendall.

Sammie passed him a Chevy Chase Pathology Associates specimen form and he wrote: ? mole, ? scar, r/o atypical lesion. Passing it back to Sammie, he said, "Let's make sure that one goes out today."

"I'll call them for a pickup," she said, reaching for the next specimen bottle. "Bernstein. Right dorsal hand."

"Squamous cell. Metropolitan Diagnostics."

They finished the last specimens and Sammie started entering the insurance information on the forms. Kendall gathered up his stack of charts from the morning and headed to his desk. He checked his e-mail, returned a few, and took off his phone messages. For a moment then he sat still, staring at the computer monitor. He had led a relatively quiet professional life. He gave some lectures here and there, belonged to all the right medical societies, went above and beyond in his continuing medical education. His opinion in town was respected and, not infrequently, attorneys on both sides of the aisle paid for it. He himself had never been sued, nor had he ever had any terrible untoward events in his office. Much of this was diligence, he knew, but some of it was simply luck. One never knew what package of psychopathology could walk through the office door and begin a chain of events that could spiral out of one's control. And though he was quite confident in his abilities, there was always the possibility of an error. Not of commission, but rather unintentional omission. The melanoma hiding in a crease of skin, or beneath a head of hair, that he simply did not see. It was the ultimate nightmare of any practicing dermatologist.

He sat for a few more seconds, as if he were about to enter an important game, as if somehow he knew that his equilibrium was about to be rearranged. Then, almost against his will, and certainly against his better judgment, he moved to his keyboard, scrolled into a search engine, and slowly began to type: Drew Garrett, Attorney, Connors and Murphy, Washington, D.C.

*   *   *

The afternoon held much of the same: cancer screenings, rashes, acne, warts. He had performed five more biopsies of suspicious lesions and was going over the specimens and charts with Sammie when Laurel, his receptionist, buzzed him on the intercom and said that Dr. Williams was on line two and wanted to speak with him. Dr. Chad Williams was the skin pathologist at Chevy Chase Pathology Associates, the local pathology lab that that had been started almost fifty years ago by Chad's father Bob Williams. Bob's eldest son Sam had joined him in practice thirty years later, and Chad had followed a few years after Sam. The eldest Williams ran a good lab, and Kendall used them almost exclusively whenever he had a choice of laboratories for his biopsy specimens. Generally a personal call from Chad was not good news, and Kendall thought back over the prior week's biopsies. He didn't remember anything that was obvious telephone-call material, but he had done a lot of surgery and biopsies and occasionally there were surprises.

A moment later Laurel slid a chart in front of him. He glanced at the name and frowned. "Shit," he said aloud. Not only was Lindsey Browning a neighbor, but she was only twelve and the lesion he had so carefully removed was from the tip of her nose.

Kendall picked up the phone and said, "Don't tell me that's a problem, Chad. Jesus, it's the tip of her nose. It looked like a little normal mole."

"Hard to say," said Dr. Williams. "I think it's just a Spitz Nevus, but you know how it is. It's a little atypical in a few spots. Best send it out for a second opinion, I think."

"Jesus."

"Sorry, Ryan. I think it's benign, but . . ."

"I understand, Chad. I'm just whining. She's a neighbor, her parents are friends, it's her nose. Shit."

"Well, hopefully they'll just call it a Spitz. If they do, it doesn't look like there's much left. It might even be clear. I'd probably want to stain it up before I said so, but she could probably get away with a very conservative excision. Maybe even just watching it."

Kendall sighed. "Okay, I'll let them know what's going on. Let me know as soon as you can, will you?"

"Sure. I'll fax you the consult as soon as I get it. I'll overnight the slides up there, too. The deeper cuts stained up great. I'll send them a bunch. I was going to send it to Will Ammerman. Is that okay?"

"Sure. Thanks, Chad."

Kendall hung up, shook his head, and returned once more to his stack of charts.

"Didn't look like much to me," said Sammie. "That was that real cute girl in room four the other day?"

"Yeah. They don't sometimes. Shit. Her mother's going to freak out."

A Spitz Nevus was a type of mole most commonly found in children. It was often banal appearing on the skin, and its biologic behavior was thought to be benign, but it also often appeared very atypical when looked at under a microscope. So much so that sometimes it was difficult for a pathologist to distinguish a Spitz Nevus from an actual melanoma. It was not unusual then for local pathologists to get another opinion from a pathologist who specialized in melanomas and other so-called pigmented lesions. Will Ammerman, Chief of Dermatology at the New York Hospital for Special Diseases, was just such an expert on Spitz Nevi and melanoma.

Kendall closed the last chart in his stack, slid the pile across the counter to Sammie, and started to go through his phone messages. Some were simple requests for prescription refills that the nurses could handle; others were patients asking for their pathology results, or with questions about their medications or problems. He took the messages that he had to answer himself and headed for his office. The first message was from Donna Browning wondering if Lindsey's pathology report was ready yet. She had left three phone numbers where she could be reached.

Kendall sighed and dialed her cell phone. "Hey, Donna."

"Oh, I'm so glad you called. I was getting worried."

"Well, I actually don't have a report yet. The pathologist did just call me, though." He paused to let that fact sink in.

Silence for a few more seconds, then Donna said, "Ryan, you're scaring me. There's nothing wrong, is there?"

19

"I don't think so, Donna, but unfortunately it's going to be a few more days before I have a definite report. As it turns out, it's a type of mole that most of the time is normal, but it can look a little peculiar under the microscope. The pathologist wants to be extra careful, so he's sending it up to a specialist in New York for another opinion."

"Oh, my God, I knew it. How did I know it? Oh, my God. Is she going to be okay? You don't have to do anything else to her nose, do you?"

"I don't think so, but I won't know until we get this second opinion. I'm very hopeful that we won't."

"Damn. Damn, damn, damn. I don't want to say anything to her. Should I? What should I do, Ryan? It's not cancer, is it? Tell me it's not cancer."

"I don't think you should say anything to her right now, Donna. Try to sit tight for a few days. We're overnighting it up there so we'll have an answer pretty quickly. I think it's going to be okay. Try to relax."

"'*Relax*!'" Donna paused, and Kendall wasn't sure if she was catching her breath or if she'd started to cry. "God, I don't even want to tell Bernie," she went on. "He won't know what to do. What did you say it was? A type of mole?"

Kendall didn't answer right away. This was not an entity that Donna Browning wanted to be reading about on the Internet. The term juvenile melanoma was still often attached to the modern nomenclature, and between the old name and the actual few reported cases of childhood melanoma, she'd be hysterical in minutes.

"Why don't you wait until we see exactly what it is."

"I won't be able to sleep, Ryan. Oh, God. I just knew there was something wrong since you hadn't called."

He had done the biopsy only two days before and had told her it would take at least several days to get a report.

"Can you call up there and see if they can do it faster? We'll pay for it. We'll do whatever it takes."

"I'll call them tomorrow, Donna. They won't have the slides until then."

"Thanks, Ryan. I really appreciate it. Oh, God, I'm going to start crying when I see her. She's going to know something's wrong."

"Hang in there, Donna. I really do think it will be fine."

Twenty minutes later he'd finished his calls and dictated his referral letters for the day. It was 6:00 PM. He had a county medical society meeting in an hour and needed to leave the office about twenty minutes before then.

He'd managed to put Garrett's Internet search out of his mind for most of the afternoon, but now, with a few free minutes, it was almost a palpable presence in the room. With a few quick taps on the keyboard it was before him again. There'd been over fifty results from the search, a number of them duplicates from the same newspaper articles or alumni magazines. What was there was more than enough, though. Drew Garrett, as suspected, was a rather successful trial attorney. He had received his undergraduate degree from Washington and Lee University, and his law degree from the College of William and Mary. He'd then clerked for one year for a Federal Circuit Court Judge named Tim Mahoney, which meant nothing to Kendall, but the way it was presented in both the Washington and Lee and William and Mary alumni magazines, it was a prized clerkship. He must have also grown up in the D.C. area since one of the articles referencing the clerkship billed his return to the Federal Court as a hometown boy makes good. From the clerkship he'd gone onto Connors and Murphy where as a young associate he had cut his teeth as the junior attorney on several prominent cases with Brendan O'Donoghue, the most known and respected litigator in the firm.

Until Kendall clicked on the last two entries, none of what he read about Drew Garrett surprised him. In fact, he admired the man's achievements and style. In all of the third party reporting there hadn't been one negative observation about the man or his work, which was an achievement in and of itself for most attorneys who made it into the press. It was the last two search results that he had feared, though. Kendall read the *Washington Post* every morning before he exercised and he had a pretty good memory, particularly for anything to do with physicians or the practice of medicine. All morning long he'd been uneasy, sensing this fragment of memory trying to break through. Now it was there in front of him, ready to ruin his evening.

Two years before, in the Prince George's County Circuit Court, Drew Garrett, representing Oscar Sanchez and his family, had successfully litigated a six million dollar settlement against two local hospitals and Dr. Luis Benitez, one of the finest obstetricians that Kendall knew. The case had made headlines for a number of reasons, one simply being that the firm of Connor and Murphy rarely took on medical malpractice cases. There were a number of specialty law firms in the D.C. area that fed like sea birds on any possible bit of medical wrongdoing, but Connor and Murphy had remained above that fray. This particular case was about more than malpractice, though. Or at least that was the publicity spin, which ultimately turned out to be quite successful. The case in the long run was more about race, socioeconomics, and the disparity in health care between rich Montgomery County and the poorer adjacent Prince George's County. Dr. Benitez had in fact gone out of his way to try and facilitate the normal delivery of Oscar

Sanchez, but after two suspect hospital transfers, Oscar's oxygen-deprived brain was useless by the time Benitez finally did bring it into the world. Benitez, by association, was slammed about in the papers for weeks; Garrett, the high-powered white-collar protector of the innocent and the discriminated, earned invaluable press for himself and his firm.

Kendall closed the search and leaned back in his chair. Once more in his mind he went over every inch of the man's skin. He inspected the slightly irregular moles, the lesion on his shoulder. He had performed thousands of skin examinations, thousands of biopsies. He had done nothing different with Drew Garrett. The man had received the same careful attention that everyone received—the same careful attention that had thus far left Kendall with an unblemished history in the national medical data banks.

Still, in this town of overachievers, where reality could be turned and molded by those with the know-how and power, this Drew Garrett put him on edge. He was a man who most likely got nothing but his way and who most likely rarely lost, whether in a court of law or on the golf course. Life had been good to Garrett, as had his health.

Kendall took out a pen and made a note for tomorrow: call Chad Williams re Garrett.

THREE

Tuesday, June 5

Judge Paul Mancini was the youngest judge in anyone's memory to be appointed Maryland's Chief Judge of the Court of Special Appeals. He had been on that track most of his life: valedictorian at St. Francis Preparatory School, Phi Beta Kappa from Holy Cross, Law Review at Georgetown's School of Law. He had the strongest intellect that Kendall knew, and he was also one of the most firmly grounded men that Kendall knew. There was nothing pretentious or ostentatious about him; he had nothing to prove to anyone except his inner self, with which Kendall believed he toiled more frequently than he let on. Particularly as he had advanced up the judicial ladder. The farther he had progressed, the more intellectual and complex were the questions of the law and the people. And unlike the safe and orderly havens of St. Francis and Holy Cross, the answers were rarely written in black or white. They were almost always gray, wrestled from legal opinions of the past and merged with the ones of the future that he himself was helping to create. For a perfectionist, though, with one brother a priest and another a missionary, it was often a maddening, tortuous process. The more cerebral the question or the case, the easier it was for the skilled attorneys, or in the higher courts the judges themselves, to create opposing valid arguments from identical sets of facts. The simple rights and wrongs of grade school were now refuted, sometimes even reversed in the cases that were decided on technicalities. God did not reign here, as he had before. Though the Ten Commandments might still rule the Catholic universe, they were twisted and warped in the courts of law and within the reality of big-time judicial and legal politics.

"Catholic guilt," Mancini would utter from time to time. It was both his suffering and his solace. Unlike some other life afflictions, though, this particular one did not abate with the years. Like a broth simmering on the back burner, it was both out of the way and omnipresent, biding its time, its presence wafting over his space, waiting patiently for its owner.

Mancini, indeed, was as good as they came. He was perhaps Kendall's best friend, or as close to that hallowed relationship as two men raised to keep an emotional arm's distance from the same gender could come. They played tennis twice a week for an hour at seven o'clock in the morning. Mancini had played on the Holy Cross tennis team and at the end of each session Kendall often counted himself fortunate to still be standing.

This morning they were playing at The River Club, Kendall at the net and Mancini banging balls at him as hard as he could. When Kendall netted his third volley in a row, Mancini stopped and asked him if he'd had enough.

"Yeah, I think so. I'll be better on Thursday."

They moved to the bench beside the court and sat with towels over their necks, both of them looking as if they had jumped into a pool in their tennis clothes. Though it wasn't quite eight o'clock yet, the temperature was already pushing eighty and the humidity added another five degrees.

"What's up?" said Mancini. "You stay out too late last night?"

"I wish. I had a county medical meeting. Pretty boring, actually. I can't get too excited over insurance reform any more. I don't thinks it's happening in my time."

Mancini was quiet for a moment. "Probably not. It's a lot like the tax code—too many hands in the cookie jar." The judge drained a water bottle and pitched it in the trashcan. "Work getting to you?"

Kendall shrugged. "Hasn't been the best week, and it's only Tuesday." He was quiet for a moment, then said: "You know a guy named Garrett? Works for Connor and Murphy."

"Drew? Sure. He's a good guy. Tough guy, but a good guy."

Kendall nodded, but didn't respond.

Mancini cocked his head to look at Kendall. "He's not bothering you, is he? Except for that one big case, he's a white-collar guy. You don't have a tax problem do you?"

"No, nothing like that. Just wondering."

Mancini knew that meant that Kendall had seen Garrett as a patient in his office, but patient confidentiality prevented him from saying so.

"He's a fair guy. Don't worry about him. What else is up? Garrett didn't make you net three straight volleys."

Oh, yes he did, he wanted to say. But, after hearing Mancini's assessment of the man, maybe he was just being paranoid. Kendall glanced at the clock on the fence at the end of the court. "Shit, I gotta get to the office," he said, standing up. "One of the girls who lives behind me has a weirdioma on her nose that I have to call New York about. Her mother's going batshit."

Mancini slung his tennis bag over his shoulder and they headed for the locker room. Walking side by side, they looked as if they had been cut from the same mold with the same knife, but from different matter. Both were tall, an inch or so over six feet, and athletically lean. But where Kendall's hair was a graying auburn brown, Mancini's was as black as the olives his grandfather used to grow. Where Kendall's face was freckled from childhood sun, Mancini's was spotless, his Mediterranean skin having thus far performed its evolutionary job just as it was designed. Kendall's eyes were grayish, bordering on blue; Mancini's were a rich dark brown, a color many in the courtroom would never forget.

"New York?" said Mancini. "What's that about?"

"Second opinion. Who wants to be responsible for carving up a twelve-year-old girl's nose?"

Mancini smiled sadly and shook his head. "Got it. Makes sense." Then, after a moment, he said: "Wow, that is pressure. That's her face for the rest of her life."

"No shit. And that's what's so crazy with all this insurance bullshit. I've got to send cases like this all the time to pathologists I don't even know. And half of them trained in Guadalajara. It's nuts."

Mancini nodded, digesting in seconds the conundrum that he had never before considered. "Got it," he said again. "So what do you do, send everything to New York?"

"No, there are some good labs in town. We use Chevy Chase Pathology most of the time. Sometimes DermPath. They're both good."

Mancini's brow furrowed. "Chevy Chase Pathology is Bob Williams' practice, isn't it?"

"Bob's the old man. There are three of them. Chad does the skin stuff. You know them?"

"Bob, mainly. They all belong to Hidden Glen. The family's been there a long time. Bob's father was one of the founding members."

They walked the rest of the way to the locker room in silence. "Bob's a good guy," said Mancini as they stopped at the door to wash the clay off their shoes. "Salt of the earth."

*   *   *

Lindsey Browning and her mother were only part of what preoccupied Kendall as he showered, dressed, and left The River Club for his office. Equally disturbing were the sharp twinges of pain in his left knee that had returned halfway through the tennis hour. They had abated for several weeks and he'd been hoping that the presumed small tear in his medial meniscus had healed itself. Even Peter Kane, his orthopedic surgeon and friend, had advocated watchful waiting for a while. Watchful waiting, however, had not included biweekly manic tennis sessions.

Now, feeling it with every step into his office, Kendall chastised himself for being a bad patient. For between the demands of his office, and the intolerable thought of any prolonged period of physical inactivity, the last thing he wanted was the arthroscopic examination that Kane had proposed as the next step.

The Brownings quickly freed his mind from his knee.

"Mrs. Browning just called," said Laurel as he walked through the door. "She wants to know if you talked to whoever in New York."

Kendall nodded and kept walking. "I'll call her. I've got the chart."

"You got the message from Mrs. Browning?" called out Sammie from the nursing area as he walked by.

"Yes, thanks." At his door, he stopped and turned around. "I forgot to ask you yesterday, Sammie. When you get a chance, will you call over to Chevy Chase and ask them for a slide on Lindsey Browning. I want to see this thing, too."

"Sure," she said, making a note on a prescription pad. "They don't open until nine, though."

Kendall sat at his desk and went right to the American Academy of Dermatology's directory of dermatologists. Dr. Will Ammerman was both a dermatologist and a dermatopathologist—a specialist in the microscopic examination of skin and its related structures. He was also one of the world's experts in evaluating unusual moles, variants of moles, and malignant melanoma. They had met at a dermatopathology teaching seminar when Kendall was only a resident. Both had attended undergraduate school at Vanderbilt and thus had an immediate bond.

Kendall reached Ammerman's secretary who put him through to his office with the caveat that she thought he was giving a lecture at grand rounds. Ammerman was a gentle man with a soft and unhurried voice, even on his voice-mail.

"Hey, Will, this is Ryan Kendall in Bethesda. How are you? Maybe we can get together this year in New Orleans at the conference and hit some. Hey, I was wondering if you could do me a big favor. Chad Williams overnighted you a specimen yesterday from a neighbor of mine. Her name is Lindsey Browning. Real nice girl with hopefully just a Spitz on her nose. Anyway, the family is understandably freaking out and if there's any way for you to take a look at it today I'd really appreciate it. Even a preliminary verbal report would be great. If you want to call me . . ."

Kendall hung up and did some paperwork until he knew Donna Browning was out of her house driving Lindsey to school. Then he called her at home and left her a message that he had called up to New York and would call her back one way or another later in the day.

"You have a couple of patients ready," said Sammie from the door.

"I'll be right out."

Kendall stood and winced as his left knee involuntarily buckled beneath him. He let the pain subside, regained his balance, and slipped on his white coat. He'd been in great health all of his life and had never really pondered an existence otherwise. The reading glasses and magnifiers were bothersome, but mainly nuisances. The knee and the nagging shoulder discomfort were far more ominous. That his cartilage and tendons were beginning to weaken and splinter was as sobering as any birthday or graduation.

Standing on one leg, he slowly flexed and extended his knee. Give it a few weeks, he said to himself. After all, he did have good genes. His father had died in his garage at the happy age of eighty-four without ever having had any major surgery or illnesses, and Kendall, who looked just like him, had every intention of doing the same.

*   *   *

It wasn't until he was sitting at his desk eating lunch and taking off phone messages that he remembered he hadn't called Chad Williams about Drew Garrett. After the morning's conversation with Mancini, he didn't have quite the same angst about the case that he did the evening before. Kendall had already figured out the "tough" part of Drew Garrett's character, but "fair" was always a commendable trait. Still, he didn't want to find out for himself.

He finished taking off his messages, hoping that one was from Williams and he'd have a good reason to call him other than Drew Garrett. Ammerman, he knew, proper as he was, would most likely not call Kendall directly, even though Kendall had given him his phone numbers and they were friends. If he did, it would only be after he had spoken to Williams, as per proper pathology protocol. Even though Kendall was the physician who had performed the biopsy, it was Williams who had submitted the material and was in fact Ammerman's client.

He had four messages. Colleen, his wife, reminding him to bring home acne creams for Matthew, his sixteen-year-old son. Kelley, his daughter, calling from college to say hello. Mancini, confirming Thursday morning at Hidden Glen Country Club, and that he would follow-up by e-mail. Beth, one of Peter Kane's receptionists, confirming his follow-up appointment on Thursday afternoon. No Williams.

Robyn, the administrator at Chevy Chase Pathology, answered on the second ring. "Just one sec', Dr. Kendall. He starts late a lot in the summer, but I think I saw him come in a little while ago."

Kendall did not remember ever seeing Chad Williams at the Hidden Glen tennis courts. If he started late in the summer he was probably playing golf, Kendall figured while he waited for him to come to the phone.

"Hey, Ryan, what's up?" said Williams. "I haven't heard anything yet from Will. I'll call you as soon as I do. I'm sure he'll look at it today. I called him this morning, too."

"Yeah, the mother's all over me and I didn't want to bother you."

"No problem. I understand."

"Heard you got in a little late this morning," teased Kendall. "What are you doing, sneaking out for nine holes in the morning?"

"Eighteen actually, if I start early enough. I work late then. Drives them nuts, but . . ."

"Right. Sounds great—good for you. Anyway, I was mainly calling about another case that you should get today. Name is Drew Garrett. I think it's okay, but it was a little different and I just wanted to go over it with you. I think it's just . . ."

"Got it," said Williams, after Kendall had voiced his concerns. "I'll get some extra cuts and maybe show it around here if there's any question about it. I'll call you about that, too, if you want."

"Yeah, sure. Thanks."

"Oh, and Ryan, I got the message about the slide on Browning. I sent all the good ones up to Ammerman, so let me get some recuts and I'll get you one in the next few days. Is that alright?"

"Yeah, sure. No rush. Thanks, Chad."

Kendall was hanging up when he heard Williams' voice again. "Sorry, Ryan, but how old did you say this Garrett guy is?"

"I don't have his chart in front of me, but I'm pretty sure he's forty-eight."

"Okay, got it. Thanks. Talk to you soon."

The rest of the afternoon went quickly, easily, as if some pressure had been lifted from him. After years of similar such moments and days he knew it was perhaps a false sense of ease, but he also understood the nature of the brief respite, of the fragile sense of comfort. Even if it was only for a few hours, some semblance of order had been fashioned out of burgeoning disorder. Though it was true that any minute this truce could be shattered, for the moment the best in the business were doing everything they could for the Brownings, for Drew Garrett, and for himself. For the moment, there was nothing else he could do.

FOUR

Colleen was squatting in a flowerbed pulling weeds when he pulled into their driveway. He watched her straighten, throw a handful of green behind a thick cherry laurel, and brush off her hands. She was in running clothes and he could tell that she had recently run, despite the near ninety-degree heat. Her white sleeveless top was a patchwork of sweat stains, and her shoulders and legs glistened in the late afternoon sun. He slowed as he passed her and shook his head in disgust. Smiling back, she brushed away a few wisps of dark brown hair that were stuck to her forehead. After twenty-five years of marriage, her intentional running during the hottest hour of the afternoon was still an ongoing point of contention.

Colleen taught eighth grade math in the county school system and most of the year didn't get home until the mid or late afternoon. She didn't like running in the gray or dark of the early morning or evening. So, pick your poison, she would say—heat stroke or vehicular or human assault.

Kendall of course understood all of this when school was in session. But school had let out the week before, and every afternoon since then she had persisted in her three mile run at four o'clock with no regard for the temperature or humidity. Even Mandy, their young Labrador, was lying in the shade of a large yellowwood tree. As he drove closer to the garage he could see that Mandy's mouth was open and she was panting, her tongue sideways out of her mouth and flapping like a grounded pink trout.

Jesus, thought Kendall. She's going to kill the dog, too.

Colleen had been waiting for him as it turned out. "I wouldn't go out back if I were you," she said from the driveway as he got out of his car. "Donna's been watching the house for the last hour. You're supposed to call her, I guess." She came close and leaned over to kiss him. "Hi. Don't want to get you sweaty."

"So what's your excuse today? School meeting? Matthew?"

"Oh stop. It's not so simple just to rearrange everything in one week, you know." She paused for a moment. "Plus," she said, looking down at her flat abdomen, "I ate too much yesterday. More bang for the buck."

Kendall snorted and opened the back door of his car. "I'm not even going to call an ambulance."

"You won't have to. You won't be home."

"Funny. And you can explain Mandy to the kids and the Humane Society."

"She's great," said Colleen. "She would have gone another mile. I'd really like to get her into the Hartman's pool, though."

Kendall looked at her and shook his head again.

"So . . . ?" said Colleen.

"'So . . . ?'" said Kendall.

"So, is she going to be okay?"

"It's not Donna. It's Lindsey."

"I know. She told me all about it. Pretty scary."

He didn't answer as he gathered his briefcase and journals. They shared much of their days together, but his day-to-day patient care, except for occasional generalities, stayed in the office. If Donna Browning wanted to make it a public matter, or at least a neighborhood matter, that was her decision.

"I think she'll be okay," he said finally. "Everyone's paranoid these days."

"Well, you best go in the garage door if you don't want to talk to her yet."

Kendall nodded and headed inside. "Is Matthew home?" he said over his shoulder.

"He's at the pool with Trevor. He's staying there for a while. So," she said, smiling again, "why don't you change and come weed with me? We both own this yard, you know."

Kendall went into his study to deposit his briefcase and journals. Out of habit he moved to his desk to check his e-mail. Though he was not as electronically tethered as many of his friends, the habit had insidiously become an unbreakable part of his routine.

There were eight e-mails waiting for him. Jokes and stories passed on by friends, River Club news, tennis spam. He quickly deleted seven and opened the remaining message from Paul Mancini: Thursday may not work, will let you know, pls call when you can, nbd.

That might be good, thought Kendall as he walked up the stairs to their bedroom. Although the pain in his knee had abated during the day, he could tell that he was protecting it. The note to call Mancini was a little unusual, though. Mancini didn't like to talk on the phone. He conversed as much as possible through e-mail unless he had to speak with someone. His time alone in his office or his car was his time to think, reflect, ponder. However, no big deal, he'd said. Meaning it could wait.

Kendall took off his clothes and stood for a moment in his underwear. Normally on days like this he would go for a run after it had cooled somewhat, or head up to the tennis courts to play with Matthew. Bracing himself on the bathroom door, he stood on his right leg and slowly flexed his left knee, which he could see was now swollen. Tight from the excess fluid in the joint, it would only flex halfway. Running was definitely out, as was any thought of hitting with Matthew, even if he were home. He slipped into shorts and a T-shirt and headed downstairs to weed.

In the kitchen, he looked through the window to the Browning's yard and saw Donna puttering around on her deck. His cell phone was still in his car. He retrieved it—no messages. He checked it to make sure the incoming call sound was on and joined Colleen in one of the front planting beds.

"Kelley called me this morning," said Kendall. "Is she okay?"

"What time?"

"I don't know exactly. Before I got to the office, though. Kind of early for her."

"The little sneak. She wants to work at the beach for the rest of the summer. She was probably trying to feel you out. She called me later in the morning."

"I see. I thought it was a little strange. She normally e-mails me."

"She has to know by the end of the week."

"Why can't she just come home?" said Kendall. "What about the summer internship that we talked about at Christmas?"

Colleen pulled a weed, put it in the bag. "Her friends are all going," she finally said. "She doesn't want to work in an office all summer."

"Shit. That's all we need. I won't sleep all summer if she's at the beach. You know what it's like there."

Colleen didn't respond. She straightened with a handful of weeds and waited for him to open the bag.

His phone rang. He looked at the caller ID—Chevy Chase Path . . . He handed Colleen the weed bag and moved away, heading for the shade of the yellowwood.

"Ryan," said Chad Williams. "Did I catch you in the middle of dinner?"

"No, I'm fine. Did Ammerman call you?"

"Just got off the phone with him. Good news. He thinks it's a benign Spitz Nevus. He showed it at their conference today and everyone was pretty comfortable with that."

Kendall could feel himself smile. "Thanks, Chad. That's great. Really great."

"He also thinks it might be clear. My tech' is staining it up right now, so I can't say that for sure yet. But I'll call you as soon as I see those slides tomorrow. You might be okay watching it."

"Are one of you going to put that on the report?"

Williams didn't answer for a moment. "Sure," he finally said. "If the stains are clear and you've got the nuts to watch it, I'll put it on the report."

Kendall smiled. "Fair enough. Thanks a lot, Chad. I really appreciate it."

"No problem. I'll call you about that other case as soon as I can."

Donna Browning was watering plants in her back yard when Kendall walked around the side of his house and into her view. She shut off the stream of water and watched him walk towards her. He could tell she was about to cry and he put out a hand with his thumb up. She dropped the hose, put a hand to her mouth, sat in a chair, and started to cry, her body shaking the chair on the uneven bricks of the patio.

*   *   *

It was almost ten o'clock when Kendall and Colleen finally left the Browning's patio. One by one after dinner, all of the adjacent neighbors had migrated to the Browning's back yard where Donna had mixed Margaritas and told anyone who would listen about the ordeal of the last few days. She had turned Kendall into the neighborhood hero for the night, and he couldn't honestly say that he minded all that much as it seemed he gave out more bad news than good these days. In fact, with the night cooler and clear, and the fireflies lighting up the stately oaks interspersed between the houses, it had been a rather enjoyable evening. So much so that it wasn't until he and Colleen were hand in hand treading carefully through the pine bark bed separating the yards that he remembered Will Ammerman. After the good news from Chad Williams, he had left his cell phone in the kitchen.

Ammerman had called at eight o'clock. He'd left a message saying that he'd be up until eleven or so and had asked for Kendall to call him back.

Kendall went out on his back deck and sat in one of the wrought iron chairs, feet up on a bench. With each hour the air was still cooling, and with a slight breeze through the trees it was quite comfortable. It was one of those June nights that as a boy he would have pitched a tent in the back yard and slept outside.

Dr. Will Ammerman answered on the second ring. "Hey, Ryan, how are you?" he said genuinely. "It was good to hear your voice today."

"Yeah, you too, Will. And thanks a bunch for looking at that case today. Chad called me a little while ago. He said you thought it was okay."

"Yeah, sure. It's just a Spitz Nevus. Nothing to worry about. I think you got under it, too. I'll leave that up to you."

"That's great," said Kendall. He paused for a moment. "So . . . not a big deal, huh? Chad had thought it looked a little atypical. Guess he's just trying to be careful."

"Well, you know how that is," said Ammerman carefully. "There might have been a few spots in his slides. Sometimes it's a cutting artifact. I thought it was a fairly classic Spitz Nevus. Actually, it was a great one for the dermpath' fellows. I took a bunch of photomicrographs, too. I'm putting together a book on pigmented lesions and I might ask you to get the parents' permission for me."

"Sure, no problem," said Kendall. "The mom will do anything for you."

"Listen, good to talk to you, buddy. I'll get you a report this week."

"Sure, Will. Thanks again. I really appreciate it."

Kendall leaned back in his chair and closed his eyes. The crickets were chirping in a loud harmonious thrill that drowned out all of the other neighborhood noises but for the intermittent deep rumblings of a big male bullfrog. The bullfrog and his harem lived in a collecting pond at the bottom of a short waterfall set into the hill in the side of their yard. Most of the year the frogs were quiet, but for six to eight weeks each spring and summer the males bellowed all night long about their conquests and progeny.

Feeling the urge to move, to walk, Kendall opened his eyes and stood. A textbook Spitz Nevus, Ammerman had basically said. A great case for the dermatopathology fellows. Classic.

He moved off the deck, around the house, into the street. Perhaps an unnecessary consult? An unnecessary two-day torture session for Donna Browning? For a moment

Kendall found himself irritated, even angry. Being careful was one thing; being paranoid was another.

By the time he neared the end of the block his anger was gone. Put yourself in his shoes, he told himself. Who wouldn't be careful with a Spitz Nevus on the nose of a twelve-year-old girl? And as Ammerman had said, there were not uncommonly minor differences in the slides that the consultants saw and the ones that Williams had originally examined. And Spitz Nevi were known for focal areas of atypia. They were probably small and limited to one or two of the first cuts.

Probably. But it wasn't the first time that Chad Williams had given him a false alarm. Although it had always turned out to be fine in the long run, and had perhaps even made them all look good for their diligence, in the end all of the worry and angst had been for naught.

Kendall reached the end of his block and turned around. Better than the alternative, he told himself once again. Better than having to call Donna Browning and tell her he was totally surprised, that he'd missed a potentially malignant lesion that now needed to be excised from her daughter's nose. He'd rather Williams give him ten false alarms then go through that, or have Williams miss one subtle melanoma from inattention.

Back on the deck, he turned off the floodlights and sat down. With the yard quiet and dark, the proud bullfrog immediately let out a throaty bellow. Kendall closed his eyes and saw Donna Browning shaking in the chair on her patio. Opening them, through the trees he watched the last light in the Browning's house blink off.

Yes, he was quite sure that Donna Browning, who was probably about to sleep soundly for the first time in days, would say the same thing.

FIVE

Wednesday, June 6

Kendall was running late. On the way out of his house Alicia Han, another of his neighbors, had called in a panic. She'd lacerated her index finger slicing an orange and couldn't get it to stop bleeding. He'd spent fifteen minutes in her kitchen stemming the blood flow, ensuring that her blood supply and tendons were intact, and wrapping it in gauze. It appeared to be a superficial laceration, so to save her a five-hour trip to the emergency room, they'd agreed that he'd suture it that morning in between patients. He glanced at the waiting room on the way into the office and sighed. It was just going to be one of those mornings.

He put down his briefcase, reached for his white coat, and glanced at the chart that one of his staff had put on the middle of his desk. "No way," he said, stopping abruptly. "You have to be fucking kidding me." He put on his coat and picked up Drew Garrett's chart. Paper-clipped to the front was a medical records release letter with the overnight delivery envelope that it had arrived in beneath it as well as instructions on where to fax the record. No note, no explanation, no nothing. Just a one-page release that was notable mainly for its professional appearance. Most of the record requests the office received were either handwritten notes hastily scrawled on a piece of paper from a purse or briefcase, or the standard form that they kept in the office for their patients convenience. This was neither. The letter was neatly printed on Connors and Murphy letterhead, and had been formatted specifically for Drew F. Garrett and his entire medical record in relation to Ryan S. Kendall, M.D.

Kendall dropped the chart on his desk, shook his head in disgust, and headed out to his exam rooms. In and of itself, the records request was not out of the ordinary. With patients moving or changing insurance companies or just wanting a copy of their file, his office handled several requests every week. No, it was not the request that he couldn't believe—it was the timing. As hard as he tried, he could not remember a previous request from any sane patient just two days after their initial visit, and before the most pertinent part of their record—their pathology report—had even been generated. Certainly he had had odd requests before, but they had almost always been from the not infrequent patients who were essentially life-paralyzed with their various paranoias and delusions, particularly of parasites and other bodily infestations. They often wanted their records on the way out the door, sometimes before he had even had a chance to finish writing, just so that they knew nothing had been changed behind their back. Within the framework of their delusions, that he could understand. But why in the hell did Drew Garrett want his record just two days after his initial appointment? What could he already think that Kendall had done wrong?

There were three patients waiting for him. He hated running late in the office, as of course so did the patients. The retirees were generally understanding and patient, but the type A's were almost always stewing, even if these days it was more the principle of the matter than lost revenue. Cell phones and e-mail had indeed changed waiting room and office dynamics, especially for the attorneys and consultants who viewed the world in terms of billable hours and who made up a significant percentage of the D.C. area population and his practice. With the ability to generate billable hours at any time of day from any corner of the planet, what used to be an intolerable wait was now just irritating. Nevertheless, though technology might have saved him many a morning or afternoon confrontation, Kendall was still acutely aware that no one liked waiting, particularly when they were partially or fully undressed. Pausing for a moment outside of his first exam room, he took a deep breath before he went in.

For a little while, with the help of his nurses and the understanding of some of his long-time patients, the morning ran better than expected. He was able to more or less catch up in the first hour and, other than the nagging thought of Drew Garrett's record request, settle into his normal routine. Then Alicia Han arrived and took even the thought of Drew Garrett away. Alicia's finger had started to bleed again, and as it turned out she had one of the worst needle phobias that he had ever encountered in an adult. After two failed attempts to get even a thirty-gauge needle into the base of her finger, he put some topical anesthetic on her skin and let her incubate for an hour. Sometime near noon her skin was numb enough for him to get a needle into her finger and anesthetize it with a digital block.

He was tying the last of the six nylon sutures that the wound had required when Laurel knocked on the door and stuck her head in the room. "Did you get a chance to look at the chart I put on your desk this morning?" she said.

"The record request?"

"Yes. His assistant is on the phone. He was expecting it this morning, I guess."

"We just got it this morning, Laurel."

"I know," she said, making an exasperated face. "What do you want me to tell her? She's holding."

Kendall had wanted to review the chart one more time to make sure it was in perfect order before it was sent out. Though he had spent considerable time writing his note and documenting everything that had been done during the visit, he wanted nothing to be open to question.

"What's the rush?" said Kendall, finishing his knot and holding up the ends of the suture for Sammie to cut.

"He has another appointment at one today and he wants the chart before he goes."

"Another dermatology appointment?"

Laurel nodded.

Kendall made a disgusted noise and looked back to the wound. "Sure, fax it to him. What a turkey," he said under his breath. Then to Alicia, who was now perfectly content and reading *People* while they worked, "Remind me never to go to medical school. Turkey," he said again, shaking his head.

*   *   *

His knee was feeling better, so he opened Judge Paul Mancini's e-mail first, thinking that he still owed the judge a call: Think I'm okay for tomorrow. You on? How's your girl?

Kendall kept the message open and quickly went through the rest of his messages, making a mental note to call Colleen about Kelley. He answered his phone calls, checked his watch, and called home. No answer. He called Colleen's cell phone and got her voice mail. He looked outside—bright and sunny and surely hot as hell. Perfect running weather, she would say, jokingly. Like much humor, though, there was an element of truth in both of their bantering, and he was always a little uneasy until he actually heard her voice again.

One more time he went over Drew Garrett's chart. He had written a good, thorough note. Except for Garrett's own edits, there was nothing unusual, nothing to be defensive about. So why then was he on edge? Why was he letting the man get to him?

The second opinion was an obvious irritant, but the fact that patients often wanted confirmation of their bodily faults, or kept out hopes for solutions or tricks that had somehow evaded their usual physician, he had come to grips with years ago. After all, it was the same hope that fueled every other medical industry driven by a problem with no real answer. The trillion-dollar hair growth and weight loss and anti-aging industries were not only alive, but thriving. This second opinion reaffirmation was simply part of the process, part of the game, and most of the time it had more to do with the patients preconceived notions of their diseases rather than any real medical disagreement. Most of the time—once they had learned on their own that there are no secrets—they ended up back in his office, and happy to be there.

No, assuming it was a thoughtful decision on Garrett's part, it was not the actual questioning of Kendall's judgment that bothered him. It was again the timing, the immediacy. It was the visceral response from a man accustomed to power and control. Unfortunately—and in the end it was this that he feared the most—what Kendall knew from experience was that, as well planned and forward thinking as Garrett thought this decision might be, it could just as easily be his downfall.

For what if Garrett got a second opinion and the opinion was wrong? Even worse, what he if sought in consultation the services of a known malpractitioner, a physician known by his or her peers to be marginally competent, or perhaps unscrupulous. Garrett, Kendall knew, as bright as he was, and as committed as he might be to his health and self-preservation, could very well be about to enter a medical quagmire of doubt and indecision—a patient's worse nightmare.

"Turkey," he said aloud, shaking his head.

Kendall went back to Mancini's e-mail and replied: Are you there? Can you talk?

Five seconds later: 301-456-7543, call now pls

"Hey, Ryan," said Judge Mancini. "So I think I'm okay for tomorrow. See you at seven?"

Kendall flexed his knee beneath his desk. The swelling was down and it hadn't bothered him much that morning, even with all the running around he had done from room to room.

"Sure—looking forward to it."

Mancini had three daughters, the youngest in middle school and the oldest a sophomore at University of Virginia who had graduated from high school with Kendall's daughter. Through their daughters and their own friendship, Colleen had also become friends with Lisa Mancini, the judge's high school girlfriend and wife of twenty-four years. Kendall then, did not know which "girl" Mancini had referred to in his e-mail.

He took a guess. "Kelley's okay," he said. "She called yesterday. She wants to go to the beach for the rest of the summer. I don't know what to say. I'd really rather have her home. It's just trouble waiting to happen."

Mancini hesitated, then said: "I know what you mean, but be careful what you ask for. Francesca's home and it's great, but she still thinks she's at school. Different schedule, you know. She wakes me up every night coming and going."

Mancini had not been asking about Kelley. "I don't remember introducing you to my girlfriend," joked Kendall. "Is that who you were asking about? She's fine. She has a friend, too."

"Yeah, right. No, your patient. The one with the weirdi-whatever you said on her nose."

"Lindsey?" he said, surprised. Mancini was not one to ask about his patients. Something had obviously struck a chord with him, and Kendall went over the other day's conversation in his mind.

"I don't know her name," said Mancini. "You were waiting to hear from New York. You don't have to say—I was just wondering."

"She's fine, actually. The pathologist thought it was benign. I probably don't need to do anything else to it either, so her nose is safe." Kendall paused then, waiting.

"Good for you. And for her. I've been thinking about it a lot. I don't know how Theresa would handle something like that. The way they look is everything at that age."

Yes, Theresa. Mancini's youngest. She was twelve, too.

"At any age," said Kendall. "Believe, me."

Mancini laughed. "Yeah, I guess. See you tomorrow. I have to run. I'm glad that worked out."

*   *   *

Halfway through his afternoon patients, Kendall took a short break to write in some charts. He buzzed Laurel on the intercom from his office.

"Yes, Dr. Kendall?"

"You know that chart you faxed this morning—Drew Garrett?"

"Sure. I faxed it right after we talked."

"That's fine. Did his assistant say who he had the appointment with?"

"No. Just that it was a dermatologist."

"You faxed the record to Garrett's office?"

"Right. Do you want me to call and ask?"

"No, I was just wondering. Thanks anyway."

"Good, 'cause she wasn't very nice. I'll call her though if you want."

"Don't worry about it. Thanks."

Kendall stood and deliberately put all of his weight on his left knee. Not great, but it held. He'd be okay, he told himself. He didn't have to get to every ball.

He drank some water from the cooler in the office, cleaned his magnifiers with a tissue, and headed out.

Sammie stopped him at the door. "Dr. Williams is on the phone," she said, handing him a chart. "I think it's about the same guy you and Laurel were talking about this morning."

Kendall took Drew Garrett's chart and headed back to his desk. He did not know of any other biopsies or excisions that Chad Williams might be calling about, and Williams knew he was still in the middle of seeing patients. This then, was not good. Especially since it sounded like Williams himself was on the phone. Normally Robyn would call ahead and get Kendall to the phone first.

"Hey, Chad, what's up?"

"I'm sorry, Ryan, but this biopsy you called me about does not look good. It's some type of a spindle cell tumor. I think it's a spindle cell melanoma, but I don't have all the stains yet. I know you were a little worried about it, so I just wanted to let you know what I had so far."

For a moment Kendall said nothing. Though he had received many onerous pathology reports in his career, this one hit him hard. He could feel his face warming, his heart picking up its pace. Spindle cell tumors as a group were notoriously difficult for pathologists to diagnose and accurately label. They could arise from several different cell types and often required special stains to differentiate the exact cell origin, which made a difference in the prognosis and how they were treated. All hope was not yet lost, though—not all spindle cell tumors were malignant.

"Okay," Kendall said slowly. "So you say you think it might be a melanoma. Does that mean you think it's malignant, whatever it is?"

"Sorry, I should have said that first. That's why I'm calling before I have the stains. It's definitely malignant—it's full of mitoses and it's pretty poorly differentiated. I'll have the stains tomorrow probably. Obviously I'll call you as soon as I can."

Kendall cradled the phone between his shoulder and his ear, folded his hands on the desk in front of him, and closed his eyes. He could feel and hear the blood shooting through the large vessels in his head. The coming sequence of events—the phone call, the shock, the questions, the surgery—he could see it all, feel it all. His stomach began to burn. He opened his eyes and took hold of the phone.

"How deep is it?"

"It's at least 1.3 millimeters."

"I didn't get under it?"

"I don't think so. Sorry."

Shit! he said to himself. What else could go wrong?

"Do you think we should send it out?" asked Kendall. "He's a pretty tough cookie. No offense, but he's probably going to want someone else to look at it." As did Kendall himself—at this point all he could hope for was that maybe Williams was wrong. That the same man who had trouble putting his name on a classic Spitz Nevus report was now overstating a complicated benign lesion.

Williams was slow to respond. "Let me get the stains first, and then I'll leave that up to you, Ryan. It's pretty obvious, though. It might just confuse things in his mind."

Kendall had worked with Williams for over ten years now, and Williams had never been reluctant to get a second opinion. Jesus, Kendall said to himself. Drew Garrett had a malignant spindle cell tumor that was "pretty obvious" to Chad Williams. Chad Williams, who was the most careful, if not paranoid, pathologist that he knew. Jesus.

"Sorry," said Williams again. "I know it's not what you wanted to hear. I'll call you as soon as I can with the stains. Oh, and Ryan, before I forget. The first cut I got for you on Lindsey Browning was a little tangential and really doesn't show the lesion very well. They're cutting some more right now. I think the slide might have gotten sent over to you by mistake with the courier, though. Have you seen it by chance?"

"Umm, I don't think so," he said, his mind elsewhere. "I'll let you know if it turns up."

"Thanks," said Williams. "I'll get you the recut today or tomorrow."

Great, thought Kendall. Lindsey Browning was fine. Drew Garrett might be dead in a year.

*   *   *

The conversation reverberating in his mind all afternoon, Kendall somehow made it through the rest of his schedule. Like an experienced driver navigating rush hour traffic, yet simultaneously having a detailed internal discussion, he put his best foot forward until his last scheduled appointment had left with their acne prescriptions. Then he pulled his charts together and looked to Sammie.

"Sorry," she said, nodding across the room, "you're not done yet."

Kendall glanced over to the hallway that led in and out of the waiting room and saw Devon, one of his nurses, escorting an attractive, well-dressed thirtyish woman to an exam room.

"She's a referral from Judge Mancini," said Sammie. "Laurel fit her in—she didn't think you'd mind. I think she has a mole she's worried about."

"Sure," said Kendall, turning to look at his phone messages.

Devon shortly came out of the exam room and handed him the chart. "Should be quick," she said. "Sounds like it's just a tag under her arm that's irritated."

Kendall nodded and glanced at Heather Bowie's chart. She was twenty-nine, married, and employed by Hidden Glen Country Club as the Assistant Director of Membership, where she no doubt had frequent contacts with Judge Paul Mancini. Mancini was the Vice President of their governing Board and was in line to become President of the Club. Situated near the Maryland and D.C. line, Hidden Glen Country Club had a hundred year history and a long and prominent waiting list. In a few years, if she weren't already, Heather Bowie would be one of the most patronized women in town.

"Hi, I'm Dr. Kendall," he said. "I understand you know Judge Mancini."

"Oh, sure. I get to work with him a fair amount. He's such a great guy."

"Yes, he is. No doubt about that. Good tennis player, too."

"I've never seen him play, but that's what I hear."

Kendall paused for a moment, welcoming a friendly face and an easy problem for him to solve. A problem he could probably fix in a minute or so, and most likely even be thanked for.

"I just got off the phone with another one of your members, I think," he said. "Dr. Chad Williams, the pathologist."

"Sure. The Williamses have been members going way back. They're all there. In fact, Judge was in just the other day going over Dr. Williams' file. I think he plays a lot of golf. Don't tell him I said so, but I wouldn't be surprised if they want to put him on the Golf Committee."

"Don't worry. It's just business when we talk. So, how can I help you? Devon said you had . . ."

Two minutes later, Heather Bowie's inflamed skin tag was off and floating in a bottle of formalin. She profusely thanked everyone again for working her into the schedule at the end of the day and was soon on her way.

Kendall quickly went over the afternoon's biopsies with Sammie and delegated all of his phone calls to Devon. Then he sat at his desk, his face in his hands. Should he wait until he had a final report from Chad Williams, or should he alert Garrett to the situation? He had been through this before, and knew it depended on the patient. Some would be pissed if you didn't tell them as soon as you had any information; some could not handle waiting while some definitive decision was made. Garrett, he knew, would definitely fall into the "pissed" category.

He took a deep breath and lifted the phone. Garrett's administrative assistant answered and she clearly knew his name.

"Let me see if I can get him off the phone, Dr. Kendall. I think he's on a conference call."

"I'll wait," said Kendall. "No rush. Or he can call me when he's done. I'll be at my desk for a while."

"Let me ask him. I think he'll want to speak with you."

"Hey, Doc'," said Garrett a minute later, his voice cool. "What's up? Do you know what that thing is already?"

"I just got a call from the pathologist," said Kendall. He paused then, as he always did, letting this sink in.

Garrett did not seem to hear this ominous prelude. Retrospectively, Kendall knew he that he'd been too wrapped up in formulating his own delivery, which he could not help but now blurt out.

"Hey, Doc', just so you know, I saw another dermatologist today. No offense, but my wife was still worried about those moles on my back and stomach."

Kendall pretty much knew what was coming. In fact, if he'd been told the name of the dermatologist, he might have even been able to fairly accurately predict how many of the moles had been removed.

"He, uh, he had a little different opinion than you did. Not to say you're wrong, of course. Maybe he's just being a little more careful. Anyway, he was actually worried about a bunch of them. He must have taken off six or seven of them right then and there."

Petersen? Vasquez? Chang? It could be any of them. The first two had been sanctioned by the D.C. Medical

Society for the inappropriate and excessive removal of benign lesions. Chang had actually been removed from the staff of two suburban D.C. hospitals for the same, and with the additional laurel of Medicare fraud.

"I'm not sure "careful" is the right word," said Kendall defensively, even though a loud voice in his brain was screaming at him not to react. And not to ask Garret whom he had seen. "Everyone has their own level of comfort with moles like you have. In fact, if I knew who—"

"It's not a big deal, Doc'," Garrett interrupted. "Just letting you know. My wife made me go," he added, almost sympathetically, as if he were backing off somewhat. "Anyway, what were you going to say? The pathologist called you and what?"

"Well," said Kendall. "I'm afraid I don't have good news in that regard. The pathologist, who's a specialized skin pathologist, believes . . ."

Six

Thursday, June 7

Halfway through their hitting session, Mancini said he wanted to play a set. Kendall's knee had held up pretty well so far, so he thought he'd be fine even with the additional running. Now, though, Mancini was moving him from one side of the court to the other, and he could feel himself involuntarily trying to protect it. Mancini hit a ball out wide that Kendall would have normally reached, but he pulled up a few yards short and let it go.

Mancini put his hands on his hips and looked at him. "Are you okay?"

"Yeah, sure. My knee's just a little sore. I'm alright."

"Are you sure? We only have a few more minutes. We can stop."

"I'm okay. Let's finish. You're on a roll."

Mancini served wide and Kendall managed to get a lunging backhand across the net. It was a short return, though, and as Mancini rushed in to take advantage of it, Kendall planted to reverse direction. The next thing he knew he was down on the clay, holding his knee and grimacing in pain.

Mancini was quickly over to his side of the court and looking around for help.

Kendall sat up and rubbed his knee with both of his palms. "I'm alright, Paul. You don't have to get anyone."

"You don't look alright. You look like someone just shot you. You're a little pale actually."

The sharp, tearing pain that had taken him down had abated and given way to a dull deep throbbing. Kendall moved his knee an inch and it didn't worsen, so he flexed it a little more. Tolerable. He tried straightening it and made it most of the way, but it was swollen even more now and tight.

"I'm okay," he said, reaching out to Mancini for him to help him up. Standing, he flexed it again. Comfortable that he had not completely torn any major ligament, he put a little weight on it, then a little more. Okay there. He took a baby step, then another. There was definitely something wrong, but he could walk. He made his way gingerly to the bench and put his racquet away. "I think I've had enough today," he said. "Maybe next week."

"Maybe not. I think you need to go see Peter Kane."

"I'm going later today actually. Good timing, huh?"

"Can you make it to the locker room?"

"Sure. It's not that bad. Really."

Mancini raised his eyebrows and looked at him. "Let's see what Peter says."

They had been playing on one of the outer courts and made their way slowly toward the locker room, stopping as they passed points in progress on the other courts. Even though it was early, most of the courts were full, mainly with groups of older men and women playing doubles before it got too hot. They came abreast of a group of men, all of whom were sixty-five to seventy or so, Kendall guessed. It was a group he had noticed on several occasions when he played with Mancini at Hidden Glen. Not only for the fact that they were all fit and moving around the court as well as men half their age, but they were always joking and clearly enjoying themselves. When he'd passed them on the way in or out in the past, he'd always felt invigorated.

They had now stopped to watch them play out a point that lasted at least ten shots. It ended when one of the men placed a deft drop shot just inches over the net that neither of his opponents had any chance of reaching.

"Goddamn you, Jack," said one of the men, stopping to catch his breath. "Cut that shit out, will you."

"Hey, Preston, watch your mouth," said Jack's partner. "There's a real live judge over there. He might throw your ass in jail."

They all laughed and looked over to Mancini.

"Hey, Bob. Hey, Jack," said Mancini. "Doesn't bother me, Preston," he added. "My guest's from River Club, though. You know how stuck up they are. He's probably pretty offended."

They all chuckled again and waved as Mancini and Kendall moved off.

"That's Bob Williams," said Mancini. "I want to introduce you to him when they're done. I asked him about you the other day, but he wasn't sure that you two had met before.

"I'm not sure if we've actually met. I talked with him on the phone years ago when I first started out in practice, probably before Chad was even out of residency. He doesn't read any skin stuff anymore. He does mainly general pathology. The skin stuff is getting super-specialized."

They reached the locker room and Mancini took hold of his arm. "Hold on. I want to get you some ice. Even just a few minutes will help."

Mancini directed Kendall to the bench in front of Mancini's locker and went to find Henry, the locker room attendant who had worked at Hidden Glen for over fifty years. When they returned, Henry carried a disposable frozen ice pack and an ace wrap. Henry was a big man, probably six-foot-two and three hundred pounds. An African American with white short-cropped hair, a contagious smile, and a slow drawling voice that could charm anyone, Henry was hands down the most popular and beloved employee at Hidden Glen Country Club.

Henry made Kendall sit still while he wrapped his knee. "Five minutes like this, Doctor Kendall," he said. "Then after you shower I'll wrap it again." Henry moved off slowly, his weight having taken its toll on his hips and knees in recent years.

Mancini, a wet towel draped over his neck, sat next to him on the bench. They talked about Henry for a minute, how he had started working at the Club with his father when he was fifteen, and how he was slowing down. Kendall needed to get to his office and he unwrapped his knee. Undressed, they were headed to the showers when Mancini said: "So getting back to what you were saying before, do you mean that Chad has special training in skin pathology? You said skin was getting super-specialized."

"Yeah, sure. Except for the HMO's, if you're going to do skin pathology in this town you really need a fellowship in dermatopathology. He did a year in Boston, and then another six months at the AFIP."

Mancini looked at him quizzically.

"The Armed Forces Institute of Pathology. Here in town. It's a referral center for cases from all around the world."

Mancini hung his towel outside the shower and stepped in. Then he pulled the curtain aside, cocked his head, and looked wryly at Kendall. "And then you still need second opinions," he said, shaking his head. "Strange."

*   *   *

There were two messages in his office voice mail. The first, of course, was from Drew Garrett who had a number of questions after the news Kendall had delivered to him late the day before. This was expected, for no matter how bright or how consciously or unconsciously prepared a patient might be for the diagnosis of cancer, the actual spoken word was a physical blow that rendered them at least temporarily incapable of digesting any ensuing conversation. Not only were most patients unable to remember much of what had been said after the diagnosis had been delivered, but what they did remember was often tainted with their fears. Garrett would be no exception, as Kendall knew the man hadn't heard much of what he'd said after the word melanoma had sunk in. In addition, Garrett would undoubtedly have his own perspective on the situation. Please call me at my office as soon as you have a chance, he had said in his voice mail. Have my assistant interrupt me—she knows you'll be calling.

The second message was from Chad Williams. He had carefully reviewed all of Garrett's special stains and the S-100, HMB-45, and Melan-A stains were all markedly positive in all of the sections. The cytokeratin stains for epithelium and the desmin stains for muscle were negative. In addition, the special stains clearly showed that the lesion extended to the base of the biopsy and, therefore, he could only give Kendall an approximate depth of the tumor. From the regular slides he didn't think there was much left, but he didn't think that Kendall had gotten under it. He would fax over a report hopefully by the end of the day. If not by then, definitely by tomorrow. Although he didn't have any questions about the diagnosis, because he knew Kendall was concerned, he just wanted to show the slides around the office. Call him if Kendall had any questions. Regarding sending the slides out for consultation, he of course would be happy to do so if Kendall or the patient desired, but he thought it was a pretty clear-cut case. And, he had added . . .

Williams had hesitated at this juncture in his message, no doubt to choose his words carefully. For although Kendall had perhaps saved the man's life by deciding to remove the lesion, it was not a perfect biopsy specimen. When evaluating melanomas microscopically, the pathologists always wanted a full thickness specimen of skin to adequately assess the depth of the tumor.

. . . And since there most likely was residual tumor at the base of the biopsy, and because it was poorly differentiated, perhaps there should be some expediency in having the area definitively excised. That of course was up to Kendall. Let him know, Williams had said. He'd do whatever Kendall wanted.

Kendall hung up, closed his eyes, put his hands to his face. Shit, shit, shit. Though he knew he might have very well saved the man's life by recommending the biopsy, he also knew that this addendum to the report was going to be a problem. Taking a deep breath, he took his hands away and looked at his watch. It was 8:45, and there was at least one patient waiting for him already. Garrett was going to have to wait until he had adequate time to speak with him. Maybe even until he had the actual pathology report in his hands. Still, he'd have to have Laurel at least call the man's office and acknowledge the message.

"You have a couple up, Dr. Kendall," said Sammie from the door.

He nodded, buzzed Laurel on the intercom, and asked her to come to the nurses' station with Drew Garrett's chart.

Turning in his chair, he stood gingerly, buttoned his white coat, cleaned his magnifiers, and sighed.

"Game time," he said to Sammie with a half-hearted smile.

*   *   *

Garrett's assistant had called Laurel back around nine and had asked her to have Dr. Kendall call Mr. Garrett as soon as possible, even if he didn't have the actual report yet. Kendall had had a full morning of patients scheduled and, between the late start and moving slowly himself, he'd been running late all morning. By the time he'd finished with his last patient and collected his thoughts enough to pick up the phone, it was well past noon.

Garrett's administrative assistant was cool; Garrett was downright cold.

"Thanks for getting back to me, Doctor," he said.

It was "Doctor" now. No more of the casual "Doc." Kendall felt his stomach tighten.

"I have a few questions as you might imagine," Garrett went on.

"Sure," said Kendall. "Sorry I couldn't call earlier, but I was swamped here and I wanted to have time to talk."

"Busy, huh?"

"Yes, actually. It was very busy this morning."

Silence for a moment, Kendall with the man's chart before him, and Garrett, he was sure, with a legal pad full of questions before him.

"My wife and I did a lot of reading last night and obviously we're quite concerned."

Kendall had asked him not to read too much about melanoma until they had a definitive report. Almost everything Kendall would tell him was dependent on the depth of the tumor, and at least at the time that they had spoken the evening before, that was still equivocal.

"I guess my first question is, what type of biopsy did you do?"

"It's called a shave biopsy, or a tangential excision. This was actually a little deeper than tangential, but if you're asking me did I do an excisional biopsy, the answer to that is no.

"Why not?"

"Because malignant melanoma was not in my differential diagnosis."

Kendall had been on a witness stand only once in his career, and that was to defend a colleague who was being wrongly sued. But he would never forget the plaintiff's attorney, the relentless attack, and the roiling in his stomach as question by question the attorney tried to lead him into an illogical and damaging path of thoughts and decisions.

"You didn't think about it all? You said that we needed to be careful. I presume that meant that there was something dangerous that we were trying to avoid."

"No," said Kendall, his stomach clamping down, beginning to burn. Which was not entirely true, but it was true in the way that Garrett meant. Of course he had thought about a possible melanoma. He thought about it a thousand times every day. He thought about it as he examined every lesion on every patient. He had even noticed just the faintest trace of pigment in this particular lesion. But had he thought that this was a melanoma? No. Had he thought that this particular lesion required a full-thickness excisional biopsy, which was the standard of care for the diagnosis of melanoma, and which Garrett was attempting to ascertain? No.

Garrett was quiet for a moment. "Okay," the attorney finally said. "So, do you know how deep it is? Do you know the Breslow level? Do you know the Clark's level?"

"Well, yes and no. It's at least 1.3 mm and a Clark Level III." Kendall took a deep breath and went on. "But there may be some tumor left at the base of the biopsy, so until the rest is taken out we won't be able to give it an exact depth."

Silence. Kendall closed his eyes, waiting.

"Let me make sure I understand what you're saying, Doctor," Garrett said deliberately. "Are you saying that there still may be cancer in my back because you did a superficial biopsy?"

Kendall hesitated, fighting the instinctive urge to lash back. "You can look at it that way if you wish, Mr. Garrett," he said finally. "Or we can be thankful that we decided to take it off in the first place. If you remember, you were pretty sure that you'd had it all of your life. These things happen. Something about it caught my eye and I thought it should be removed. But I didn't think it warranted a large excisional biopsy. We need to be grateful that we know what it is and go forward."

Silence again. Kendall waited, imaging Garrett at his desk, evaluating his options.

"So how do we go forward, Doctor?" he asked. "I know it needs to be excised. My understanding of melanomas that are that deep is that they also require a sentinel lymph node biopsy. Is that correct?"

Drew Garret and his wife had done a whole lot of reading on the Internet. "Yes, that's correct. There are a number of excellent surgeons in town who can do both. I can help you with that and, depending on your schedule, I can probably facilitate getting it done as quickly as possible."

"I appreciate that, but I'm sure these people are busy. You're talking at least days before that's going to happen."

"Probably. We want to get it done as quickly as possible, but it still may take a week or so to get you seen and get everything arranged."

Silence. Then, said Garrett: "Maybe I misunderstood you before, Doctor. Please correct me if I did. Did you not just tell me that there most likely is residual melanoma where you did the biopsy?"

"Yes, but—"

"And can you tell me with certainty or complete confidence that between now and the time that a surgeon removes that area that the residual melanoma might not metastasize?"

Closing his eyes, Kendall could feel the hard wood of the witness stand pressing against his back and arms.

"No, I can't. This is not an uncommon situation, though. Women have breast biopsies every day that show cancer and then they have to wait for their surgery."

"Most of those women probably also had proper biopsies, Doctor. And I would imagine that that's the standard-of-care for breast cancer, is it not?"

Don't react, the voice in his head screamed at him. It will only make it worse.

"And what would you do, Doctor?" asked Garrett when Kendall didn't respond. "What would you do if it were your wife? Colleen, isn't it?"

Kendall took a moment to answer, trying desperately to ignore the lawyerly I-know-all-about-you jab. For Garrett, the attorney who was now scared for his life, did have a valid question. What would he do?

"I'd be happy to excise the rest of the lesion," said Kendall, "but even if I do that you'll still need a wider definitive excision."

"I understand that, Doctor. When can you do that?"

He hesitated for a moment. He wasn't working later that afternoon, but he had the appointment with Peter Kane and his knee was throbbing. This was more important, he decided. He'd have to get to Peter another day, or maybe catch him at the end of his patients.

"How about later this—"

But Garrett was already speaking. "Thank you, Doctor," he said. "I'll call Dr. Petersen. He seems to be a little more conservative than you." Click.

Kendall immediately hit redial. Garrett's assistant answered.

"May I please speak with Mr. Garrett? We didn't get to finish our conversation."

"I'm sorry, but he's on the phone. May I give him a message, Doctor?"

Jesus Christ, he wanted to yell at her. He never gave me a chance to answer. "Yes, please. Would you please tell Mr. Garrett that I was about to tell him that I could help him out this afternoon. Please ask him to call me and we'll work it out."

"I'll give him the message. Thank you, Doctor."

*   *   *

The appointment with Peter Kane was straightforward. He had probably torn his medial meniscus, one of the discs of cartilage between the femur and tibia. It wasn't an emergency, but the arthroscopy that Kendall had been trying to avoid was now unavoidable. Check his schedule and let him know, Peter had said. He'd work him into the operating room schedule whenever.

Colleen was out when he got home. Probably running, he figured. Mandy was gone, the house was unlocked, and the television was on in the kitchen. He limped out to the mailbox, got the mail, and went out on the back deck where he sat in a chair with his left leg up on a bench. The large oak close to the house cast a broad umbrella of shade over the back yard, and even though the ambient temperature was pushing ninety, it was tolerable where he sat.

The pile of magazines and letters in his lap, he leaned back and closed his eyes. In the last twenty-four hours Drew Garrett and his wife had clearly become lay experts in malignant melanoma. But it was also just as clear that neither of them, nor Garrett's assistant, had yet to access the national medical data bank. Otherwise, Kendall knew, the conversation with Garrett wouldn't have ended as it had. He might have still been interrogated, but he would have also been excising Garrett's biopsy site, probably at this very minute. There was no way that Garrett's wife, as careful as she seemed to be, and most likely Garrett himself, would be leaving that in Dr. Petersen's hands. Kendall shook his head in dismay. Whatever had drawn them to Petersen for the second opinion to begin with obviously still held true.

Kendall opened his eyes, sat up a little, and turned to the mail. There were a number of letter-sized pieces and a stack of catalogs and magazines. He flipped through the bills, mortgage ads, credit card applications, and paused at the two pieces of personal mail. One was an invitation addressed to Colleen; the other was a plain white envelope addressed to him and marked "Personal." He looked at it more closely. It was not a mass mailing. His name and address had been electronically printed in fresh black ink.

There was no return address. He turned the envelope over—nothing. He turned it back over. The postmark was the day before from a Washington, D.C. post office.

He looked at it for nearly a minute. Although disgruntled patients were not uncommon, he could not think of any recent incidents that might warrant such a delivery, particularly to his home. He did not have any secret business ventures, or shady friends. He was not having an affair, nor had he ever had one. Nevertheless, though all of this was true, he still had an innate sense that there was nothing good about whatever was inside the envelope.

He held it up to the light. There was a piece of paper inside. It looked like a letter.

He set the other mail aside, sat up in his chair, and carefully opened the envelope with a kitchen knife that he had brought out with him. Inside was a single folded piece of paper.

It took him a moment to grasp what had been sent to him—a photocopied page from a personal reference form. Probably the last page, he figured, because there was a signature line at the bottom. The signature itself had been covered with white-out, as had any other identifying information, including the name at the top of the form. He briefly scanned the questions. He had served for several years on the Admissions Committee at The River Club, so he was quite familiar with the nature of the form. The only question was to which country club did it belong.

He sat back and read it one question at a time.

Nominee Name: ___(white-out)___   Pg.4

Do you know the nominee personally?   Yes

Do you know the nominee's spouse?   Yes

Has the nominee been entertained in your home?   No

If not, would you invite the nominee to your home?   No

Have you ever played golf with the nominee?   Yes

Would you invite the nominee to play golf with you? No

Do you believe the nominee will be an asset to (white-out)?
No

If not, why?   Because he's a cheater.

Member's Name (print please): _____(white-out)_____
Club Number: ____(white-out)_____

Member's signature: _(white-out)_____**Date**:_(white-out)___

SEVEN

Friday, June 8

Kendall woke shortly after five with the first sounds of the morning birds. He stayed still, watching the early morning gray soften minute by minute. Through the bedroom window he could see a thick arm of the goliath oak slowly take shape, and then the birds themselves, darting between the branches and the thick summer leaves. Turning away from the window, he tried to go back to sleep, but the letter was already forefront in his mind. Sleep was futile. Who? Who? And Why? The questions once again raced through his mind; the answers—none of them good—struggled to keep pace.

The night before, Colleen had intuitively known that he was unsettled, but without his lead she had chosen to leave it be. She was on her side now, curled up and facing him. She slept soundly, noiselessly, her shoulders rising and settling, rising and settling in a calming rhythm. Her face was relaxed and comfortable, as if it did not matter what this day would bring. She was impervious in many ways to everything that he was not—a trait he envied more and more as the years went by. With each new day it seemed that she woke already knowing that, one way or another, she would manage this day, and the days to come. Somehow she would win the little wars, whether by true victory, or simple deflection of the petty angers and reactions that turned the solvable problems into lingering ones, the innocuous comments into personal barbs.

They had been together so long that he did not remember if she had always been this way. Sometimes he thought it was a learned trait, an evolutionary defense she had acquired to defend herself against eighth graders prone to exuberant and irrational actions. Eighth graders, both formidable and fragile, who would one day latch on to her wide safety net, and then the very next day rip it off with a hurtful vengeance. Other times he thought she must have always been so fortunate, that it was part of what had drawn him to her.

He watched her for another minute, wanting to stroke her hair and cheek, wanting to gently wake her, to show her the letter, to get her sane and surely wise advice. Yet, as flagrant a breach of confidence and trust as it was for whomever had sent it, that same person had also clearly and implicitly trusted him with its care, and no doubt its secrecy, tainted as it was. They had also trusted Colleen to respect the "Personal" embossing that would surely raise a question in her mind, if not frank suspicion.

The sender of the letter trusted both of them. This was clear, and it was a point to which Kendall kept returning, for it was no small matter. The letter, in the wrong hands—even the knowledge of its existence—could cause a stain on its rightful home, and on the individuals beneath the white-out, for years.

Watching her, for the first time in their married life, Kendall felt as if he had somehow strayed, as if he had broken one of the unspoken rules of their life. He watched her sleep a while longer, feeling his arms and hands slowly tighten, feeling the balance of his life once again tipping slowly out of his control. No, he kept telling himself, nothing was broken. Bent maybe, but nothing yet was broken.

He got up and quietly left the room. It was early even for Mandy, and as he reached the kitchen she lifted her head from the family room floor to watch him. The coffee maker started to gurgle, a sure signal to her that the night was over, and she came grudgingly over to lick his hand and wait for her food.

Kendall opened the door to the deck and sat at the kitchen table while the coffee brewed. Who? Who? And Why? he asked himself for the hundredth time since he'd opened the envelope. Who? Who? And Why? Why did someone want him to know that someone thought someone else was a cheater? And the someone who had filled out the form must have been a friend or a colleague, no less. No one asked for a letter of recommendation if they didn't believe it would be complimentary. Sometimes a business associate who could not tell someone to his face that he really was an asshole, or that he drank too much, or that the worst part about him was actually his spouse, would say so behind his back on paper, where they assumed it was confidential. Yet even so, negative reference letters were rarely so forthright. They usually got their point across with cautious withholding or, at the most, a lukewarm endorsement. In the hundreds of reference letters that Kendall had reviewed himself, he could not remember a single one that contained such a blunt assessment of someone's character.

Who? Who? And Why?

He poured himself a cup of coffee and went outside. Normally on such a morning, his mind racing with his office or family, he would put on his running shoes and let his body work it out. But his knee was even more swollen, and he was going nowhere this morning except to the deck where he limped to the rail. Leaning on the smooth redwood, he watched the sparrows and the occasional cardinal land lightly on the rocks of the waterfall, drink quickly, and be off again. Nature had taught them well. One or two seconds too long and they might be whisked away, just another part of the food chain.

He stayed there for a while, the cup of coffee warm in his hand, the sky now pink at the eastern edge. Rule number one, he told himself. Always remember rule number one—don't give a patient two different diseases. It was a saying in medicine that had been drummed into him during internship and residency, and that he often reflected on now with patients who had difficult problems. The premise was simple: patients who were sick with different symptoms or signs did not normally have two different diseases. Coincidence in medicine was generally a lucky phenomenon, not an unlucky one. Even though a patient's fever and malaise might seem out of sorts with their rash or joint pain, the human body did not break down in a disorderly fashion. Always look for a single answer. Genetics and evolution had come way too far to allow for happenstance.

No, happenstance was as foreign in the human body as it was in nature. And when it did happen, it was like the dallying sparrow, plucked away in an instant, forever irrelevant in the future of things.

The answer to the first of his questions then was not happenstance, he figured. For a moment he had thought it was not a coincidence that just two days before he had met Heather Bowie, the Assistant Director of Membership at Hidden Glen Country Club, in his office. Just as quickly, though, that thought had faded. Why would Heather Bowie, though she would have access to it, commit career suicide? Or even worse, risk a defamation lawsuit for herself, or her club?

No, there was no benign answer here. Just like Garrett, it was bad and getting worse, spiraling somehow out of his control.

Kendall heard the bedroom door open, then the soft padding of Colleen's feet on the carpeted stairs, then crisper on the kitchen tile. A coffee cup clinked on the granite counter; the refrigerator opened and closed. Then she was next to him, cupping her hands around her eyes to shield them from the light. Had he not gotten out of bed, he knew she'd still be asleep.

She stayed this way for a moment before putting her arms around him and staring out into the yard. "What's the matter?" she said. "Are you okay?"

"Yeah," he said. "I'm just bummed about my knee."

"I know. You just have to do it and get it over with."

He nodded, watching a robin land lightly on a rock, drink, look furtively in their direction, and take off.

"What else? Are you worried about Kelley?"

He had reluctantly given in to his daughter going to the beach for the rest of the summer.

"Well, I don't feel good about it, that's for sure. What happened to the internship we talked about?" he asked again.

"We talked about that, Ryan. She's twenty. She wants to go to the beach."

Looking out past the oak, past the Browning's house, he nodded resignedly.

"You've been a little quiet the past few days. Is everything okay in the office?"

Kendall was quiet for a moment. "I'm in the middle of a few tough cases. It's getting tiring."

Colleen rested her face on his shoulder. "You're not alone, you know. Don't forget that."

One of the sparrows landed, slipped away. Landed, slipped away.

Don't give the patient two diseases. There is no happenstance.

He turned and put his arms around his wife.

Yes, Heather Bowie had been in his office, but it was not Heather who had sent the letter. And he thought he had a fairly good idea about the file from which it had come. The one that had been out in Heather's office just the other day. The only question was why.

"I know," he said, stroking her hair.

"Can I ask you something?" she said.

"Of course."

"I saw the mail yesterday before I went out to run. You don't have to tell me if you don't want to. I . . . you know I trust you. It was just a strange looking letter, that's all."

He hesitated and she moved away.

"Forget it," she said. "I shouldn't have asked."

He pulled her back. "It's nothing," he said. "It's from Paul. It's just a club thing I'm helping him with. It's nothing."

*　　*　　*

At 9:00 AM, Laurel called into exam room number four over the telephone intercom.

Kendall was bent over a patient draining an abscess. Sammie picked up the phone. "Hey, Laurel, can it wait? He's got gloves on." Sammie listened for several seconds, then turned to Kendall. "Mr. Garrett's on the phone. Laurel said he sounds a little upset. Do you want to speak with him or call him back?"

Kendall straightened. Blair McAllister, eighty-two years old, was one of his long-time patients. He'd understand. Kendall took off his gloves, told Blair he'd back in a few minutes, and went to his office.

"Good morning, Doctor," said Garrett. "I have a couple of questions if you don't mind."

"Sure."

"Do you have my final report yet?"

Kendall looked in his "In" box. Garrett's chart was not there.

"No, but I'm sure I'll get it sometime today. They're very reliable. I'll call you as soon as I get it."

"Who's very reliable, Doctor?"

"The lab where we sent your biopsy. In my opinion, they're the best in town."

"That's the next question which I'm presuming you can help me with. There's no record of my specimen at American Laboratories. My understanding is American Laboratories is the laboratory that has a contract with my insurance company. I guess I'm confused. Is that not where you sent it?"

Tighten, burn. The wood pressing into his back, the room warm and stuffy.

"No, it's not. I had the specimen sent to Chevy Chase Pathology Associates. American Labs is a very large operation. It's mainly a contract lab and the pathologists come and go. They're also very slow in generating reports. Chevy Chase Pathology is much faster and I know the pathologist, who I think is excellent. I thought that's what you would have wanted. I apologize if I was wrong about that."

Garrett was quiet for a moment. "I suppose I understand your reasoning, Doctor, and I do appreciate it, but perhaps you should have checked with me before you made that assumption."

"You're right, Mr. Garrett. I should have asked you. I wrongly assumed that's what you would have wanted me to do. I didn't think the cost was important here. It's my mistake. Our office will cover the cost."

"I'm not concerned about the cost," said Garrett. Then after a few seconds, his voice perhaps a touch softer, he said: "So help me understand, Doctor. If you believe this Chevy Chase laboratory is superior, then why wouldn't Dr. Petersen use it as well?"

"I can't speak for him, but perhaps it's easier for their office. Then the patients don't complain about their insurance not covering the cost of the lab."

"I see. Well, now I understand why there's no record of my biopsy at American Laboratories."

"As I said, I apologize for the confusion."

"Do you have any of my pathology slides in your possession, Doctor?"

"No."

"Do you have anything related to my case in your possession other than my original medical record?"

"No."

"May I please have the exact name and address of the laboratory where you sent my biopsy?"

"Sure." Kendall flipped through some charts on his desk and found one with a Chevy Chase Pathology Associates report in it. He gave Garrett the address and the telephone number. "Would you like me to fax you the final report when I get it today?"

"I don't think so. I'll get it from them. Thanks anyway."

"Do you want me to call you?"

"Not unless the report says something different than what we've already discussed."

"Okay. But we still need to talk about a surgeon and most likely a sentinel lymph node biopsy. You might want to see an oncologist as well. I'd be happy to help you with any of it."

"I think I'm all set, Doctor. Thank you, though. I'll be in touch." Click.

Kendall set the phone down and stood. There was nothing else he could do now. In a strange way, he even felt relieved.

Sammie was on the phone in the nurses' station when he came out of his office. "I swear to God, Robyn," she said, laughing, "we don't have it. I don't know what to tell you. All I know is that it never came here."

Kendall motioned for her to hurry up. In addition to Blaine McAllister who was still waiting for him with his partially drained abscess, there were two charts up on exam room doors.

"Gotta go," said Sammie. "Let me know what happens." She hung up and made a face as she hurried to catch up to Kendall.

"What's that about?" he said.

"They're missing a slide and Dr. Williams is going nuts."

"Why is she calling us?" said Kendall, his hand on an exam room door.

"I guess it's one of the slides on that girl with the nose thing. They can't find it anywhere. By the way, the courier brought your slide this morning. I'll put it on your desk as soon as we're done."

Kendall shrugged. "I never saw it. Forget it—I have to finish up in here."

EIGHT

By the time Kendall had recovered from the phone call with Drew Garrett, it was almost time to start seeing his afternoon patients. He ordered lunch for his staff and ate a sandwich at his desk, where there were six charts with phone messages waiting for him. He put the phone on speaker and made the calls and wrote in the charts as he ate. Those done, he accessed his voice mail and checked his e-mail at the same time. Delete, delete, delete. E-mails from Colleen and Kelley to open. The phone messages were playing. Paul Mancini checking in with him about his knee. Had he seen Peter Kane yet? Let him know how he was doing. Chad Williams letting him know that he had faxed over Drew Garrett's pathology report and would Kendall please call him back as soon as he had a chance. There was a different quality to Williams' voice the farther Kendall got into the message, and when it was over he replayed it. Irritation maybe? Anger? The message played out and he erased it. Colleen wanted face cream; Kelley and her friends had found a house at the beach to rent and she needed a deposit.

He looked at his watch—fifteen minutes before his first afternoon patient. He needed to speak to Colleen and then to Peter Kane. With all the walking and bending he'd been doing, his knee was getting worse by the hour. He was going to have to clear his schedule the next week and just get it done. And he wanted to speak with Peter anyway. Peter was a native Washingtonian. He had gone to St. Francis Preparatory School, Georgetown University, and Georgetown University Medical School. His family also belonged to Hidden Glen Country Club, and Peter had grown up there playing golf.

But the sound of Williams voice was nagging him, and there wasn't enough time to make both calls. He looked outside—it was clear and bright. Chad Williams was probably headed for the golf course. Odds were he had a better chance that Peter Kane would be in his office later on a beautiful Friday afternoon. He tapped out the main number for Chevy Chase Pathology Associates. While the phone was ringing, he took the plastic cover off the microscope he kept on his desk and opened the slide tray that Sammie had put down with Lindsey Browning's chart.

Robyn answered. "Oh hi, Dr. Kendall," she said. "I'll get him for you. And *please* let me know if you see that slide. I swear he's going to fire me if I don't find it. Now, don't tell him I told you that. Hold on."

With the phone on speaker, he slipped Lindsey Browning's slide onto the microscope stage. Even with modern technology, the process from living tissue to formalin to glass microscope slide had not changed much over the years. It was a meticulous and labor-intensive undertaking requiring the formalin-fixed tissue to be dehydrated and then embedded in a small block of paraffin wax. Once the tissue was embedded in the wax, this so-called tissue block was then attached to a plastic cassette half the size of a credit card for handling and storage. From the tissue block micron thin sections of tissue were then shaved off with a microtome and placed on a glass microscope slide. These were then stained, permanently mounted with xylene under a glass cover slip, and labeled with the patient's name, the biopsy site, and the laboratory's accessioning number.

Two things were thus accomplished. First and perhaps foremost, a glass microscope slide holding stained tissue was produced. This stained tissue could then be interpreted by a pathologist, who could then render a diagnosis and generate an official pathology report. Secondly, the process memorialized the biopsy specimen within the tissue block. Properly labeled with the laboratory's accession number for identification, the tissue block was then available for sectioning for as long as the lab wanted to store it. For medical-legal purposes, laboratories were always loathe to discard tissue specimens, so it was not uncommon for them to be stored for twenty or thirty years. This embedding process was also how teaching institutions preserved interesting cases. Kendall could remember from his own residency the thousands of tissue blocks stored in the rows of steel cabinets tucked away in the back of the pathology lab.

"Hey, Ryan," said Williams. "I faxed you that report. Did you get it?"

Kendall had seen Garrett's chart in his "In" box while he was making phone calls. "I did," he said without looking up from the microscope. "Thanks. What's up? You sounded a little peeved."

Lindsey Browning's slide was well-prepared with multiple cuts from the specimen. Kendall looked at the first cut under low power so as to get a feel for the overall architecture of the lesion. It was definitely symmetrical, which was always good. Nature and the human body did not order themselves randomly. Their aberrations, however—their cellular malfunctions and cancers—paid no attention to protocol. They spread upwards, sideways, downward—they did whatever they wished, for they were rogues without bounds. Benign growths on the other hand, though they might stretch the limits, did not break the rules. They stayed within their boundaries, neat and proper, as did this small growth that he was now studying under his microscope. This small growth that even he could see looked like a Spitz Nevus. And even under low power he could also see that the entire lesion seemed to be contained within the biopsy specimen. Williams was right—it did look like he had taken off the whole thing with the biopsy.

"Goddamn right," Williams was saying, his voice booming out of the speaker. "What the hell's the matter with him? You probably saved his life."

Kendall lifted his head from the microscope, looked at his door which was partially open, and picked up the receiver.

"What do you mean?" said Kendall. "Are you talking about Garrett?"

"Goddamn right. Ten minutes after I faxed you his report this goddamn young lawyer shows up at our door with a release for all of the slides, the block, and quote 'any and all reports.' Not just the slides mind you. He wanted the whole goddamn block. Shit, we hadn't even put it away yet. Jesus Christ, what an asshole."

I guess Garrett was right, Kendall said to himself—the attorney didn't need him to fax the report. That would have been too easy.

"He's desperate, Chad," said Kendall. "We might feel the same way. You never know."

"Yeah, I guess. But the block? Jesus, I would've given him all the slides he wanted. What if he loses it? What if this case goes to court for some reason and he loses the goddamn block. Jesus Christ, my ass'll be grass."

"You had him sign a release or something didn't you?"

"Damn right. But still . . ."

"Then you're covered," said Kendall. "Don't worry about it. Someone's obviously telling him what to do or else he wouldn't have asked for the block. You know he's getting a second opinion on the slides. Whoever's doing that probably wants to cut their own. I don't know who's helping him, though. I can't believe it's Petersen. He's a wimp."

"Petersen? You mean George Petersen? The slicing, dicing machine? What does he have to do with it?"

"Garrett went to see him after he saw me because he didn't like what I said. Petersen took a bunch of moles off him. Five or six, I think."

"Shit, he got off lucky. He sent me twelve once. It was unbelievable. Specimens A through L. Twelve goddamn bottles."

"Look, Chad, we're both in the same boat. There's nothing we can do. He's a smart guy. He'll figure it out."

"I hope so. It's a bad tumor. Lots of mitoses."

"Speaking of tumors," said Kendall, putting his head back to the microscope. "I'm looking at Lindsey Browning's slide right now. Looks like a Spitz to me. I give up after normal moles though. That's your job."

"Yeah, that's a good cut I sent you. Listen, I hate to even bring it up because I don't want you to think we're sloppy, but that slide we can't find is one of hers. It's driving me goddamn nuts. I've never lost a slide before."

"*You* didn't lose it, did you?"

"Well, you know what I mean. I'm responsible for what happens here. Anyway, it looks just like that one except it's a tangential cut like I said before. So, if you see another tray around with her name on it, you can just send it back."

"Sure. No problem," said Kendall, taking the slide off the microscope mount. "I don't remember seeing it though, and neither does Sammie. I'll check with the rest of the staff—you never know. We do have a temp' helping Laurel out front. And let me know if you hear anything else from

Garrett, and I'll do the same. Don't worry about it though. No one's done anything wrong—there's nothing he can sue us about. He's scared, and this is all he knows. It's just how these guys do things."

Kendall hung up and sat back for a minute. "Cheater" was perhaps an overstatement, he thought. Williams was just paranoid, and obviously terrified of any legal confrontation. Maybe he had been sued before. Most pathologists were at some point in their career.

He put Lindsey Browning's slide back into the cardboard slide tray, and put the tray and her chart in his "Out" box. There certainly weren't any more questions about her nose. Unless Chad Williams wanted to show him the slide with the atypical areas in it, the lesion he had removed was a "textbook Spitz Nevus, just as Will Ammerman had said. Actually, thought Kendall, that's probably the slide that's missing. That's why he's so worked up. It's probably the only slide with any semblance of atypical areas warranting all of the emotional upheaval and a three hundred dollar consultation from a specialist in New York.

*   *   *

At 3:00 P.M., with Kendall in the middle of a skin cancer screening, Devon stuck her head in the room to tell him that Dr. Williams was on the phone.

"Ask him if I can call him back, please. Get his back number."

Devon came back a moment later. "He said that's fine, Doctor Kendall. I'll put the number on your desk. He said he'd be there all night."

Kendall looked up. "'All night'?"

Devon shrugged. "That's what he said."

Kendall finished with Mrs. Bishop and paused outside the room. It was fairly slow for a Friday afternoon. He only had one chart up and he'd been on time since he'd started. "I'll be right back," he said to Sammie and headed for his office. Whatever it was, with the sky blue and the golf course green, it had to be pretty bad to keep Chad Williams in his office late into a Friday evening.

"Hey, Chad. What's up now?"

"Let's see, "What's up now?" said Williams. "For starters, how about another lawyer with a stick up her ass with forty-eight slides for me to read from American Labs."

"What? On Garrett?"

"That's right. Forty-eight slides from Mr. Drew Garrett for me to read on Friday fucking afternoon. That's in addition to my normal stuff to sign out."

Kendall was truly confused and for several seconds said nothing. "I don't understand," he finally said. "I didn't see any scars from previous biopsies. In fact, I'm not sure that he'd ever seen a dermatologist before."

"Jesus, Ryan. These are all from this week. Four from each of the six moles Petersen took off, and fourteen from the excision he just did yesterday for Christ's sake."

"Hold on. You're saying this is all the stuff from Petersen?"

"That's right. Oh, and you haven't heard the best part. Miss Stick-Up-Her-Ass also told me that Mr. Garrett would greatly appreciate a preliminary report by the close of business today. And if that was not possible, at the latest by Monday at noon."

"Whoa."

"Right. So that's what's up. Are you with a patient? You need to hear what he did over at American. It's pretty funny, actually."

Kendall looked out his door. No more charts had been put up.

"I'm listening."

"He went over there himself and raised holy hell. All kinds of shit about the standard-of-care for getting reports out and blah, blah, blah. He even used us as the 'gold standard' in the D.C. area. How the hell he knows that, I don't know. Anyway, he got to the lab director somehow and had him trace out the route of the specimen bottle from accessioning to the histo' lab to the pathologists' offices. Sure as shit, he found the slides from his moles in a pile waiting to be read with a thousand other ones. His excision specimen hadn't even been processed yet and then he really went nuts. We know all the tech's over there. He had the director stumbling over himself and the pathologist was literally in tears. She's fresh out of residency and in way over her head anyway."

"Jesus," said Kendall, imagining the scene. "I can see him doing it. He'd be pretty good at it, too.

"Believe me, they're shitting in their pants right now. Anyway, he left and some other fuck-nut went over and stayed there until the excision specimen was processed and the pathologist read every damn one of the slides and printed reports. Then he took all the slides, the reports, and all of the blocks."

"What's the excision report say?" said Kendall.

"Are you kidding? He wouldn't let me see that. He wanted me to look at everything fresh. But she did report it as clear," Williams added. "I know that. I talked to her about it, and I'm looking at those cuts now. It looks clear to me, too. It's not a very big excision, though—I hope that's not all the treatment he's getting."

Kendall did not have the time or energy to explain the size of Petersen's excision, that it was simply a prelude to definitive wider one. "So can you issue an addendum saying that there's no more visible depth to the tumor?"

Williams hesitated. "Yeah, sure. It's still a bad one, though. It's very blue. He still needs the full-court press."

Kendall felt himself getting irritated. Williams' job was to interpret the slides and issue a report, not to treat his patients.

"'Very blue,'" said Kendall. "Sorry, you lost me there. What do you mean?"

"Oh, nothing. Just talking to myself. You know, most tumors stain up some shade of blue. This one was pretty dense."

"What about the moles?"

"She said they were normal, but I could go either way so far. I've only looked at three of them, but there's some junctional activity. I couldn't make anything more than mild or moderate atypia out of them, but . . ."

Kendall straightened. But what? he said to himself, waiting for Williams to finish. But it would serve him right?

"It's your call," said Williams. "I can go either way."

"What do you mean, Chad? It's not my call. They're either atypical, or they aren't."

Williams didn't respond right away. "I need to look at them some more," he finally said. "I think most of them are fine. One or two might be borderline."

"Okay," said Kendall. "I have to go. Fax me an amended report as soon as you can, please."

He sat back for a moment. Yes, he definitely needed to call Peter Kane. And not just about his knee. But what about Garrett? he asked himself. Should he call him? Should he see if he could help him in any way? Obviously the man was just as unhappy with Petersen and American Labs as he was with him.

No, he said to himself on the way out to the exam rooms. Garrett was on a roll. A steamroll. Best let him work it out himself. If Garrett wanted his help, one way or another—by phone, courier, or subpoena—he would surely ask for it.

*   *   *

At 5:00 PM, Kendall picked up the phone and held it in front of him for a moment. It was not a difficult call. Peter Kane, soon to be on the other end of the line, did not have a transmittable disease, or cancer. He made many more difficult calls than this every week. Still, it was a lie, a ruse. He was getting sucked into the vortex of this force, almost against his will. He had not asked for the letter, had not gone looking for it. In many ways, he did not want to know who some unnamed country club member thought was a cheater. Someone else wanted him to know, though. And it was most likely his closest friend, Judge Paul Mancini.

But why? If indeed it was Mancini who had sent it to him, certainly it was for a good reason. Which was what? Now that he had been drawn intentionally and irrevocably into the heart of this puzzle, how was he to answer that question? How was he to find his way?

"Hello," said Dr. Peter Kane.

Kendall had called him on his private line. "Hey, Peter. It's Ryan Kendall. Do you have a minute?"

"Sure. What's up? Do you have a date? I've got my schedule right in front of me."

"Sort of. I'm going to figure it out with Colleen tonight. I think I'd like to do it next week, though—maybe Wednesday. Would that work?"

"Sure. I'm in the OR all morning on Wednesday. Call me first thing Monday, or even over the weekend if you want. I'm on call, so I won't be doing much except working. Wednesday's a good day. Plan on taking Thursday and Friday off. You'll be able to get around by Monday."

"Right. That's what I figured. Okay, I'll call you. One more thing, Peter. I, uh, I have sort of a strange question. I think you said I could probably be back playing tennis or golf in a few weeks."

"Yeah," said Kane hesitantly. "Within reason. Don't push it."

"I won't. Promise. What I'm wondering is, I've never played in our member-guest golf tournament, and I was hoping to give it a try this year. It's not until the middle of July."

"You might be okay by then."

"I understand. Well, if am okay by then, here's my real question. I was thinking of asking Chad Williams, but I've never played golf with him before. I talk with him on the phone about cases, and I see him around at conferences occassionally, but I've never really been out with him. Three days on the golf course is a long time, if you know what I mean."

Peter did not answer right away.

"I don't care if he's any good or not. But, you know, besides the golf there are the dinners and . . ."

"I know what you mean," said Kane. Then, after another long moment of silence: "Well, he's a decent golfer, so you don't have to worry about that. He plays a fair amount."

Besides knowing the Williams family from Hidden Glen, Peter was also on the staff at Fairfield Hospital where Chevy Chase Pathology did a lot of the hospital's pathology work.

"Ummm, what can I say, Ryan. Uh, do you have anyone else you can ask?"

"You. I can still write that off, I think."

"Thanks. Maybe next year."

Kendall was silent.

"You have to make a decision, huh?"

"Yeah. I have to block the time off."

"Well, what can I say. I wouldn't do that if I were you," he said finally. "He's a nice enough guy, but . . . geez, Ryan, this is a tough one. Umm, geez, so . . . so I guess you haven't heard that story," he said tentatively. "Which is good, I suppose. I thought everyone in town knew."

"Not me," said Kendall, closing his eyes. Tighten, burn. "But maybe I should. I work with him a lot, too. Don't worry—I won't tell anyone. I know the ropes."

"I know you do. Still, I hate to even talk about it, because I don't really know the details."

Silence.

"My understanding," Kane finally said, "is that he almost didn't get into the Club. Even if your parents are members you still have to put in an application. Most of the time it's just a formality, so I think this was a pretty big deal. His Dad might have even been on the Board at the time. Anyway, I heard there was someone who didn't want him in, and it was a, uh, a very contentious discussion."

"He's in though, isn't he?"

"Right. His dad's a great guy, as is his brother. And his grandfather was one of the founding members. I don't really know much more."

"Wow," said Kendall after a moment.

"Right. As I said, it was a big deal for a while. It's settled down now, but . . ."

"But not really."

"Right."

"Wow," said Kendall again. "Double wow. Sure you don't want to play?"

"Maybe next year. Call me this weekend. The sooner you get that knee done, the sooner you'll feel better."

"I will. Thanks."

Kendall hung up, turned in his chair, looked out the window. Okay, so fine. He didn't have to send any more specimens to Chevy Chase Pathology Associates. Mancini had made his point, as had Peter Kane, as had Chad Williams himself. Certainly it was sometimes difficult to make a definitive diagnosis of mild atypia in a mole, but for Williams to infer that he might make the diagnosis of an atypical mole on Garrett out of spite was almost incomprehensible. Chad Williams would take it personally and probably not very well, but these things happened. Business was business.

He looked at his watch—it was getting late. He'd been preoccupied with Drew Garrett all week and he needed to get home and pay some attention to his family. He went through his "In" box, leaving Garrett's chart for last.

Ready to leave, Kendall opened the chart and scanned the report. He had seen a hundred such verdicts and other than the fact that this was Drew Garrett's, it was no different. In fact, as far as pathology reports went, it was a good one—it was professional, complete, and contained all of the necessary histologic information. Unfortunately, none of it was good. In fact, this smallish red bump, a bump that might have been there for years, could very easily send Drew Garret to an early grave. And at this point, there was nothing that Kendall could do about it.

CHEVY CHASE PATHOLOGY ASSOCIATES

4200 Wisconsin Ave * Chevy Chase, MD 20815 * 301-654-6500 tel * 301-654-6505 fax

Robert S. Williams, M.D., F.A.C.P.
Samuel M. Williams, M.D., F.A.C.P.

Chadwick P. Williams, M.D.
Myra P. Green, Ph.D.

Physician: Ryan Kendall, M.D.
6500 Kirkwood Rd., Suite 400
Bethesda, MD 20817
Date of Surgery:06/04/10
Date Received: 06/04/10
Date Reported: 06/06/10

Pathology Report Number: **26859-10**
Patient: **Drew Garrett**
6587 Old Meadow Dr.
Chevy Chase, MD 20815
DOB: 2/26/1959 Sex: M

Source: Right upper back
Pre-operative Diagnosis: ? Nevus, ? Scar, R/O atypical lesion
Clinical Information: Unknown duration

Gross Description: Received in formalin is a dome-shaped piece of tissue from the right upper back measuring 8 x 7 mm with a tan granular elevated hair-bearing surface. The specimen is marked with blue ink, sectioned into 6 pieces and submitted in total.

Microscopic Description: A cellular proliferation of spindle-shaped cytologically atypical cells fills the included portions of the dermis and extends to the base of the submitted tissue. Tumor cells demonstrate atypical nuclei and mitotic activity. Tumor cells are strongly and diffusely S-100 protein-positive as well as HMB-45 and Melan-A-positive. Tumor cells are cytokeratin-negative and desmin-negative.

Final Diagnosis: Malignant Melanoma, Spindle Cell Type—Deep Margin Involved
        Clark's level: III
        Approximate Maximum Thickness: 1.33 mm To The Base
        Growth Phase: Vertical
        Mitotic Rate: 8 per High Power Field
        Ulceration: Absent
        Lymphocytic Host Response: Sparse; Noninfiltrative
        Precursor Lesion: Not identified

Note: The included measurements of Breslow thickness and Clark's level should be regarded as preliminary because tumor extends to the base of the submitted tissue.

_____
Chad P. Williams, M.D.

NINE

They were sitting at a corner table in *Bella Luna* watching the waiter serve their entrees when his phone rang. He glanced at the caller ID: 301-469-4589. It wasn't a number he recognized so he let the call go through to voice mail. If someone really wanted to speak with him, particularly on a Friday night, they would leave a message.

"So you were saying Kelley found a job as a lifeguard," said Kendall. "That's a great job for a dermatologist's daughter."

Colleen rolled her eyes. "If you don't stop it she's never going to come home."

"I don't make up all the skin cancers I see. She's pretty fair—she needs to be careful."

"She knows, Ryan. She'll use her sunscreen." Colleen took a sip of wine and looked at him. "It's the summer, she's at the beach. What do you want her to do, stay inside?"

"I want her to come home and do an internship with Gary Young over at KPWarwick. Just like we said at Christmas. That was the deal when she went to Florida for spring break. Remember? Where she got burned I might add."

His phone started to vibrate, and then the message icon began to blink. "Why don't you see who's calling?" said Colleen. "And then we'll start over."

"Good idea."

Halfway through the message, Kendall frowned and stood. He pointed outside to Colleen and she nodded, returning to her wine.

He was gone for several minutes. When he came back, he said: "That was Donny, the building manager for our complex. The cleaning crew told their boss that there was a man in my office about an hour ago that they didn't recognize. He didn't seem to be taking anything, so apparently they didn't call security. By the time Donny and the crew chief got there he was gone."

"That's weird. They should have called someone earlier."

Kendall picked up a fork and toyed with his asparagus. "They do a good job, but I suspect a lot of them are illegal. The company is basically three families from Nicaragua."

Colleen nodded. "Still, that's a little strange, particularly if they said something later. I'd still look around pretty carefully. They just might not have seen him taking something. Why else would someone go in?"

Kendall shrugged. "Money and drugs. That's about it. We hide the money now and we don't have any street drugs. The last time we got broken into they took syringes and needles, too." He was quiet for a moment. "I do worry about one of our old employees going in and looking for their file or pay records, though. Especially someone we let go. I should probably go by tonight."

"I still don't understand. How did he get in? Did he break in?"

"I don't think so. Donny said the doors and the locks looked okay."

"Does the building have security cameras?"

Kendall shook his head no. "It's an old building and the management company is cheap. They just put on the electronic security system for the entrances last year. If you know what you're doing though, it's not very hard to get in most of the offices. The lab couriers are coming in and out at all hours, so it's easy to get into the building. And when the cleaning crew is in the office they leave the doors open so they can get their stuff in and out. And all the trash. They lock up again when they leave, but I've left my office lots of times at night when they're already cleaning and the doors are wide open."

"So . . . ?"

"The crew chief is going to talk to the workers who were in the office again and try to get some more information. I don't think any of them speak English. Donny said he'll call me if they find out anything."

His phone was vibrating again.

"Remind me to marry a lawyer next time," said Colleen, picking up her fork and separating a small piece of broiled rockfish.

It was another number that Kendall didn't initially recognize, this one with a Chevy Chase exchange. When he looked at it again a minute later, though, he wondered if it was the back line for Chad Williams that he had dialed earlier in the day. He took the phone off the table and put it his pocket. There was nothing that Chad Williams had to say that couldn't wait thirty minutes.

"So," he said, "you know how I've been talking about playing in our member-guest tournament one year?"

Colleen cocked her head. "That's in July. What about your knee?"

"Peter thinks it will be okay by then."

She nodded and returned to her rockfish.

"So, this pathologist that I work with a lot has really helped me out with some tough cases. Especially this year. It would be nice to do something special for him."

"So ask him."

"I'm thinking about it. But I don't really know him. Three days on the golf course with someone you don't know very well is a long time. And then there's the stag dinner, and the spouse's dinner. You'd have to sit with his wife."

"I'm a big girl."

"Okay. I'm just giving you the chance to check it out before I ask him. I'm sure some of the women you play tennis with know them."

"Why do you say that?"

"They belong to Hidden Glen. Doesn't your team play over there?"

"What's his name?"

"Chad Williams."

"I know a Bunny Williams. I'm pretty sure her husband is a doctor, but I don't what kind."

"There are several Williamses at Hidden Glen, and at least three of them are doctors. They all work in the same office, actually."

"Well, I know Bunny, and she's as sweet as can be."

"Well, maybe you can just make sure it's the right Williams then. And if you can, see what you can find out about him while you're at it. I don't want to spend three days on the golf course with a nudge."

*   *   *

He listened to the voice mail while they drove to his office.

"Hey, Ryan. Sorry to bother you on Friday night. Just wanted to let you know that I finished reading all of Garrett's slides and I went ahead and signed them out. We'll print reports on everything first thing Monday morning. The excision that Petersen did is clear, but as I said before, it's pretty small. He only got around the biopsy site by two or three millimeters. For everyone's sake, I certainly hope that's not the only treatment the guy's getting. Anyway, I don't see any tumor left, so I dictated another report with an addendum that after review of subsequent submitted materials the reported depth of 1.33 mm probably represents an accurate measurement of the true tumor depth."

"*Probably*," said Kendall under his breath with a smirk. "Jesus, what a wimp."

Williams was still talking. "So that's that. The moles were basically okay. I thought four of them were just run-of-the-mill compound nevi. Two of them had mild junctional atypia and I signed them out as atypical, but the margins are clear so I don't think they need to be treated. I'll fax you the reports Monday. Let's see . . . it's nine o'clock now. I'll be here a little while longer and then I need to get home. Call me if you want. Thanks, buddy."

"That was Chad Williams," Kendall said to Colleen. "He's just leaving his office."

Colleen looked at her watch. "Pretty late for a pathologist, isn't it?"

"Yeah, it is. It's a long story. Long week, actually."

There were only a few cars in the parking lot and Kendall parked just yards from the front entrance. The front door was locked for the night. He swiped his security card down the electronic reader on the wall beside the door, and a moment later the doors parted. The lobby was deserted, the tile floor still moist in spots from the night's cleaning. One of the elevator doors was open. Kendall swiped the same card to activate the elevator and they rode to the fourth floor.

The hall was quiet, the only sounds the background hum of the air conditioners and fans, and then the soft padding of their shoes on the carpet. His office was around the corner from the elevator and they slowed as it came into view. The lights in the waiting room were off; the lids to the specimen containers in the hallway were up, signifying that their contents had been removed.

They paused to study the door to the waiting room and then the employees' entrance—there was no evidence of tampering on either of them. Kendall unlocked the employees' door and they moved into the reception work area. Lights on, pause again. Monday's charts were out on Laurel's desk as they had been when he'd left just hours before; the billing manager's door was open, her desk neat, the cabinets closed. He no longer kept a safe in the office, for it was the first thing that intruders looked for. They hid the small amounts of petty cash that they kept in a different place each night. He in fact had no idea where it was this night, but nothing looked out of order. It if weren't for the phone call from Donny, nothing seemed different.

But somehow it was. This was his space, more so than his home in many ways, and he felt somehow violated. Even though he had no idea who had been there, or what had really happened, it was as if someone had broken into their home and gone through his most personal drawers, his papers, his belongings. And not just his own. Each of the thousand charts that lined the walls contained bits and pieces of a life—bits and pieces that were implicitly entrusted to him by their owners. This office was a private affair, a personal affair, and someone, in some way, had tainted the sanctity of it.

Colleen, familiar with the office, moved ahead of him. She turned the lights on in the nursing station, then in each exam room one by one. Careful, he wanted to yell out to her. Who knew what lurked back there. But he knew that they would be wasted words. She had already shown what her answer would be.

They met up in the nursing station.

"All the exam rooms look fine," she said. "But how would you ever know if anyone took some needles? They're out loose in the drawers."

"We wouldn't."

He checked the cabinet that held the injectables and prescription pads—it was still locked.

They moved into his office and turned on the light. For a minute they stood still, scanning every drawer, every file, every shelf. Kendall's gaze settled on the short filing cabinet near his desk where he kept the employee files in a locked drawer. It wasn't often, but every couple of years he made a bad hire, every one of which was a potential legal problem. Within the drawers were also all of the employee reviews and pay records. He walked to the cabinet and pulled on the drawers—they were locked. He opened them with his key—all of the records were in place as he remembered them.

He stepped backwards and looked at his desk. Everything looked the same as when he'd left it. Two surgery charts for Monday were in the center; a note pad with a list of calls to make was in the upper right hand corner. He was about to turn around when the microscope caught his eye. The cover was in place, and it was pushed up against the wall in front of his blotter as it always was when it wasn't in use. But something wasn't quite right—it wasn't quite where he'd left it. The workspace on his desk was small, and over the years he had come to a careful arrangement of telephone, computer monitor, keypad, microscope, blotter, and space for his coffee cup. An inch here or there and he could not type comfortably, or worse, risked knocking an entire cup of coffee across the desk. The microscope had its own resting place, and it was not in it. It was just an inch or two off, but it was not where he had moved it after looking at Lindsey Browning's slide.

He moved closer to his desk and opened the drawers. Nothing looked out of place.

"What's the matter?" said Colleen.

"I don't know. My microscope's not where it normally is. They probably moved it when they cleaned tonight."

He looked at the stack of plastic trays to the side of the blotter. Nothing seemed different. Then the other side of his desk. His "In" box was empty; the "Out" box was full, as he had left it. In fact, it was sagging from the weight of the charts and Lindsey Browning's slide tray. He picked up the pile and set it on his desk. Garrett, McKenna, Kravitz, Chen, Browning, slide tray, O'Keefe, Dunn. He stopped, put them back in the order he had found them, and did it again.

"Give me a sec'," he said over his shoulder. "I just want to make sure all my charts are here."

He sat down at the desk. Closing his eyes, he took himself back to the phone call with Williams, to Lindsey Browning's slide that he'd been studying while they talked, and to the irritation he'd been feeling with the pathologist. He had put Lindsey Browning's slide in the cardboard tray, closed the lid, put the tray on top of her chart, and put both in the "Out" box at the same time. He would not have done it any other way. The tray was smaller than the chart, and he wouldn't have been able to hold the tray if it had been beneath. He took the tray and the chart and did it again. He opened the slide tray—the one slide was in the same slot that he remembered placing it in.

He put Dunn and O'Keefe's chart back in the "Out" box. One more time he took hold of Lindsey Browning's chart and the slide tray. He placed them on his desk, picked them up together, and put them in the box. Then Chen,

Kravitz, and McKenna. The only chart left was Garrett's. He opened it—the pathology report was still loose inside, waiting to be filed into the chart by Laurel. He put it back on top of the pile.

"Let's go," he said, still looking at his "Out" box, which was not in the order that he'd left it. "I'll call the manager again and see if he found out anything else from the crew chief."

Colleen didn't answer.

He turned around. Lights were blinking off in the exam rooms, then the nursing station. "I'll be outside," she called from the hallway.

*   *   *

Kendall called Sammie from the car. "Sorry to bother you at night," he said. "When you have a chance this weekend, will you run by the office and take a look around. Donny said someone was in there, but I can't see that's anything been taken. I don't want to wait until Monday to call the police if something is missing, though. Can you just swing by and make sure we're not missing any specimens or reports or instruments? . . . Sure, tomorrow is fine. I'll meet you there if you want. Just give me a call . . . . Yeah, check your work area carefully. See if anything's out of place . . . . Okay, thanks a lot."

They rode in silence for a while. When it became too uncomfortable, Kendall called Donny. "Hey, Donny. Have you heard anything else? . . . Yeah, about my age. That old, huh? . . . I know—don't worry about it. Thanks. Let me know if anything else comes up. I went by there and I think everything's okay . . . . Okay, thanks again."

Colleen was looking out the window. "Well?" she said.

"The workers aren't saying much. Donny thinks they're afraid."

"He told you something."

"They said it was a man. Sounds like about my age. White. Acted like he knew what he was doing."

She turned and looked at him. "What about your desk? What were you looking at?"

"Nothing, probably. They may have moved some stuff when they cleaned."

Colleen nodded and looked away. When she looked back, she said, "So what's the deal with this member-guest tournament? You've never played in it before."

"Right. And I'm fifty-one-years-old."

She nodded. "Fair enough." For a moment she was quiet, looking out the window. Then, "So what's going on, Ryan? Why do you need me to snoop on this guy? If he belongs to Hidden Glen, why don't you just ask Paul or Peter? They should know him."

"Nothing's going on. I am going to talk to them. I just wanted to give you the chance to check out his wife. If you don't like her it could be a long night."

"Yes, it could," she said slowly, still gazing out the window. "It could definitely be a long night."

TEN

Saturday, June 9

For Colleen, it in fact turned out to be a short conversation and a long night's sleep. They had watched the news for a while in bed, and then she'd abruptly turned on her side, back to him, and gone to sleep. He'd been awake until well past midnight. Garrett and Williams, Mancini and Kane, his office, his knee, Colleen. Without any good solutions for any of them, his mind had jumped from one to the other until it had tired and he'd finally fallen asleep.

When he woke, nothing had changed. He lay in bed, listening to the birds, an early dog barking down the street, the soft rushes of Colleen's breaths. Though he trusted her implicitly, at what point was it morally acceptable to question aloud another physician's most basic trusts? What if he were wrong? What if the reference form wasn't on Chad Williams? Even if there was a question about his membership at Hidden Glen, it did not necessarily mean that he was the "cheater" on the form. And it was certainly a long and almost preposterous stretch that Williams could be so worried about Lindsey Browning's missing slide that he would actually come to his office looking for it. Plus, Williams had been in his own office reading slides and dictating until nine o'clock.

Still asleep, Colleen rolled over in the bed to face him, as if she knew that he was thinking about her. So, he asked himself once again, when was the trust of his marriage worth more than the trust of another physician? What if he were to confide all of this to Colleen and he were wrong? What he would tell her could never be retracted and whether it was right or wrong, she would forever look at Chad Williams, and perhaps his wife, in a different way. Williams, as far as he knew, had done nothing wrong. Paranoid, yes. Spiteful, perhaps. But nothing in regards to this dreadful reference form, this most horrific of accusations whether it be professionally or socially, had yet to have any bones to it.

Someone knew the answer, though. Or at least they thought they did. And if indeed it was Paul Mancini, if in fact it was he who had sent him the reference form, then Mancini himself had undoubtedly struggled with the same question. True, he had tempered the transgression with white-out. Nevertheless, he had violated one of the most trusted processes at Hidden Glen Country Club, an institution with a hundred-year history and an unspoken honor code among its custodians.

When then? When did wrong become right? When was it okay with God, or whomever one looked to in the time of need, to cross the line? Wide awake now, Kendall got up and sat on the edge of the bed. A flock of sparrows zipped through the branches of the oak tree as if they were being chased, followed by two large crows. When the consequences of not crossing it were more dire than the transgression, he thought. In the end, whether the answer to the question came from a priest in reconciliation, or from a physician standing by an ICU deathbed, it was the same—wrong became right when the risk of inaction outweighed the risk of the action.

He stood and limped to the bathroom. Colleen he was still unsure about, although he felt the tensions of the past week as a tangible presence between them, a presence that had to be settled. Mancini he was not unsure about. He needed to call him. He needed to speak to him directly, frankly. For if Bob Williams was "the salt of the earth," then what was Chad?

* * *

He was sitting out on the deck reading the paper when Sammie called him at eight o'clock. "I'm going to the beach today so I went in early this morning," she said. "I don't think anything's missing, but someone was definitely in the nursing station going through stuff."

"How do you know?"

"'Cause I look around before I leave every day. Remember a couple of years ago when they changed cleaning people for a while and we were missing change and pens and all kinds of little stuff. They even caught one guy taking food out of the refrigerator."

"Yeah, sort of."

"Anyway, I look around before I leave. I like to know where things are."

"So what do you think they were going through?"

"Some of the path forms were moved. And we have that whole stack of charts that we're waiting for labs and path on. It wasn't where I left it. I don't know. Just some little things like that."

"Yeah, that's sort of what I thought. Oh well. Thanks for going in. Have fun."

"Are you going to call the police?"

"I don't think so. Nothing's missing that I can tell, and I don't want to get the cleaning crew involved if I don't have to."

"Okay. See you Monday."

He hung up and looked through the trees. Lindsey Browning was out in her back yard kicking a soccer ball into a regulation-sized goal her father had erected. He waved to her and she waved back. A moment later Mandy came tearing around the corner of the house chasing a squirrel, followed by Colleen who still had her on a leash. Colleen had gotten up at seven to take Mandy for a walk. One of the neighbor's dogs had died the day before in the heat, and she'd decided to give Mandy a break from the afternoon jaunts for a while.

Colleen loosed Mandy, who took off up the hill toward the trees as fast as she could run. Then turning toward the deck, she turned on the back hose, filled a watering can, and began to water the potted flowers that were on the steps to the deck. "I saw Wendy Pittman when I was walking," she said. "She lives up by the Walkers."

"I don't think I know her."

"I play tennis with her sometimes. She belongs to Hidden Glen. Anyway, I looked in her Club directory. Bunny is married to Chad, Janet is married to Sam, and Pat is married to Bob. So go ahead and invite him if you want. Bunny and I will be fine. The rest is up to you."

*   *   *

Around ten o'clock he moved into the shade and called Mancini.

"I was wondering when you'd get around to calling me. How's your knee? Peter said it wasn't good."

"So much for patient privacy. Are you familiar with HIPPA?"

"Yeah, well . . . I feel bad. We should have stopped playing. I should have stopped."

"It wouldn't have mattered. I just need to get it done. I'm going to call Peter today, actually. Hopefully it's just a small tear and I'll be as good as new before you know it."

"Where are you going to have it done?"

"Fairfield, I think. Peter likes it there. What else did he tell you?"

"Nothing much. That you're procrastinating."

"Wouldn't you?"

"I guess."

"Did he tell you about my member-guest tournament?"

"Yeah, he did mention that."

"Well?"

"I think you're being a little ambitious. That's a lot of golf."

"What about Chad Williams?"

Mancini was quiet for a moment. Deliberately so, thought Kendall.

"How well do you know Chad?" he finally said.

"I don't. That's why I'm asking. I started using their lab years ago when I first opened my practice. In fact, I think Peter's dad referred me to them. He's probably the same age as Bob. Anyway, back then, Sam used to sign out the skin stuff. Then Chad came and he started reading all the skin because he had just finished his fellowship. I think I told you that. He did a fellowship somewhere in Boston and then another one at the AFIP. I think I've only talked to him face-to-face once or twice though. At derm' meetings in town."

"Peter and Chad are the same age," said Mancini, "so Peter knows him pretty well. Both from the Club and from school."

"Chad went to St. Francis?" Kendall asked. "I wouldn't have guessed that."

"No, he went to Somerset. So did Bob and Sam. But you know how it is around here—all the kids get to know each other. They were in the same class, at least when they started, so they know a lot of the same people."

"What do you mean when 'they started'? Don't tell me he was held back. He's not stupid, is he? Jesus, you're scaring me."

"No, he's not stupid. At least I don't think he is. I don't know that he was ever on track to be a rocket scientist, but stupid, no."

"So what did you mean?"

"I don't really know the story. All I know is that he started at Somerset, but I don't think he graduated from there. He might have gone to boarding school."

Silence.

"So what about my question?" said Kendall.

"Which one?"

"About asking him to my member-guest tournament."

"I thought you talked to Peter about that."

"I did. I'm asking you."

"I think you should talk to Peter."

"I already talked to Peter."

"I think you should talk to him again."

* * *

Maureen Kane, Peter's wife, told him that Peter was in the emergency room at Fairfield Hospital. He'd been there all morning evaluating his eighty-year-old uncle who had fallen and broken his hip, and a ten-year-old girl who'd fractured her wrist playing soccer. She gave him her husband's cell phone number and said that would be Kendall's best bet.

When Peter had left the house, he'd told her he had no idea when he'd be home.

Kendall called Peter Kane's cell phone and left a message. No rush, he said. Call him when he had chance. He knew Peter was busy.

The sliding glass door opened behind him, and Matthew came out in gym shorts and a T-shirt. Kendall smiled. He hadn't seen him in two days.

"Hey, boy, where have you been?" he said. "The day's half over."

Matthew, a junior at Riverview High School, still looked half asleep. He was shielding his eyes from the sun, and looking around as if he hadn't ever seen the back yard at this hour of the morning.

"Where's Mandy? I'm going to kill her. She woke me up with all that barking."

"She's working on the squirrel population. She actually got one this morning."

"Gross."

"It wasn't pretty."

"And you let her lick your face?"

"I've had worse."

"Gross." Matthew pulled a chair into the shade and sat down. "Mom says your knee is really messed up now."

"Peter Kane's going to take a peek in it on Wednesday."

"You mean open it up?"

"Yeah."

"That sucks."

"Yep."

"So no more tennis or golf for a while, huh?"

"A little while. Hopefully not too long."

"Double suck."

"Yep."

"Geez, what are you going to do?"

"I don't know. Bother your mother."

He was quiet for a moment. "Who's going to cut the grass?"

"You."

"That's what I was afraid of."

Kendall's phone rang. It was Peter Kane from his cell. Kendall lifted a finger to Matthew and answered the call.

"Hey, Ryan," said Peter. "I've got the Fairfield OR schedule right in front of me. Shoot."

"Wednesday morning? Does that still work?"

"You've got it. First case. One of our staff will get some pre-op stuff over to you on Monday. You need to be here early—around six or so. I'd like to put you to sleep so I can fix anything that's there. Is that okay?"

"No local or twilight, huh?"

"We can do it that way if you want, but I'd rather put you to sleep."

"Okay."

"And you're going to take Thursday and Friday off, right?"

"Yes."

"Great. Anything else?"

"I know you're busy. If you have a minute this weekend would you give me a call?"

"I'm okay now. They're just taking my uncle to the OR. He tripped on the steps to the first tee this morning. Poor guy. It's a bad break, too."

"Geez, that's too bad. Maureen said he's eighty. Is that right?"

"Yeah, and he's really pissed, too. He had a big bet with the pro that he was going to shoot his age. He's already done it twice. So what's up?"

Kendall hesitated. Although clearly Peter had spoken with Mancini about their prior conversation, it still wasn't the easiest of subjects. "Well, Paul said maybe I ought to talk to you again. About Chad Williams. Forget the golf part. I'm more concerned about my patients."

"Right. Well, there are lots of pathologists in town, aren't there?

Jesus fucking Christ, Kendall said to himself. Then, "Well, sort of," he said slowly. "Skin is different, though. You need special training."

"There's always DermPath. That's where we send our skin when we take things off."

"Right. I use them some, too. Who do you use at Fairfield? I thought Chevy Chase did a lot of their pathology work."

"They do. For our group, though, the hospital sends it out to DermPath."

Jesus. Maybe he was the only guy in town who didn't think Chad Williams was a moron. "Okay," said Kendall. "So what happened with Chad at Somerset?"

Kane didn't answer right away. When he did, he seemed to have the same careful tone that he had the other day. "I don't know the whole story. All I know is he left about halfway through his second year. Maybe it was even his first year. I think his father tried to get him into St. Francis, but that didn't fly. He finished high school at some boarding school in Massachusetts."

"He must have done okay," said Kendall. "He went to Blakemore College, didn't he? I thought I remembered seeing that on some promotion they did once."

"He did. So did his father and his brother."

"Oh. And Washington Med?"

"The same."

"Residency?"

"Washington. They all trained there."

"I see."

"And he did a year of grad work between college and med school," added Kane. "While he waited to get in."

"Right."

"Anything else?" asked Kane. "I think they're ready for me upstairs."

"I don't think so. I think I've got the picture. I, uh, I feel like an idiot. I—"

"Hey, it's not your fault. Glad we could help. I'll see you Wednesday. Piece of cake—don't worry about it."

*   *   *

They ate dinner out on the deck that night. Colleen seemed to have put aside the letter and the trip to his office, and the only talk was of Kelley, Matthew, and the remains of the dead squirrel that Mandy had hid up in the bushes, presumably for a late night snack. The Brownings saw them out on the deck and came over for a glass of wine that turned into a bottle. Into her second glass, Donna dragged Lindsey over to show Kendall how great her nose looked. It had indeed healed well—the biopsy site was barely visible.

When the Brownings had left and it was dark and quiet except for the crickets and the gloating of the bullfrogs, Colleen asked him if he had decided about the member-guest tournament.

"Do you mean about Chad, or at all?" he said.

"Chad."

"Chad would be a no. Paul really wouldn't say, but Peter Kane didn't think it was such a hot idea."

"Good," she said. "Neither did Wendy."

ELEVEN

Monday, June 11

The call came from a number he did not recognize. He knew it was a Chevy Chase exchange, but it was a different number than any of the ones he remembered at Chevy Chase Pathology. He let it go through to voice mail. Most calls early on a Monday morning were patients needing to be worked into the schedule with acute problems, or patients canceling appointments. Either way, he was only a few minutes from his office, and Laurel or Sammie could take off the message, along with the other one he'd received about ten minutes before.

The phone rang again—same number. A minute later it rang again.

Kendall activated his hands-free receiver. "Dr. Kendall," he said. "May I help you?"

"Good morning, Doctor. Drew Garrett here."

"Good morning," said Kendall. "How can I help you, Mr. Garrett?"

"Drew, please. I'll still call you Doctor, but you can call me Drew."

"Okay. How can I help you, Drew?"

"My wife and I would like to meet with you today. We were hoping you'd be available around noon, or whenever you take a break for lunch. I'll pay you for your time, of course."

Jesus. He was fitting in patients all morning to clear his end-of-the week schedule, and he knew he'd be lucky to finish before one. But he could feel himself smiling, not so much with satisfaction as with relief. It was as if a sudden weight had suddenly been lifted from him and he could now go on with his life again. For the tone of Drew Garrett's voice was now unmistakable—he was scared and he wanted help.

"I'd be happy to meet with you and your wife. And I'm not concerned about getting paid. Could we possibly make it 12:30 or so? Monday mornings are usually a little hectic."

"We'll see you at 12:30, Doctor. Thank you in advance for your time."

Sammie was waiting for him. "I looked all around again," she said. "I don't think anything's missing."

"Okay," he said as they walked to his office. "Ask everyone else to check their space when they have a chance. And do me a favor, please. Call over to Chevy Chase and tell Robyn that I have to have the reports on Drew Garrett before noon. Tell her Dr. Williams dictated them Friday night."

"Friday night?" said Sammie.

"Right. It's a long story. And Mr. Garrett and his wife are coming in to see me today at 12:30, so I need to be done with patients by then."

"We'll do our best."

They reached his office and he put his briefcase down. "Hold on, don't leave. Two more things." He handed her his phone. "I have at least one message on there that's from a patient, I think. See if you can take care of that one. Mr. Garrett may have left a message also, but I've taken care of that."

Sammie was looking at him. "What's the second thing?"

"Try to keep me in the rooms closest to my office today," he said. "I'm not moving real well."

At his desk, Kendall took Garrett's chart from his "Out" box and put it back in his "In" box. He checked his voice mail—there were no new messages. He had a few minutes left before his first patient and he took out the *Washington Physicians Directory* and a piece of office letterhead. There were two surgeons to whom he referred most of his complicated melanomas. Both were experienced and skilled surgeons, and both were capable of performing the sentinel lymph node biopsy that Garrett was most likely going to require. He wrote down the two names, their addresses, and their telephone numbers. Garrett, he knew, was going to want all of this done as quickly as possible.

"Your first patient's ready, Dr. Kendall," said Sammie.

Kendall stood and gently flexed his knee. Though he knew it was going to be a crazy morning, a morning that just a little while ago he was dreading, he was now looking forward to it. Game time, he said to himself. Play to win.

*   *   *

His knee was throbbing by mid-morning and he went into his office for a quick break. Four e-mails: Mancini wishing him well on Wednesday; Peter Kane reminding him not to take any aspirin or anti-inflammatory drugs; Kane's OR scheduler with pre-operative forms attached to the e-mail; Colleen saying that the more she thought about it, the less she liked the idea of this member-guest tournament no matter who he took. Funny, he thought. She who ran in the ninety-degree heat was worried about his knee.

His desk phone said he had messages. The first was from Chad Williams. The reports had been printed and he'd get them over right away. He was still worried about the size of the excision that Petersen had done on Drew Garrett. Was Petersen really that incompetent? Didn't he know that a 1.33 millimeter melanoma needed a wide surgical excision and a sentinel lymph node biopsy? They all had their names on this case and Petersen was going to screw it up. Maybe Kendall should call him before they all got sued. And oh, by the way, he'd been planning his week and had been over at Fairfield Hospital looking at the OR schedule. There was a Ryan Kendall scheduled for Wednesday morning in room eight for arthroscopy under general anesthesia. His dad had told him the other day that Kendall was having a problem with his knee and most likely was going to need a 'scope. Was that him? If it was, sorry. He had a good surgeon though—Peter Kane was one of the best in town.

The second message was from Will Ammerman. He'd received the case that Felix Kozloff had sent up from Duke over the weekend. As an aside, he said, he didn't really like looking at outside materials without the initial pathology report or a preliminary diagnosis from the consulting physician. He liked to know what the issues were. He understood that the patient wanted him to look at the slides and give an opinion without being biased, but he always did that anyway. Nevertheless, Felix was a good friend and he'd gone ahead and read the slides. He'd already called Felix with a verbal report, but since Kendall's name was on the request as one of the consulting physicians, he wanted to let him know that it definitely was a spindle-cell melanoma, and he wouldn't be surprised if clinically it was amelanotic, since there was only a trace of pigment in the specimen. He had measured it at 1.32 mm, and although it wasn't a full-thickness biopsy, he didn't think it was any deeper than that. But it did have a vertical growth phase and a high mitotic rate, so he'd probably be pretty aggressive with treating it. Call him if Kendall had any questions. A written report would be issued by the end of the day. Oh, and before he forgot, he'd actually like to use the case for his book. He wanted to cut some new slides, though. The ones he had received were certainly good enough to read, but he wanted some better ones for the photomicrographs. Did Kendall know who had the tissue block? Could he possibly help him get it? Thanks.

Duke, thought Kendall as he hung up. He'd suspected that Garrett had had some help in navigating the complexities of the labs and the reports. He did not know the name Felix Kozloff, but other than Will Ammerman, he didn't know many dermatopathologists outside of the Washington, D.C. area. He was sure he would find out more about Dr. Kozloff shortly, though. Mr. and Mrs. Garrett were due in his office in two hours.

Sammie looked upset when he went back out to the exam rooms. "What's the matter?" he said. "We're pretty much on schedule."

"I called over to Chevy when you took your break. Robyn's gone. One of the other girls said she quit, but I don't believe that for a second. I bet he fired her. She said he was going crazy about that slide and he kept saying that she better find it."

"That's too bad," said Kendall. "I liked Robyn. She was always great on the phone."

"You should hire her," said Sammie. "I bet she'd be great."

*   *   *

Drew Garrett offered him a wan smile when Laurel brought him and his wife back to Kendall's office at 12:40. "Thanks for seeing us today," he said. "We know you're busy. I brought the boss."

"That's what we're here for," said Kendall, shaking his hand, and then his wife's. "I'm Caroline," she said. "I'm really glad I finally have the chance to meet you."

As expected, she was an attractive woman, probably Garrett's age, who looked as fit and healthy as he did. As expected, she also looked as if she'd been crying recently, perhaps as recently as a few minutes ago.

Kendall sat in his desk chair facing them.

"You know, Doc'," said Garrett, "this isn't quite what I had in mind last week. I was just trying to make Caroline happy."

"I know. It's not what I had hoped for either. But all we can do now is go forward. Let's just be grateful that she sent you in."

Garrett nodded, the slightest trace of a glaze in his eyes.

"So, Dr. Kendall," said Caroline, "we realize that we've probably made some mistakes since Drew last saw you. We're past them so to speak, and we hope that you can start fresh with us. We'd like you to help us get this taken care of. Right, Drew?"

Garrett nodded. "Have you spoken with anyone at Chevy Chase Pathology Associates?" he asked.

"Dr. Williams," said Kendall.

"How about at American Laboratories?"

"No. But Dr. Williams did."

"I figured that. So you know about Friday?"

"I think so."

"We got a little hyper'," he said, with a trace of a sheepish grin. "We got a lot accomplished, but I don't want that to scare you off. We don't work at the same pace that some of these labs obviously do. Frankly, I wouldn't have any clients if I did, but that's a different matter."

"I understand," said Kendall. "It drives me nuts, too. Have you seen your reports?"

Garrett nodded. "I have a couple of questions, but overall they seem pretty straightforward. I'm getting to be an expert."

"So tell me about Duke," said Kendall. "Who's Dr. Kozloff?"

"My brother Dan is a hematologist down there," said Caroline. "Dr. Kozloff is one of their pathology specialists. Dan had him look at all of Drew's slides. In fact, my understanding is that several people in the department looked them. They all agreed about the diagnosis."

Coast to coast, this communal sharing of microscopic material was a ritual repeated in pathology departments every day, whether with a simple two-headed microscope, or a teaching behemoth that allowed ten sets of eyes to look at a single slide. For although the vast majority of human pathology was easily recognized and named, sometimes, no matter how many tens of thousands of slides a pathologist had reviewed, the genetic cesspool created an anomaly that defied every attempt to label it. Two sets of eyes then were always better than one, and often it was even more. Even expert pathologists like Kozloff and Ammerman were prone to these group intellectual dissections. Often it was in the name of teaching, but Kendall sometimes wondered if it was more to share the blame in the rare instances that they erred.

"So did the specialist in New York," said Kendall. "Are you aware of that?"

Caroline blinked hard several times. "No, we hadn't heard that yet. Dan told me he was overnighting the slides up there, but we hadn't heard anything."

Kendall worked the days in his head. "How did the slides get to Duke so fast?"

"We drove down there Friday night," said Caroline. "Dr. Kozloff looked at them Saturday morning and I guess he sent them out that afternoon. They said they could do the surgery and everything else down there, too, but we just didn't want to do that. This is our home."

"Okay, Doc', so who's the best in town? Let's get going."

"Well, here's what needs to be done. As you know, the area needs to be definitively excised. What Dr. Petersen did was only a temporizing procedure. Because of the depth of the tumor, the surgeon will also probably want to do a sentinel lymph node biopsy, which I know you've read about. It's potentially a little more complicated on the back, but they'll still probably want to do it. I also think you should see an oncologist and have a PET scan. Do you have an internist?"

Garrett shook his head no. "I've never needed one."

"We'll get you one. So here's who I like to use . . ."

Ten minutes later, he handed Drew Garrett the names of the surgeons and the names of two internists and two oncologists that he had added to the list. He had starred his first choice for each and he also told Garrett that he would call those offices as soon as they were done here and tell them that Garrett would be calling. "See what kind of appointments you can work out," said Kendall, "and I'll touch base with you later today. I'll call them again or the other offices if you're having a hard time getting in." He looked at each of them. "Any questions?"

"Why did you say the lymph node part was harder on the back?" asked Caroline.

"Because the lymph drainage on the back isn't as clear-cut as say on the arm or the leg. The sentinel lymph node, or the first lymph node that drains that area, may not be as accessible."

Caroline stared at him blankly.

"It might be inside the chest," said Kendall. Then, when it was quiet, he said: "I do have one question if you don't mind. Out of curiosity, why'd you pick Dr. Petersen? If you wanted a second opinion, I would have been happy to give you several names."

The Garretts looked at each other. "It was all just a shock," said Drew. "I thought you were nuts about this spot and my sun damage."

"And I wanted him to get a second opinion on those other moles," said Caroline. It's my fault. One of my friends said he was great. She loves him." She shook her head in true disbelief. "How does that happen? I mean, how does someone like that stay in practice and get a good reputation?"

Kendall nodded thoughtfully. "Because he makes you feel good," he said. "He tells you what you want to hear."

"It's not your fault, Caroline," said Garrett. "I should have looked him up before I went. He's got quite a rap sheet," he added, looking at Kendall and then at the floor. "Pretty stupid on my part. Oh well. Live and learn."

"We'll get you through this," said Kendall. "One step at a time. I'll call you later today." He rose from his chair, as did Caroline, but Drew Garrett stayed put.

"What about the other guy, Doc'?" he said, the contriteness from just a moment before now gone. "There's a discrepancy in the reports about my other moles."

Kendall looked at him and sat back down. "Which other guy?"

"Dr. Williams," said Garrett. "You said you thought he was good, but I don't know what to think any more. That Petersen asshole is on every best doctors list around here."

"I think Dr. Williams is a good dermatopathologist," Kendall said carefully. "Honestly, sometimes he's a little too careful, so with the initial report on your back, just because of the diagnosis, I would have recommended getting a second opinion. And just so you know, I would have recommended Dr. Ammerman in New York, which is where Dr. Kozloff sent the slides. You did that on your own, which is great. So, I don't think there's any question about that diagnosis since we now have two expert consultations that agree with everything he said. In regards to your other moles, there was a slight difference of opinion, but unfortunately that's not that uncommon."

Garrett stared at him. Answer the question, his look said.

Kendall paused, trying to formulate in his mind a rational explanation of an inexact science. The microscopic pathologic examination of human tissue was one of the last in laboratory medicine that was left to the human eye and brain. It was still part science, part art, and part judgment. There was no computer to fall back on, no machine to analyze and compute. It was the just the pathologist and the slide—mano y mano.

"This is not the same as putting a tube of blood into a computerized machine," said Kendall. "It's a person looking at a pattern under a microscope and constructing his or her own opinion. That's not to say it's a random process—normal tissue has a repeatable and orderly appearance, and most cancers are fairly clear-cut. There are gray areas though, such as atypical or dysplastic moles, where the lesions aren't cancer per se, but they're not quite normal either. The pathologists don't like taking chances with these, so depending on their comfort level, some moles are read out as normal and some are read out as mildly atypical. When they're only mildly atypical like yours and the margins are clear, I usually leave them alone."

Garrett's face had hardened as Kendall spoke, and by the time Kendall was finished there was a flush in his cheeks. Looking at the man, Kendall could not help but see Williams in his mind as well—Williams flushed with anger over the forty-eight slides delivered to his office on Friday afternoon. They were even about the same age, he figured.

"Do you know Dr. Williams?" asked Kendall. "He grew up around here, too."

Garrett looked at him with surprise. As if only attorneys knew how to use Internet searches. "I know who he is," he said. "Call me later. I want to get going on this."

TWELVE

Tuesday, June 12

Kendall got to his office early. With his knee surgery less than twenty-fours away, and the realities of leaving his office for three days piling up, there was plenty to do.

Sammie arrived a few minutes later. The door to his office was open and he could hear her putting her purse away, unlocking the cabinets, taking the instruments out of the autoclave. Then she was in his office and next to his desk with a yellow sticky-note in her hand. She gave him a smile and stuck it on his blotter.

"I think you ought to call her," she said. "She'd be a lot better than that temp' who's helping Laurel out up front. She could help with the billing, too. Karen gets behind sometimes."

Kendall looked at the note with Robyn's name and phone number.

"Do you know her?"

"Not really. She seems real nice, though. And like you said, she's always been very helpful."

Kendall nodded. "I'll call her."

"You have nothing to lose," said Sammie on the way out. "That girl up front is a cretin."

He caught up with his dictation and lab reports. With his e-mail and phone messages clear, he made a list of things to do for the day. Drew Garrett was at the top. Garrett had made considerable progress the day before. With the introductions from Kendall, he'd managed to get an appointment with an internist this morning, and a surgical consultation in the afternoon. He needed some more help with the oncologist and the PET scan, and Garrett was hoping he could get that scheduled for him on Wednesday. He added Robyn to the list, and then after a moment, Will Ammerman.

Ten minutes before his first patient. He called the oncologist's office, but their phones didn't turn over until nine o'clock. He looked at his list—Robyn was next and Sammie's yellow note was still there staring him in the face. If nothing else, he thought, Sammie was right about the temp' working out front. That was a problem he needed to fix.

Robyn did not seem surprised to hear from him. "Hi, Dr. Kendall. Thanks for calling. I talked to Sammie for a while yesterday. She's so nice."

"Yes, she is. Listen," he said, "I'm sorry to hear about you leaving Chevy Chase. I guess I'm still a little unclear about what happened. Did you quit or were you fired?"

"Probably a little of both. I just couldn't take it anymore. I mean, I don't want to speak badly about anyone, and I have a lot of respect for Dr. "C," but this whole slide thing is making him crazy."

"You mean the slide that's missing?"

"Right. He's told me a hundred times now that he's never lost a slide in his life. And although he hasn't come right out and said it, he obviously thinks I lost it. I think he thinks I sent it out to your office by mistake, but I didn't. I know I put it on his desk in a tray."

"What's the big deal? He has the tissue block. He can always cut more slides."

"Believe me, I know that. And so does everyone else. He says it's just the principle of it. That their reputation is built on trust and if they look sloppy no one will ever send them cases. He's always worried about that, you know." Robyn paused. "He's a little different about those things."

"What do you mean?"

"Oh, just about all the paperwork and the technicians and everything. He's a real micromanager. He's always checking the slides and he won't even let poor Yvonne—she's the receptionist—put together the consultations he sends out. He does it all himself. I don't know—maybe it's normal. I'm just comparing him to the other doctors. They're much more laid back. They just come to the office and read their slides and go home. Dr. 'B' called me last night, actually. That's the father."

"Why did he call you?" asked Kendall when she didn't elaborate.

"He likes me. I think he's pretty upset about me leaving. I've been there eight years, you know. That's a long time. Longer than anyone else, I think."

"Does he want you to come back?"

"I think he's going to talk to Dr. 'C,' but honestly, I'm not sure if I want to go back."

"I understand. Well, we're looking for some help up front and maybe in the billing office. Do you want to give it a try over here?"

"Sure, I'd love too."

"I'm going to be out the rest of the week. Why don't you take a few days off and start next Monday. Does that work?"

"Sure. Thanks, Dr. Kendall. I really appreciate it. I can't afford to be out of work."

"See you Monday. Try not to worry about it."

Maybe we'll see you Monday, Kendall said to himself as hung up. Bob Williams had been running an office for a long time, and he knew that good staff were hard to find. In addition, the senior Williams was a genuinely nice and sincere man. Mancini had formally introduced them in the locker room the day Kendall had injured his knee and they'd had a few minutes to chat. Bob Williams would surely speak with his son and try to get Robyn to come back.

Chad Williams was a bigger question. The more Kendall learned about him, the odder he seemed. And he still didn't understand why he was making such a big deal about the slide. Okay, so maybe it wasn't a very atypical Spitz Nevus. Maybe he was taking careful to a ridiculous extreme. Paranoia wasn't the worst sin for a doctor. None of them wanted to see the Drew Garretts of the world anywhere but in their own office.

Still, it did not sit right. One disease, he thought. Not two or three or four. And still there was that letter, sitting in his desk, lurking like a hidden rattlesnake. He added Mancini to his list. The judge was going to have to step up to the plate.

*   *   *

Joseph McKenna, his 10:30 surgery appointment, had suffered a minor myocardial infarction over the weekend and canceled his appointment. Kendall asked Sammie to get him when his next patient was ready and then limped to his office. He crossed Robyn off his list, called Will Ammerman, and got his voice mail. He thanked Ammerman for the phone call the day before and told him that he already had the patient hooked up with a surgeon. The tissue block he was not sure about. They might still have it down at Duke, but it was also possible that the patient had it. He would find out and try to get back to him today. He also had a personal favor to ask, but he'd go over that with him when he called again.

He hung up and immediately dialed the office of Dr. Hector Fernandez, an oncologist with offices in northwest D.C. and Bethesda. The receptionist was happy to accommodate Drew Garrett first thing Wednesday morning in the D.C. office and agreed that Dr. Fernandez was most likely going to order a PET scan, and perhaps a chest CT scan. Better to schedule both and cancel them if need be, she said. She scheduled Garrett's appointment for nine-fifteen, the PET scan for eleven o'clock, and the CT scan for one o'clock.

Kendall was feeling good about the Garretts and wanted to let them know. Hopefully they were between appointments. The day before the Garretts had given him all of their phone numbers which were now stored in his phone. He dialed Caroline's cell phone. Caroline, he knew by now, took care of all of the scheduling.

She answered, but her voice was hushed. "We're in the lab getting his pre-op bloodwork," she said. "After that he's going for an EKG and a chest x-ray, and then we're headed to Dr. Uhle's office for the surgical appointment."

Kendall gave her the appointment times for Wednesday.

"That's great," she said. "I can't tell you how much we appreciate it."

"A couple more things," said Kendall. "Do you have a minute?"

"Yes. We're still waiting for the lab tech' to draw his blood."

"Dr. Ammerman, the specialist in New York who did the second consult, would like to make a few more slides. He needs the tissue block to do that though."

"Why?" said Caroline immediately, a trace of hope in her voice. "Does he see something different?"

"No, I'm sorry, I didn't mean to imply that. He runs a teaching program, and it's an instructive case for the residents." Caroline was in no frame of mind to handle the concept of her husband's cancer being a case worthy of being entered into a pathology textbook. He'd deal with that after Garrett's surgery.

"That's okay, I guess," she said.

"Do you know who has the tissue block? Drew checked it out of Chevy Chase Pathology last Friday."

"I'm not sure I know what you mean, but we have a bag of papers and slides at home. I'll look later if you tell me what I'm looking for."

"It's a plastic cassette, about half the size of a credit card. One end will be tapered and the other end should have some numbers written on it. Actually, if you look at the initial report from Dr. Williams, the numbers on the cassette should match up with the accessioning number on the report. There will also be a small block of wax stuck in the middle of the cassette. That's where the tissue is."

"Oh. That's why they told me not to let it get hot. I guess the wax will melt."

"Right."

"I'll look later. Do you want me to call you?"

"Sure. It's probably best if you call my cell phone. That's the second thing. I'm not sure if I told you or not, but I'm having a minor surgical procedure done tomorrow morning and I'll be out of the office for the rest of the week. We can keep talking by phone, though. Either on my cell or at home. You have both numbers. I should be home by early afternoon tomorrow."

"I'm sorry. Are you okay?"

"Yes, thank you. It's just my knee."

"Okay, I'll call you. They're ready for Drew—I need to go."

*　　*　　*

At 6:00 PM he was almost ready to leave the office. His "In" box was clear, he'd made all of the necessary phone calls on pathology reports and laboratory results, Sammie had cleared his "Out" box, and his desk was clean. The only unfinished business was the remnants of his list.

He was thinking about Mancini when his desk phone rang. It was Will Ammerman.

"Hey, Ryan, I got your message. That would be great if you could get me the block. That's not a good tumor. Let's hope for the best."

Burn, tighten. "I'll get it for you, Will, and again, thanks for everything. Listen, I hate to put you on the spot, but I have this difficult situation here that I need to try and resolve."

"Shoot. How can I help you?"

"It's Chad Williams. I've been sending him cases for years, and overall I think he's done a pretty good job. He might be a little careful, maybe even paranoid, but it hasn't really been a problem. But I really need some help now. I've had a couple of problems with his lab, and I'm not so sure I trust him anymore. I've got a lot of years left here, if you know what I mean."

"Sure, I know what you mean. Umm, what can I say? The cases he sends me are generally fairly clear-cut, so I think he is on the cautious side. As far as him personally, I've only met him once or twice at conferences, so I don't know what else I can tell you in that regard either."

"He did his path' residency at Washington Medical School," said Kendall, "and my understanding is he did one fellowship in Boston and another at the AFIP. I'm sorry to put you on the spot, but I was hoping you might know someone at one of those places who you could touch base with. I'm just curious about what he was like during his training. I seem to be the only one down here who doesn't know that maybe he's not the sharpest tool in the shed."

Ammerman was quiet. Doctors did not do well dealing with the inadequacies of other doctors.

"I know it's a tough question, Will, but this is serious business. I can't be worrying about my reports for the next ten years."

"I can make a few calls," said Ammerman. "No problem. I'll give you a call later in the week. Is that okay?"

"Sure, Will, that's great. Thanks."

Mancini was still in his office.

"Are you ready?" said the judge.

"As ready as I'll ever be."

"You'll be fine. Peter's great."

"Do you have a minute? I need to ask you something."

"Sure. What's up?"

"Well, let's just say that I'm this dumb doctor, which I am, and I don't really know anything about snooping or things like that. And let's just say that I was curious about someone, say about where they were at a certain time, say maybe whether they were in a certain office building or not. And let's say that office building was in town, say Wisconsin Avenue, perhaps even the same building with Bob Williams' path' lab, and that maybe it had cameras in the lobby or outside, or that there was a guard in the lobby, or that there was some way to check and see if this person had left that building. How would someone like me go about trying to find that out? What would someone need to look at the video or the logs or whatever?"

"How long ago are you speaking about? Surveillance cameras only have so much memory. And a lot of them aren't even real—they're just for show."

"Last Friday night."

"I don't know. I'd have to check with one of the state's attorneys. How about if I do that and get back to you?"

"That would be great. I'd appreciate it."

"Give me a time window so I can be more exact when I speak with one."

Kendall picked up his cell phone and scrolled through his "Received" calls. Williams had called at 8:42. "Between six and nine."

"Good luck," said Mancini. "I'll call you."

Kendall hung up, crossed Ammerman and Mancini off his list, and sat back in his chair. Paranoia, maybe he could accept. But spite, and perhaps deception, or even downright lies, he could not. Something had to give.

He picked up the phone and called Chad Williams' back line. As he had hoped, Williams was gone. He listened to Chad's voice-mail message, then left his own.

"Hey, Chad, sorry I missed you. Just wanted to let you know that I may have found your slide. I think the temp' we have up front put it in the wrong lab box when it came in, and it might have been sent back to that lab because Laurel thought it was a mistake. Anyway, I'm going to be out of the office for a couple of days. My staff will be looking into it. If that's what happened, we'll get it back and then I'll get it back to you. Sorry. Talk to you soon."

THIRTEEN

Wednesday, June 13

It was still dark outside when they left their house. The neighborhood streets were quiet and most of the houses were still unlit. He drove slowly, deliberately, curving their way through one wooded housing development after another. Along the way they passed only a solitary runner and a group of deer grazing nonchalantly in a front yard flowerbed. When they reached River Road, he stopped and turned toward the city. Fairfield Hospital was technically within the D.C. limits, but just barely. It was in reality a suburban hospital with a city address.

With each mile the traffic increased, and by the time the hospital came into view, though it was only just light enough to see past the arcs of the streetlights, the roads were full of cars. With the third worst traffic in the nation, much of the city and its outlying suburbs got an early start.

"You're being awfully quiet," said Colleen.

"Yeah," said Kendall. "It's not like we're going fishing, you know."

"It's going to be fine, Ryan. You have to try and relax."

"It's easier being the doctor."

"I'm sure it is. It's good for you."

"Probably," he said after a moment.

They pulled into the patient parking lot and she put a hand on his arm. "Relax. We'll be out of here in a few hours, and then you can concentrate on getting better."

Kendall turned off the engine and faced her. "I know," he said. "It's just different when you've been there on the other side. You know everything that can go wrong."

Colleen lifted his chin with an index finger and smiled at him. "Half-full, remember?"

Kendall gave her a forced smile.

"Actually, I was thinking some more about that member-guest," she said. "I know what I said the other day, but if your knee is okay, maybe you should play in it. We're not getting any younger."

"We'll see."

"Think about it."

Kendall looked at her, took a deep breath, and unbuckled his seat belt. "Game time," he said. "Let's go."

The check-in area for outpatient surgery was already busy. Many surgeries that only a few years ago would have required an overnight stay were now done routinely on an outpatient basis, and the waiting area was full of imminent rhinoplasties, tonsillectomies, arthroscopies, and hernia repairs. There were mothers holding children as young as two and eighty-year-olds struggling with the clipboards and forms. Kendall took a clipboard from the receptionist and they took seats directly across from the check-in desk close to the entrance. Between the two of them, they were done with the necessary paperwork within a few minutes and he gave it back to the receptionist. Take a seat and his name would be called, she told him without looking up.

The preoperative suite was off an entrance that led to the east wing of the hospital. The east wing housed the emergency room, the operating rooms, and both the surgical and medical intensive care units. The staff parking lot was directly outside the east entrance doors, and the physician's lounge was down the hall and around the corner. Kendall knew his way around from the many conferences he'd attended there, and he also knew most of the medical staff through the conferences, various medical societies, and patient interactions. He also took care of many of their families.

He sat down for a minute next to Colleen, then stood and looked through the glass squares in the waiting room door. It was 6:30, and the physician traffic through the east entrance was noticeably picking up. He watched Doctors Karpinski, Latimer, Jaggers, and Sullivan hurry through. He moved closer so that he could see out the entrance as well. Peter Kane was coming up the sidewalk, briefcase in one hand, cell phone to his ear in the other. Kendall started to push through the door, then stopped. Peter was focused and obviously in a hurry.

"Sir, would you mind taking a seat," said the receptionist. "You're in the way there."

Kendall moved around the corner from her and looked out the window. Victor Pablo, Janice Abood. For a moment he was jealous, missing the early morning operating room banter and camaraderie. Solo practice was a lonely endeavor at times, absent of the people and the energy of the hospital.

Tony Pecora, Jennifer Cantwell. A black Lexus pulled in and he watched Thomas McCarey, the most senior and respected general surgeon in town, get out of his car. McCarey was tall and slim, with an angular face and a full head of white hair. He walked steadily towards the doors, a briefcase in his left hand, his right hand clasped over his left wrist in front of him. Watching him, clad in a navy blue blazer and tie, his gaze on the ground in front of him, Kendall thought he could just as easily be walking up the steps of St. Benedict's Catholic Church where Kendall knew he attended mass every Sunday, and every other day of holy obligation. McCarey paused about ten yards before the doors and adjusted his tie. Then for another few seconds he stayed there, his right hand back over his left, his briefcase held in front of his legs, his gaze still down towards the ground. Kendall moved his face right up to the window. McCarey was praying, he thought. Before he went through these sacred doors. Before he began his day of work. He who had seen every bodily miscreation that God could think of, he who had witnessed every misfortune that vehicles or falls or violent human beings could inflict, was praying to God.

Kendall was so engrossed in watching him that he almost did not see Bob Williams come along side and pat him on the back in greeting. There was another man behind Williams, twenty to twenty-five years or so younger, but without a doubt cast from the same gene pool. Though Kendall did not remember ever having met Sam Williams, this must be him, he thought. Then they were gone.

He moved away from the window, hoping that Chad was not soon behind them. Kendall had no desire to discuss the missing slide or Garrett or anything else related to the youngest Williams pathologist at the moment. Recalling Chad's message from the other day, though, he presumed Chad would probably be at the hospital this morning. The morning OR crunch was when most of the tissue specimens and frozen sections were generated.

The receptionist now had a line in front of her. He moved to the side of her desk, behind an entire family waiting with a crying toddler, and looked at the OR schedule taped to the wood laminate. He was looking at it upside down, so it took a few seconds to get oriented. There he was: Ryan Kendall at 7:00 AM in Room 8; arthroscopy with possible meniscus/ ligament repair; general anesthesia/Burke. Ed Burke, one of the senior anesthesiologists, was Peter's doing, he thought. Kendall knew that Peter and Ed were good friends, and that Ed was his anesthesiologist of choice.

A heavy-set nurse wearing a surgical cap and scrubs came into the room holding a clipboard. "Dr. Kendall?" she asked, looking around.

He turned to face her and raised his hand.

"Come on back," she said. "Let's get you ready to go. Dr. Kane wants to start right at seven."

Colleen had stood when she came in. "You can come too," said the nurse. "Then you can go to the surgical waiting room when he goes back to the OR."

They followed her to a large room with multiple cubicles partitioned by heavy green drapes. The room doubled as the preoperative dressing room and the outpatient postoperative recovery room. She gave him a hospital gown and within minutes he was on a bed and she was bending over him slipping an intravenous line into his arm.

"No meds?"

"Nope."

"No allergies?"

"Nope."

"Nothing to eat or drink after midnight?"

"Nope."

"Do you have any questions?"

"Nope."

"Okay. All set? Dr. Burke's waiting for you inside. He'll go over a few more things with you." The nurse handed Colleen a bag with his clothes and told her how to get to the waiting room.

Colleen leaned over and kissed him. "Relax," she said, patting his arm. "I'll see you in just a little bit."

Then they were moving, the gurney sliding on the gleaming tiled floor, the fluorescent overhead lights so bright he had to turn his head. A set of broad double-doors opened and they were into the operating suite proper, everyone now in scrubs and surgical hats, masks hanging around their neck. He could see a large bank of x-ray reading lights to the left, with a group standing in front of a row of black films and someone pointing to a large bone. Peter was there, he thought, but he wasn't sure.

They turned a corner and stopped in a holding area next to another rolling bed. Two more nurses appeared and helped him move to the new bed. One checked the intravenous line in his arm; the other checked the clipboard hanging on the end.

"Dr. Kendall, right?" she said. "Social number 217-67-9845?"

"Right."

"Dr. Kane is working on your left knee today?"

"Correct."

She took a label and wrote left knee in big blue letters on a label and stuck it on his leg.

Ed Burke was suddenly there, standing beside him, his hand on his arm. "Hi, Ryan. Long time no see."

"Hey, Ed."

"It's fun being the patient, huh?"

"It's a blast."

"Do you need to pee or anything?"

Kendall shook his head no.

"All right, let's go. Room eight," he said to one of the nurses. Then, patting Kendall on the shoulder, "I'll meet you there in just a minute."

Peter Kane was indeed in the group standing by the X-rays. He waved to Kendall as they rolled past.

The operating room was even brighter and he shielded his eyes. Before he knew it he was next to the table and moving again, this bed rigid, harder. He looked to the bank of lights on the wall and recognized his own x-ray films. The operating room scrub nurse was talking to him. She verified one more time that it was his left knee that Kane was "scoping" and started scrubbing it with Betadine.

He let his head fall back to the table, then lifted it as the swinging double-doors opened and a nurse backed in pulling a tray of anesthesia medications and equipment. A gurney rolled by in the hall, followed by a nurse holding a tray of tissue specimen bottles. The doors closed, then opened again. Ed Burke walked in, followed by Peter Kane. They stood on either side of him looking down, surgical caps covering their hair, masks over their mouths. Kendall could tell that they were smiling at him behind the masks, and Peter was saying something to him, but he didn't hear him. His mind was on the specimen bottles, on where they were going, on who was going to process what was put into them, on who was going to read the slides.

"I saw Bob and Sam Williams come in this morning," said Kendall, looking at Peter Kane.

"They read a lot of the frozen sections," said Kane.

"What about Chad? Is he here much?"

Kane looked at Ed Burke. "Not as much as he used to be. What do you think, Ed, once a month maybe?"

"Sounds about right. A lot of the skin cancers that they used to do here are done out in the offices with Mohs surgery now."

Kendall's face was getting warm, and he knew he must be flushing. Planning his week. Room eight. Why did

Chad Williams care? Why did Mancini care and send him that letter? Why would Paul Mancini, on track to be the most influential judge in the state of Maryland, soon to be President of Hidden Glen Country Club, violate his conscience, his club, his God? One disease, not two.

"What's the matter, Ryan?" said Ed Burke. "Are you okay?"

Kendall nodded.

"You look a little hot. Are you getting faint?"

Kendall shook his head no. "I'm okay."

"Because he's a cheater," a friend of Chad himself, or perhaps his father, had written. "I'd talk to Peter again," Mancini had said. And even this Wendy woman, this friend of Colleen's, what could she possibly know?

Kane was shaking his arm. "I'm going to go ahead and fix it if it needs it, okay?"

Kendall nodded.

"He's going crazy," Robyn had said.

Ed Burke looked down at him. "I'm going to give you a little 'vitamin V' now."

Versed, Kendall knew. He'd be in never-never land in seconds.

"Umm," said Kendall. "I, uh . . ."

Kane was nodding at Burke. Burke looked down at him again, and then his face turned fuzzy, faint. Kendall could hear the clatter of instruments, but everything else was getting dark. A warm glow spread through him and the noises faded. For a few seconds he thought he had never felt so wonderful in his entire life. His head was moving, tilting. Then came a ripping and tearing deep in his neck Then again, and somewhere in the most primordial layer of his consciousness he felt himself bucking. But nothing seemed to be moving. Not his eyes, his arms, his legs. There was something in his windpipe, tearing and pushing its way in, and he screamed, but no one heard him. He felt himself bursting inside, bucking against the pain. And then there were voices over his head.

"What the fuck?"

"Jesus, Ed, what's the matter?"

"I don't know. He's not getting the gas. He's not asleep. Goddamn it!"

He felt a hand on his arm, then his chest, trying to keep him down. His throat was on fire, choking him, but his eyes would not open. He screamed, he thought. Air, he needed air. He bucked and bucked.

"Hold him down, goddamnit! Give me the Fentanyl from the cart, Patty! Hurry up! I've gotta put him out! I've gotta get this tube in!"

Pressure on his arm, his chest. His head pushing against a wall, his throat on fire. A knife went into his arm. The pressure faded. Then he felt the air, sweet blessed air. Then, darkness.

FOURTEEN

Someone was leaning over him. He blinked several times and the face slowly came into focus. It was Ed Burke, just a foot from his face, staring into his eyes. Burke must have seen something that he liked, for he smiled and put a hand on his arm. It was a warm, thankful smile. Unusual, thought Kendall, both for Burke and a simple arthroscopy. Later he would realize that Burke was simply grateful that Kendall's pupils had constricted with the first rays of light passing through to his retinas as they were supposed to do. Burke was simply grateful that his pupils were not fixed and dilated.

He coughed. His windpipe burned and his throat ached. He'd had general anesthesia once before and did not remember this pain. His field of vision broadened and he saw that there was a group of masked people standing around his bed. Kane was there, his forehead pale, his eyes filled with worry. The rest of the group he did not recognize. A tall man came up beside him and looked down, his deep blue eyes steady and gentle. Tom McCarey, he realized. Why in the name of God was Tom McCarey standing over his bed? And looking at him with his emergency room eyes? Looking back at McCarey, he sensed suddenly that something had gone terribly wrong and he tried to lift his head. McCarey put a hand on his forehead and calmed him. Then he patted his arm and moved away.

"There was a problem, Ryan," said Burke. "Can you hear me?"

Kendall moved his head. It was pounding, the blood rushing through it in deafening waves.

"There was a problem with the anesthetic—we couldn't get you to sleep right away. Your trachea and your throat probably hurt like hell."

Kendall lifted his head an inch, put it back. He wiggled his fingers, his toes.

"We think you're okay." Burke's face turned hard, his eyes full of anger. "The hoses weren't holding gas—we think someone tampered with them. Squeeze my hand."

Kendall squeezed his hand.

"What day is it?" asked Burke.

"Wednesday," Kendall managed, the breath burning as it came out.

"Where are we?"

"Fairfield."

Burke nodded. "Let's get you out of here. Colleen's waiting for you in the recovery room."

Peter Kane stepped to the bed, his eyes glazing. He took hold of Kendall's hand and squeezed it. Kendall managed a slight smile and Kane wiped his eyes. Then he stepped back as Burke guided the bed out of the operating suite.

Double-doors opened in front of them and they were into the recovery room. There was a crowd of people around the nursing station, and another crowd at the other end of the room. Somber, he could tell. Somber and hushed. Then Colleen was there, her face over his, as pale as he had ever seen it. She took his hand and held on.

"I told you," he said. "Everything always happens to the doctors."

Colleen didn't smile. She shook her head no and said, "I'm afraid not." She looked down to the crowd at the other end of the room. "There was an older man having a hernia done. They couldn't get him intubated and they think he had a heart attack."

The words didn't make sense. He was in Fairfield, in the recovery room now. "Someone had a heart attack? I don't understand."

She nodded and started to cry. "It was awful. I was sitting next to his wife in the waiting room when they called her out."

Her words slowly registered.

"She's down there with him now," said Colleen. "I think they're still working on him."

"Jesus," said Kendall, trying to see down to the end of the room. But his neck was stiff and it hurt and he put his head back down.

Burke came back. "How do you feel?" he said.

"Like a truck ran over me."

He nodded. "We're not sure what to do with you, frankly. I don't think you were without oxygen for more than ten or fifteen seconds. But as you can understand, we want to be careful. We're going to have a neurologist take a look at you."

Kendall blinked, looked around. He repeated his social security number to himself, then his birthday and his anniversary. "I'm fine," he said. "I don't think it's necessary."

"Sorry, my friend," said Burke with a wan smile. "We want to make sure. We need to keep you a little longer anyway. We need to see you pee, too, so try to drink some of that water."

"I still don't understand," he said to Colleen when Burke had left. "What happened?"

"I think everything was fine and then I guess you weren't getting the anesthetic. You were partially awake when you were supposed to be asleep. Do you remember any of that?"

He looked at her. His throat burned and he did feel like he'd been run over, but he did not remember anything past Ed Burke injecting him with Versed.

"I think the neurologist is a good idea," said Colleen. "They were pretty worried about you."

"I'm fine. I want to get out of here. Would you hand me the water, please." Kendall sat up a little and took several sips of water. Leaning back, he looked at Colleen and said: "I guess I didn't get my knee done."

She shook her head no, tears in her eyes again. "No member-guest for you, buddy." She took his left hand in both of hers and held it. "You're going to have to stay home with me and stop some of this nonsense that's been going on. You almost died, you know."

* * *

Peter Kane also insisted that a neurologist evaluate Kendall before he left the hospital. Melissa Khoury arrived around eleven o'clock and put him through forty-five minutes of questioning and neurologic maneuvers. The entire time a parade of people walked in and out of the recovery room and the operating suite. Two groups went into the operating suite carrying boxes of equipment with the Maryland State seal on the side. Another group had cameras slung around their neck and portable lights in their hands.

"I think you're fine," Khoury said near noon. "You're lucky."

Lucky? he said to himself. I don't think so.

Ed Burke came back and officially cleared him to leave the hospital. He also suggested that they go out the rear entrance. He said they were trying to keep everything within the hospital until they understood what had happened, but just in case, he didn't want a microphone shoved in Kendall's face. He'd call him later at home. The police had found a note in the employee lounge. It sounded like a disgruntled employee. Someone who'd been fired recently.

Colleen got their car and drove it around to the back of the hospital. In the bright sun he felt wobbly and he held onto her arm until he was in the passenger seat. Settled, he put his head back against the headrest and closed his eyes. The sun through the window was warm on his face and he turned his head toward the window. He took himself back in his mind to the preoperative area. He felt the bed, remembered rolling into the OR, seeing Kane by the X-rays, rolling back to room eight, moving onto the firmer operating room bed, the cold Betadine on his knee, the operating room doors opening and closing, opening and closing. He remembered the hallway. When the doors had opened he'd seen the anesthesia cart come in, and the gurney go by in the hall, and the nurse in the hall with the tray of specimen bottles. And talking with Peter Kane and Ed Burke about the Williamses, about Bob and Sam and Chad, and how Chad now only came to the hospital once a month or so, because much of the bigger skin surgery was done out of the hospital. He remembered suddenly feeling nervous, and wanting to stop the surgery because he just didn't understand anything that had happened to him in the last ten days. And then as hard as he tried, he could remember nothing else except for Ed Burke leaning over him with a syringe of Versed.

His cell phone was ringing. He opened his eyes and reached for the center console where he'd left it early that morning.

Colleen put a hand on his and stopped him. "There's no one you need to speak to right now. Put your head back and relax."

It rang a few more times, then stopped.

But there is, he said to himself, taking his hand away and settling back in the seat. There most definitely is.

*   *   *

When he was settled on the couch and had a little more color in his face, Colleen brought him his cell phone with a note pad and a pen.

There were two messages. The first was from Caroline Garrett, her voice worried. Drew had seen Dr. Fernandez and his exam was fine. Dr. Fernandez agreed with the surgeon's plan and didn't think Drew needed any other treatment. Unless of course the sentinel lymph node was positive, and then they'd have to regroup. His blood tests were fine, too, and they thought his PET scan was normal. But there was a question about his chest CT scan. One of the radiologists thought that one or two lymph nodes deep in his chest were enlarged, and there was also a spot in his lung that they weren't sure about. Please call her when he had a chance. She knew he had his surgery today and she hoped it went well.

The second was from Paul Mancini. He hoped everything went well and wanted to let Kendall know that he would call or send him an e-mail later in the day about his question. He was still waiting to speak with one of the state attorneys.

Kendall erased both messages and made a note to call the radiologist himself about Garrett's report. Then he called his office.

"Hi, Dr. Kendall," said Laurel. "Are you done already?"

"Sort of. How's it going there?"

"Fine. We're catching up on a lot of paperwork and doing some cleaning."

"Anything on your end that I need to know about?" asked Kendall.

"I don't think so. I let the temp' go home. I hope you don't mind."

"No, that's fine. I should have told you that before I left. In fact, unless you need her, she doesn't need to come in the rest of the week. I might have someone new for you on Monday. Did Sammie tell you?"

"Yeah. She sounds good. And you might want to speak with Sammie. She was on the phone a lot this morning with one of the labs. I'll get her."

"Hey, Sammie, how's it going?"

"Fine. How was your surgery?"

"It was okay. Any problems?"

"Just Chevy Chase and that slide thing again. Did you say something to them about us sending it back to a different lab?"

"Yeah, I'm sorry. I had a lot going on before I left and I forgot to tell you. But I didn't tell them that we definitely did it. I just left a message for Dr. Williams that we'd make sure that it didn't happen."

"Now I understand. One of their tech's called over here first thing and wanted to know all the different labs we used so they could call them."

"That's fine," said Kendall. "Don't worry about it. Would you do me a favor, please? Can you check my phone and see if I have any messages. Thanks."

"Yeah, you do," Sammie said a minute later. "Do you want me to take them off?"

Kendall thought about it for several seconds. "No, thanks anyway. I might try and come in for a couple minutes tomorrow. All right, Sammie. Try and get out a little early today. See you tomorrow."

Kendall found the number for Bethesda Chevy Chase Radiology Associates and got connected to the CT department. Dr. Jeff Overman had read Garrett's CT scan.

"Thanks for picking up," said Kendall. "I know you went over the results with the Garretts, but they're a little overwhelmed right now. Mrs. Garrett told me you saw something on the CT scan."

"There are some hilar nodes that are a little enlarged," he said. "And there's a density in his left lower lobe. But you know how it goes. Without any prior films it's hard to say if any of it means anything. It could all be normal. His PET scan looks clear, which is good. But if the melanoma's on his back, I'm a little hesitant to write the nodes off. Or the lung density. We can do a MRI, but I don't think that's going to add much at this point. If his sentinel node is negative, I'd probably just follow it."

"I understand. Thanks, Jeff."

Caroline Garrett picked up on the second ring. "Okay," she said after Kendall had explained it again. "I talked with Drew about it but he doesn't remember ever having a chest x-ray let alone a CT scan."

"This happens all the time," said Kendall. "Try not to worry about it. Do you have a surgery date?"

"Sort of. Like you said, the surgeon wants to see where the sentinel node is before he schedules the surgery. So Drew's actually going in tomorrow or Friday for the dye part. We're still waiting to hear on that. Then the surgery will be early next week."

"Okay. Let me know when the dye injection gets scheduled."

"I will. And I found that block thing you were asking about. What do you want me to do with it?"

"Let's talk later today. I may go into my office tomorrow. I might be able to meet you somewhere."

"Okay," she said. "Maybe you can call Drew at some point, too. He's feeling pretty down."

*   *   *

Kendall was sitting in front of his computer watching his monitor when Ed Burke called at 5:00 PM.

"How are you feeling?" said Burke.

"Better. My throat's a little sore."

"I bet. Stay inside tonight. We're trying to keep your name out of it, but it's gotten out to the press. There are reporters up the wazoo here."

"Great. That's just what I need. So what's happening?"

"It's a zoo. We've looked at all of the hoses and connections. Someone cut the hoses in three rooms. We think it must have been with an eleven blade, because the slits are so thin that you'd never see them. There are probably thirty slits in each hose."

"Jesus."

"Yeah, it's just unbelievable. I think I told you—the police found a note in the employees lounge. Poor Theresa. She's the head OR nurse. It sounds like it's someone she fired. It was a pretty vicious note."

"How's the old guy doing?"

"He's hanging in there. He's still on a ventilator, but he's out of his arrhythmia."

"That's good. When I was in the recovery room I saw a bunch of people going in with police equipment. Did they try and get fingerprints?"

"Yeah, but our prints are all over everything. Plus, you know whoever knew enough to get in and do this had gloves on."

"The note they found," said Kendall after a moment. "Did you see it? Was it handwritten or typed?"

"Typed. On blank paper. Why do you ask?"

"Just curious. Someone might have recognized the handwriting."

"No, afraid not. Listen, I know it's not at the top of your list right now, but we still need to get your knee done. I'll talk to Peter. I'm sure he'll be calling you also. I've never seen him so upset."

An e-mail flashed on his monitor. It was from Mancini. Kendall opened it while he spoke. "I'll call Peter," he said.

Are you there? Mancini had typed.

Yes, Kendall typed back.

I'll call you, typed Mancini.

"Hey, Ed, I've got another call coming in. How about if we talk again later or tomorrow?"

"Sure. Get some rest. I'm sorry, Ryan," Burke added, his voice faltering. "I'm sorry you had to go through that."

"Stop it, Ed. I should be thanking you."

The call waiting tone on the phone sounded.

"I have to go, Ed. I'll call you."

Colleen came into the library and sat in a chair across from his desk. Kendall looked at her—she wasn't leaving. He pressed the call-waiting function on the phone and said hello.

"Ryan," said Mancini. "Peter just called me. Jesus, are you okay?"

"I'm alright. Thanks."

Thank God. Peter's a wreck. Listen, I spoke briefly with one of the state's attorneys last night." Mancini paused then, as if to give Kendall a moment to absorb what he was saying. "One of tenants in that building you asked about left at six forty-five and didn't get back until eight-thirty."

"Umm, okay," said Kendall, absorbing the odd tone in Mancini's voice.

Mancini was quiet again for a moment, then added, "He was gone an hour and forty-five minutes."

Kendall closed his eyes, his stomach suddenly queasy. "Thanks, Paul," he said. Then, after a moment, "Maybe we need to talk."

"I was thinking the same thing. Let me think about this tonight. I'll call you tomorrow."

"Okay. Thanks."

Kendall hung up and looked at Colleen. "Where's Matthew?" he said.

"At Colin's. I just spoke with him."

"And Kelley? Have you talked with her today?"

"About an hour ago. She's fine."

He looked around the library, his lips pursed. Then he slowly shook his head and said, "Do me a favor, please. Will you close the garage doors and make sure the gates are closed and locked."

She nodded. "And then are you going to talk to me?"

"Yes," he said, opening his desk drawer and taking out the letter. "Then I'm going to talk to you."

FIFTEEN

Thursday, June 14

Matthew was a counselor in a junior tennis camp from nine o'clock to three o'clock. Colleen drove him to camp and was back by nine to get Kendall. She had already said first thing that morning that she would be driving Kendall wherever he needed to go, and by the look on her face when she stepped back into the kitchen, she hadn't changed her mind. She knew he had not slept well, and she still had reservations that he might have physical or cognitive sequelae from the day before's ordeal. Earlier that morning she'd also said that during the night he'd awakened almost every hour frightened and gasping for air, and that when she'd tried to calm him he'd made no sense, rambling about dreaming and drowning.

Kendall thought for a moment about attempting to dissuade her from driving him, but he in fact felt no better, and perhaps even worse. He had a dull, nagging headache, and his larynx burned with speech and his throat with any food or liquids. He got up from the kitchen table and went into the entry hall bathroom to look in the mirror. The shower had not helped much. His eyes were still lifeless, his face drawn. He looked closer. He hadn't noticed it in the upstairs bathroom mirror, but he was starting to bruise around his mouth. Maybe she was right.

Colleen took one more trip around the house to make sure all the windows were closed and locked. She called Mandy, put her outside with plenty of food and water, and checked both gates to the back yard. Back in the kitchen, she looked at him and said, "Ready?"

"Yep."

She locked the back door and they went out through the garage. It was just a few minutes past nine o'clock, but the sun was already halfway up the sky and bright. Kendall put on sunglasses and pulled out an index card full of phone numbers that he'd written down the night before.

"We're going to your office first?" said Colleen.

He nodded, studying the card. He'd spoken with Drew Garrett for a while the night before and he wanted to follow up with Caroline. The Internet had surely changed the world, and it was a wonderful source of medical information both for patients and doctors, but it was also the source of untold angst. There was a reason that the patient-doctor visit had evolved over time and that, no matter how much information was available at one's fingertips, most doctors did not practice medicine other than face to face. One quickly learned that it was often not the breadth of the information that mattered as much as the delivery and the relevance. Drew and Caroline Garrett had spent the evening before trying to understand the lymphatic drainage of the back and its implications for his sentinel lymph node biopsy, and by the time he'd called they had both been ready to throw in the towel.

He was getting ready to dial their home number when his phone rang. It was Caroline Garrett.

"Hi," she said, a trace of optimism in her voice. It was an emotion he had not yet heard from her and for a moment he, too, felt better. "I just wanted to let you know that Drew got his dye study scheduled this morning at eleven. We're on our way over there now."

"Okay, good," he said, coming back to ground. "At Roosevelt, right?"

"Right. I'm not sure if Dr. Uhle will be there or not. A doctor named Brigham is doing it in the radiology department."

"I'm going to try and come over. Anything else?"

"No. I have the bag with me with everything in it."

"Thanks. I'll see you there."

Dr. Uhle, the surgeon, wanted to know exactly where the sentinel lymph node or nodes were for this tumor site before he went into surgery. More often than not, the lymph fluid study was done at the time of surgery because the lymph drainage was straightforward. But on the upper back, lymph fluid could flow to the neck, or deep into the chest. It could also unexpectedly cross the midline, a double-cross of sorts, fooling everyone. Uhle had probably learned his lessons the hard way. If he needed to go into Drew Garrett's chest early next week, he wanted to be prepared. So today Garrett was only having the lymphoscintigraphy done, the injection of a radio-labeled dye around the tumor site which would then be tracked in the lymph flow. The first node it reached—the sentinel node—would then be targeted for removal at the same time that Uhle excised the melanoma site. The sentinel lymph node would also have frozen sections examined by a pathologist at the time of surgery. If the node was free of tumor, no more lymph nodes would be removed. But if the sentinel node contained melanoma cells, then the entire chain of lymph nodes in that area might be removed in an attempt to limit any further metastases.

They reached his office building and walked to the elevators in silence, Colleen looking around for surveillance cameras.

"They need to get cameras," she said. "Even if they're just for show. You need to bug them."

"Add it to the list."

Laurel looked at Kendall when he walked in and frowned. "Hi, Mrs. Kendall," she said. "Are you okay, Dr. Kendall? Can I get anything for you?"

"No, thank you. I'm fine. I just want to check my mail and my messages. Anything going on?"

"No, it's pretty quiet. A doctor called for you yesterday. I put him into your voice mail."

In his office, Kendall put his mail to the side of his desk and picked up the phone. He had three messages.

The first was from Will Ammerman getting back to him about Chad Williams. Best to talk in person, he said. He'd call back later.

Chad Williams' voice came next. Thanks for the call, but he didn't want anyone at Kendall's office to have to do any extra work. Just let his office know which lab it was and they'd take care of it. He hoped Kendall was doing well after his surgery. Peter Kane was the best.

Ammerman again. He'd spoken with Laurel at Kendall's front desk and heard that he was out for a few days. No big deal. Call him when he was back in the office.

Kendall hung up and made a face. "I forgot to tell Will Ammerman that I'd be out for a couple of days. He's got my cell number, but he probably didn't want to bother me at home."

"So call him."

"I am. Would you lock the door, please?"

While Colleen got up and walked to the door, Kendall put the phone on speaker and dialed Will Ammerman's back line.

"Dr. Ammerman."

"Will, this is Ryan Kendall. Thanks for calling."

"Hey, no problem. Are you okay? I heard you're out for a couple of days."

"Yeah, no biggy. Just a little knee thing."

"Geez, sorry. Hope it doesn't keep you off the court very long. So, I did speak with a couple of people. Can you hold a second? I want to close my door . . . Sorry. So, I spoke with Harvey Plummer at Washington. He's the chief there now, but he trained with Chad. I'm afraid you might be right. How did you put it? That he might not be the sharpest tool in the shed?"

Kendall rolled his eyes at Colleen. "Right."

"Harvey said he wasn't necessarily bad, but he just had trouble making decisions."

"That's a great attribute for a pathologist."

"Right. And he was a little bizarre at times. Harvey said he had all these little rituals, maybe idiosyncrasies is a better word. He was very particular about how he wanted the tissue cuts oriented on the slides. Apparently he wanted them just so, and if they didn't come out the way he wanted he'd make the tech's get recuts. He actually learned how to process tissue specimens and cut slides himself so if the tech's couldn't get it right he'd eventually just do it himself." Ammerman paused and actually chuckled. "This really isn't funny, but Harvey said he also had this scale of blues that he would use to diagnosis tumors."

"'Blues'?"

"Yeah, he would hold slides with tumors on them up to the light and try and make a diagnosis by how blue it was. Weird, huh?"

Kendall's eyes were now closed, his mind ringing with Williams' voice. "But he's certified," said Kendall. "I know he passed his dermpath' board exam."

"The second time."

"After the second fellowship?"

"Right. It was a prerequisite by the Chair of the Pathology Board."

"I'm an idiot," said Kendall. "I've been working with him for years."

"Hey, don't be so hard on yourself. It's not like he never passed them. I know lots of people who took their boards twice."

"Yeah, but—"

"Forget it, Ryan. I didn't know, and I'm in the business. Listen, I have to run. I was going to call up to Boston where he did his first fellowship, but I wasn't sure it was necessary. What do you think?"

"No, this is all I need, Will. Thanks. And by the way, I'm going to get the block on that spindle cell melanoma today. Do you want me to send it up?"

"Soon as you can. I'll get it back to you pronto."

Kendall hung up and looked at Colleen.

"That's pretty scary," she said.

He didn't hear her. "It's pretty blue," Williams had said on the phone the week before. The fucking asshole had actually said that aloud.

* * *

Drew Garrett was lying face down on a table in the scintigraphy suite. A tall man in scrubs was bent over him with a syringe in his hand. Through the windows of the cubicle that housed the equipment controls, Kendall could see the biopsy site on Garrett's upper back marked with purple surgical ink. A baseball-sized purple circle had then been drawn around the site and divided into four quadrants.

"Is that Dr. Brigham?" asked Kendall.

"Yes. He's one of the interventional radiologists," said the technician sitting at a small desk in the cubicle. "I'll get you some scrubs if you want and you can go in."

Kendall's knee was swollen and it had been hard enough getting dressed that morning. And his head was pounding again. He needed to get home soon and get some rest.

"No, thanks. I'll just watch from here for a little while."

Dr. Brigham finished injecting one of the quadrants with a syringe and picked up another from a surgical tray next to the bed. The syringes contained a colloid or fluid that would be absorbed by the lymph vessels. The colloid was tagged with technetium, a radioisotope that could then be visualized by a nuclear scanning machine. After all four quadrants had been injected, the radio-labeled colloid would be given about twenty minutes to find its way, and then the first images would be obtained. Then they'd have Garrett walk around for an hour or so and take a second set of images. All in all, it would be well over an hour before Garrett was done, and probably not until later in the day that the nuclear medicine physician would sign off on the report.

Kendall wrote his name down on a piece of paper and gave it to the technician. "Would you please let Mr. Garrett know I was here," he said.

"Sure. We should be able to do the first shots in about twenty minutes or so."

"Okay, thanks."

Colleen and Caroline Garrett were sitting next to each other in the waiting room. Caroline had seemed eager for the company when Kendall and Colleen had arrived and found her sitting by herself, staring at her hands in her lap.

"How's it going?" she said as soon as Kendall came into view.

"Fine. They're just putting the dye in now. He'll be out in twenty or thirty minutes, and then they'll probably have him walk around for a while."

"That's what they said before." She reached beside her and handed him a plastic bag. "All yours."

He looked inside—there were a dozen small plastic containers with glass slides in them, and in the bottom of the bag, a larger plastic case that he could see contained a green plastic cassette. He closed the bag and thanked her. Caroline did not need to see a piece of her husband permanently memorialized in paraffin wax.

"I think we're going to head home," he said to Caroline. "Call me later if you can."

She nodded and moved instinctively to hug him, then seemed to think better of it and pulled back.

Kendall stepped closer and put his arm around her. "Hang in there," he said, squeezing her shoulder. "Let us know if you need anything."

Colleen was quiet as they made their way out of Roosevelt Hospital. Outside, she said: "She's very nice. God, what a nightmare. They've got three kids—six, eight, and ten."

Kendall nodded. Who knew the answers to the hardest questions of this game? Who ever knew?

He'd felt his phone going off several times while they were in the hospital and he checked the calls when they were outside. Burke, Kane, Mancini, Burke, his office.

"And by the way," Colleen was saying, "Caroline wanted you to know how appreciative they are of everything you've done for them. Particularly setting them up with all of the doctors. I guess he didn't have an internist and she'd been bugging him for a while to get one. As it turned out, he knew the guy you sent him to and he really likes him."

"Joel Lieberman," said Kendall. "He is good. I should go see him, actually."

"Yes, you should. I've been telling you that for a while now."

And I've been telling you to quit running in the ninety-degree heat, he said to himself. "Add it to the list," he said aloud.

"I will," she said. "Believe me. Anyway, he sounds really nice. They went to high school together, and I guess they hadn't seen each other since then."

They reached the car and Kendall scrolled through his calls again, deciding whether to listen to the messages or simply call them back. The former, he decided. But not until he got home. His head was pounding and his eyelids wanted to close. He put his head back and closed his eyes. "Yeah," he said, "where'd they go?"

"Somerset," she said.

He didn't flinch, although it felt as if she'd punched him. Garrett had looked at him the other day without batting an eye and only said, "I know who he is." Not a word about going to the same school, even if it had only been for a short time. Just, "I know who he is."

"As a mater of fact," said Colleen, "maybe I'll call his office when we get home. You're going to have some down time."

Kendall didn't answer, his thoughts racing around her words and Garrett's. Don't jump the gun, he said to himself. Garrett's statement didn't necessarily mean that they did know each other. All Garrett had said is that he knew who Williams was. Maybe they hadn't overlapped at the school. Drew Garrett, Kendall was sure, didn't forget many names or faces.

"Somerset Preparatory School for Boys," added Colleen, imitating the British receptionist in the school's admissions department. They'd briefly looked at the school for Matthew and they both knew the mantra. "'Boys for life,'" she said. "Maybe it's true."

*   *   *

He slept for two hours, his body demanding it. When he woke his neck was even stiffer and his head still throbbed, but his mind was clear. He got up, showered, and went to his desk. Notepad before him, he went into the voice mail on his cell phone and started taking off the messages. He could hear Colleen and Matthew in the kitchen, and he told himself he needed to spend some time with Matthew. His son had been given a cursory explanation of a surgery that didn't happen, and he was naturally curious. And afraid in a way, Kendall knew. Although it was not an emotion that sixteen-year-old boys readily acknowledged, Kendall had seen it in his eyes—the primordial fear of losing a parent, a provider, before their time.

Ed Burke, asking how he was. Peter Kane, the same, and wanting to reschedule the arthroscopy. Judge Mancini, wanting to talk at some point later in the day. Burke again, saying apologetically that the police wanted to speak with him. Sammie, letting him know that Dr. Williams' office had called again wanting to know if they had figured out which lab they had sent the slide to. Caroline Garrett, her voice despondent.

He had no desire to speak with the police, nor to reschedule his surgery any time soon. Williams was no surprise. Yes, he definitely needed to speak with Mancini. But the tone of Caroline Garrett's voice was worrisome. Whatever it was that was causing it, he already knew was not good.

"Well, I guess it's good that they did the dye study ahead of time," she said after answering her phone on the first ring. "Like you said might happen, the lymph node that they were looking for is in his chest near his aorta. Para-something, I think he said. I don't know. I wasn't really listening by then. I just can't take any more."

"Paraaortic?"

"I think that's right. Drew would know. Dr. Uhle called him afterwards. He may have a thoracic surgeon help him with that part."

"So, what are you going to do?"

"What do you mean?" said Caroline Garrett. "I don't understand."

"Well, he doesn't have to have the sentinel node biopsy done. It wasn't that long ago that we didn't do them at all. I just don't know how difficult it is to get to that lymph node."

"I'm sorry, Dr. Kendall," she said, a sudden edge in her voice. "Are you asking me if he might not have that part of it done?"

Kendall felt his face warming. "Well, no, not exactly. You just always have to weigh the benefits and the risks." How do you say to Colleen Garrett that nicking the aorta is like rupturing a fire hydrant? That even good doctors make mistakes?

"Well, I'm sorry, but I just don't understand what you're saying. If it's not necessary, then why is it done at all?"

"I didn't say it wasn't necessary. It's a matter of relative risks. I wasn't trying to confuse things."

"You gave us the surgeon's name," she went on. "Are you not confident in his ability? Or whoever else he might bring in?"

"I didn't mean that, Caroline. And I'm sure Dr. Uhle will go over this with you also. All I meant is that there are risks with any surgery, even in the best of hands, and you have to weigh that against the benefit of doing the node biopsy."

"Well, if it was done safely, is it not better to know if the node is positive or not? Particularly with whatever they saw on his CT scan."

"It is."

"Isn't that the key piece of information in determining whether he needs any more treatment?"

"It is."

"Then why are you asking what he's going to do? He's at baseball practice now with our ten-year-old son, and then he's going to practice with our other two sons." Caroline's voice was rising as she spoke. "He's forty-eight years old. Why would you ask that? Why would he not do everything possible to—"

"Caroline, I'm sorry, it was a bad question."

She was quiet. "I'm sorry," she said. "It's been a long day. Listen, why don't we touch base over the weekend? I need to get dinner ready."

"Sure," he said. "I'll call you. I'm sorry."

He closed his eyes for a moment, then opened them. He had a new e-mail from Mancini: Are you there? Bob Williams would like to speak with you. We can talk later.

Yes, he typed. Call on home number.

Kendall got up and walked through the kitchen, pausing to squeeze Matthew's shoulders.

"Do you feel any better?" said Colleen.

"Good as new," he said, taking the portable phone from the wall. "Chad's father is going to call me. I'm going to take it outside."

She nodded and turned back to Matthew, who was working on his third bottle of vitamin water. He had Kendall's auburn hair and complexion, and his face was still flushed from tennis camp.

Lindsey Browning was in her back yard with a friend, kicking a soccer ball from one end of the yard to the other. Watching her, Kendall thought it seemed like months since he'd taken the mole off the tip of her nose. Thinking back, he figured it was just a little over two weeks ago. And he still wasn't through with her yet.

The phone rang. Kendall took a deep breath and answered it.

"Thanks for speaking with me, Ryan," said Bob Williams. "I know you've been through a lot in the last two days."

"My pleasure. How can I help you, Bob?"

"Well, a few things. They're all hard."

"Nothing's hard, Bob."

"That's kind of you. Listen, I talked with Robyn for a while, and I hope you can understand that she's been with us for a long time. I don't really know what happened with this slide but—"

"Bob," Kendall interrupted. "I expected you to call her. I totally understand. For both of you, I hope she goes back to your office. No hard feelings whatsoever."

"Thanks. Paul said you'd understand."

"Absolutely."

Silence.

"This slide that's missing," Williams finally said. "I don't know what to tell you. It happens sometimes. We process fifty thousand specimens a year, and occasionally something gets misplaced."

"I know, Bob. It's not like I've never had a problem in my office. It's Chad making the issue, not us."

"I realize that. And I guess that's what I'm concerned about." Williams paused and emitted a sigh that Kendall could hear. "I'm a little worried about him, Ryan."

"What are you worried about?" asked Kendall when he didn't go on.

"I don't know. I can't put my finger on it. How can I say this? Paul said I could talk to you, so I am. I've been covering up for Chad since he was in grade school. I just can't do it anymore. My wife and I . . ."

Kendall thought he was crying, but he wasn't sure. "Covering up for what?" he asked. "I don't understand, Bob."

"For having a kid who can't live up to everyone else. For having a kid who can't get anything right, but who's been expected to get everything right from the time he was four. This is a tough town, you know. Maybe it's been a tough family."

"I understand. I have a son." Kendall paused. "I appreciate your confidence, but why are you saying this to me?"

"Because Paul is my friend, my good friend, and he thinks you have some reservations about Chad. Something's not right, and I don't know what it is."

"Neither do I. But I agree with you. Frankly, I think he's so worked-up about this slide that he went into my office looking for it." And he might have tried to kill me, he wanted to say, but this was his father, and he really did not know if it was true or not.

"Well, if he did, I'd fire him, son or no son. But why would he do that?" said Williams. "We always have the tissue block. We could cut a thousand new slides on that case if we needed them."

"I don't know, Bob. Did you ask him why it's such a big deal?"

"Sure I did. But he always has an answer—he always has. He said it just makes us look sloppy. It bothers him."

"That's what Robyn said, too."

"You've worked with him for a while," Williams went on, his voice now clearly strained. "I can't check his work. I don't know what half the things are that he's looking at. Is he competent, or is he incompetent? Please, tell me what I need to do. I'll turn the lab upside down to fix whatever is wrong."

"I don't know, Bob. He's careful, maybe even paranoid. I don't know if he's incompetent, though. I've been trusting his reports for years, and I've never really had a reason to ask that question. My sense with this slide is that it doesn't really show the atypical areas that he said it did, and he's afraid of me seeing it. I think he was just being overly paranoid with a run-of-the-mill Spitz Nevus, and in the process he caused a lot of heartache. I suspect he feels bad about that."

"That would be just like him," said Williams. "Make a big-to-do about nothing, and make himself look good in the process. That's his modus operandi. He's done it all his life."

"Great."

"Listen, my wife and I are going down to our bay house tonight to talk. I'll call you tomorrow. My tennis group is counting on me in the morning, so I'll be back early."

"Okay. I'll be here or on my cell. Just out of curiosity, bob, how old is Chad?"

"He's forty-five."

"And why didn't he graduate from Somerset? Why did he go to boarding school?"

Williams didn't answer for a moment. Finally, he said, "You'll have to ask Chad that question, Ryan."

SIXTEEN

Friday, June 15

Staring intently at the computer monitor on his desk, he searched every combination of Drew Garrett and Somerset School for Boys that he could think of. A few more entries besides those from his original search on Drew Garrett the week before came up, but still nothing about Garrett and Somerset. Finally he found it on the Somerset website. Drew Tyler Garrett, class of '76, was a past president of the Alumni Society, and was currently on the school's Board of Trustees. That didn't leave much to question about his status at the school, thought Kendall.

He searched for Chad Williams as well, but found nothing except a few cursory items about pathology roundtables and entries in staff directories at Fairfield and Eastern Washington Hospital. Going just by age though, if Williams was three years younger than Garrett, then he was probably in the high school class of 1979. Perhaps Garrett really didn't know him any better than he had let on. Three years was an eternity in high school.

His cell phone rang—an exchange and number that he now recognized as belonging to Fairfield Hospital. He'd already let two of Ed Burke's calls go unanswered, and Burke wasn't even leaving messages anymore.

"Hello," said Kendall.

"Oh, hi, Ryan. You are there. Ed Burke here. How are you today? Are you feeling any better?"

Well, it depends on why you're asking, he thought. He tried to make his voice sound hoarse, but he wasn't sure it came across very well. "My throat hurts and it's hard to talk, but otherwise I'm okay."

"Are you up to speaking with one of the detectives today? I don't think I can put him off any longer."

"Do I have to?"

"Yeah. They have to do their job. As much as that note makes it sound like it's someone we fired, there's no one on their radar screen right now. They want to make sure that someone wasn't after one of you and did three rooms just to make it look better."

"Is the old guy still hanging in?"

"Yeah. We got his tube out today. I think he's going to make it, but you never know at his age."

"I never really heard about a third person. What happened to them?"

"It was a guy—an attorney. He was lucky. He wasn't back in the operating room yet when we found his machine."

"So what do you want me to do?"

"I have his name and number. Will you call him today?"

"Sure. I understand."

Burke gave him the information and also told him that Peter really wanted to get him back on the OR schedule. Kendall politely agreed and said he'd give Peter a call as well.

Colleen came into the library and waited until he was off the phone. "I'm going to take Matthew to camp. Do you need anything?"

He shook his head no. "A detective wants to speak with me. I'm supposed to call him."

Colleen pursed her lips. "Let me take Matthew and then we'll think it out before you call."

The phone rang again. The caller ID said Hidden Glen CC.

"Hello."

"Bob Williams, Ryan. Do you have a minute?"

"Sure."

"Are you free this morning?"

"All morning. I was supposed to be recuperating so I'm booked out of my office."

"I have a slide we need to look at. Do you have a microscope at home?"

"No," said Kendall. Then after a moment, "Have you looked at it yet?"

"No. I'm at Hidden Glen. I just got it."

Okay, thought Kendall. You can explain that later. "Do you want to meet me at my office?"

"Tell me when. I have to shower, but then I can head right over."

Kendall looked at his watch. He wanted a few minutes to speak with Colleen. "How about ten?"

"I'll see you then."

"Bob?"

"Yes?"

"Does it have a name on it?"

"No. But it has an accession number on it. Do you want it?"

"Yes, please."

"23587-07"

"Thanks. See you at ten."

*   *   *

"You really need to think this all the way through," said Colleen. "If you give the detective his name then you're going to have to explain why, and you're also going to have to be comfortable with them investigating him. Which if he tried to kill you is exactly what needs to be done."

"But if he didn't I'll be up shit's creek."

"Well, do you think he cut the hoses in your operating room?" asked Colleen. "You have to be able to answer that question."

"I don't know—it's not that simple. On the one hand, I can't imagine that he did. I mean, think about it. He'd go to jail forever. Why would he ever do that?" He paused, staring at the remnants of his computer search that were still on the monitor. "On the other hand, I think he's scared shitless for some reason, and somehow it has something to do with me."

"If he tried to kill you, he'll try again. Maybe you should talk to the detective sooner rather than later."

Kendall shook his head in disagreement. "If he really wanted to kill me, if he really had the guts to do that, he would have done it already. And what if wasn't him? They've got a note, remember? What if I get this detective all pumped up and it turns out to be some guy they fired six months ago. He'll sue the hell out of me. I don't have enough insurance to cover accusing another doctor of attempted murder."

"And what if you get him all pumped up and they find out it was him?"

"But what if it's not? Plus, as soon as the detective starts talking to him he'll get paranoid, and then Bob will never find out what's going on over there. Bob trusted me enough to call me about his son. I can't just turn around and point a finger at him without something more concrete to back it up."

"You need to talk to Paul again. If he's really the one who sent you that letter, then you need to know why."

Kendall shook his head again. "I can't do that either. What if by chance it wasn't him? He's going to be president of that club—he'll go batshit in the admissions office. And if it was him, he sent it to me by mail for a reason. There's a reason he just didn't pick up the phone and call me. Besides having gone to all that trouble with the white-out."

Colleen was silent.

"I need to see this slide, is what I need to do," said Kendall. "And I need to hear what Bob has to say. Then I will call Paul just to touch base and hear what he has to say. Why don't you come to the office with me? I don't want you here by yourself."

She looked at him and rolled her eyes. "I'm glad you're not worried about him."

*   *   *

Laurel answered the phone at his office.

"Do me a favor, Laurel, and pull Lindsey Browning's chart," he said.

"Sure. Are you coming in today?"

"I'm on my way in now. Dr. Bob Williams will be coming over around ten. If he happens to get there before me, go ahead and let him have a seat in my office."

"Okay. Sammie told me Robyn's probably not coming here anymore. Is that true?"

"Probably. I think her leaving Chevy Chase was mostly a misunderstanding."

"So I have to get that temp' back, huh?"

"I don't know. We'll figure that out. Maybe Robyn has a sister."

"Maybe. I have the chart. Do you want it on your desk?"

"Yes, but first will you look inside and tell me what the accession number is on the path' report from Chevy Chase. There's only one path' report in there from them."

"Hold on. 23587 dash 07."

"Thanks, Laurel. Go ahead and put it on my desk." Kendall took off his earpiece and looked at Colleen. "It's Lindsey's slide."

Colleen shook her head, her lips pressed tight to each other. "There better not be something bad on that slide, or Donna is going to absolutely die."

"There won't be," said Kendall.

"How do you know? Why would he care so much about it then?"

"Because as his dad said, that's his modus operandi. Make a big-to-do about nothing, and somehow make himself look good in the process. Besides, Will Ammerman looked at a bunch of her slides and he said they were fine."

"I think you're underestimating him," she said. "I think you need to call Detective Finotti."

*   *   *

Bob Williams hadn't arrived yet, so Kendall went ahead and called Paul Mancini. He'd just let him know he was meeting with the elder Williams, he figured. Mancini's phone went through to voice mail and Kendall left a message that he would call back. He checked his e-mail. Peter Kane's scheduling assistant asking him for dates to reschedule. The rest was junk. Nothing from Mancini.

Laurel called on the intercom to tell him that Dr. Williams had arrived. Colleen went out to the waiting room and Kendall moved the microscope from his desk to a small conference table.

"Morning, Ryan," said Bob Williams, his face grave. He was dressed in a white shirt and a blue seersucker summer suit. His bald scalp was tanned and sweating slightly, and the short gray hair on the sides of his head was still partially wet. The three Williams doctors were all fairly short. Bob was probably five-foot-eight or so, and Sam and Chad were at the most an inch taller. Bob was in the best shape, though. Sam had looked a little paunchy the other day, and that was how Kendall remembered Chad as well.

"Morning, Bob. Have a seat." Kendall placed Lindsey Browning's chart on the table next to the microscope.

Williams looked at the chart. "Is that the patient?"

"I believe so."

"May I see the chart?"

Kendall picked it up and handed it to him.

Williams opened the chart and quickly found Lindsey's pathology report. Kendall watched his jaw tighten, his eyes get hard. He closed the chart and placed it back on the table. "Will Ammerman is the pigmented lesion specialist that I've heard Chad talk about?"

Kendall nodded.

Williams took out a single glass microscope slide from the inside pocket of his suit jacket and set it on top of the chart.

Kendall looked at the slide. Resting on Lindsey's chart, it had its own presence, almost as if she herself were sitting between them. He took it in his fingers and turned it over. It was cracked. A thin break ran diagonally almost the entire length of the slide. And as the elder Williams had said, there was no name on it. Normally there would have been a small piece of white adhesive on one end with a name printed on it. The other end of the glass was covered with a film that would hold pencil or ink and the numbers 23587-07 were written on it. Kendall put the slide back on the chart and looked at Chad's father.

"Henry found it," said Williams. His voice was now as hard as his eyes.

"Henry?"

"You know Henry. Our locker room attendant."

Henry. Big Henry.

"He has an exterminator come in every couple of months and he was cleaning out behind the lockers and in the nooks and crannies to get ready. It must have fallen out of Chad's pants or shirt and dropped behind the locker."

Kendall nodded slowly. "So, you haven't looked at it?"

"He just gave it to me this morning."

For several more seconds then they both just looked at the slide. Finally Kendall said: "Go ahead, Bob. It's yours."

"Not really. That's part of the problem." He tapped Lindsey's chart firmly with an index finger. "It's this young girl's. We're just middlemen, like a bank. And we're to be trusted like a bank."

"I understand. It's disappointing."

Williams took a pair of glasses out his coat and wiped them with a cloth. Over his forty-plus years of pathology medical practice, he had gone through this routine countless times. This time his fingers were trembling. He picked up the slide, managed to get it onto the microscope stage, and clamped it into place. Putting his face to the microscope, he first adjusted the focus for his eyes. All pathologists followed a set routine when looking at stained tissue under a microscope. They first examined the specimen under low power so as to study the architecture, the symmetry, the overall pattern. That first glance for an experienced pathologist often told the entire story—it was a microscopic gestalt, one of the brilliant kaleidoscopes that the human body uniformly replicated over and over.

Williams was a pro, and Kendall watched with admiration as his fingers now delicately focused the lenses on the tissue. When he had the focus just right he quickly moved the slide around the stage. Left, right, up, down. There were three cuts of tissue on the slide and he repeated the sequence with each cut under low power. Finished with the third cut, he swung in the high power lens, his jaw shut and clenched. First cut—left, right, up, down. Then onto the second and third cuts. Swiveling the low power lens back into place, he looked up. His face was pale, his eyes dead as if some part of his life had just been sucked out of them. He turned the microscope around and slid it towards Kendall without saying a word.

Kendall adjusted the lenses for his eyes, then focused down on the first cut. Although he was not a dermatopathologist, a significant part of his dermatology residency had been spent learning skin pathology, and it had accounted for a full third of his dermatology board examination. He also routinely looked at many of the slides that were generated out of his own office. He was fully capable of evaluating most normal lesions, and many abnormalities as well. One thing he certainly knew was what a normal mole looked like, and that was exactly what he was looking at now. Confused, he glanced up at the elder Williams. Williams was staring out the window, looking more sad now than angry.

Maybe it was a mistake. Maybe a piece of tissue from another biopsy had been left on the microtome. Kendall put his head back down and moved to the second cut—normal mole. Third cut—normal mole. He quickly swung in the high power lens. Normal mole, normal mole, normal mole.

Kendall lifted his head and turned off the power to the microscope, his stomach burning again, his heart thumping like a first date. The slide showed a normal run-of-the-mill mole. There was no Spitz nevus, no atypia, no nothing other than normal mole cells. Pretty much what he would have guessed when he removed it from Lindsey Browning's nose. It was only her mother who had really questioned whether it had changed. Lindsey had only wanted it off because she didn't like it.

"As I told you yesterday," said Bob Williams, "it's one of the ways my son has managed to get himself through life. That and his father helping him every step of the way," he added, his eyes tearing. "My wife and I were up most of the night. Somehow we knew that even with everything we've given him and done for him he'd still manage to hang himself."

"I'm sorry, Bob," said Kendall, watching the man and trying to put himself in his place. Williams didn't respond and for a moment Kendall wasn't sure if he had heard him. Then the pathologist's face suddenly changed.

"May I use your phone?"

"Sure. Use the one on my desk."

Williams got up, sat down at the desk, and dialed a number from memory. "Men's locker room please," he said. He covered the phone while he waited and spoke to Kendall. "Chad's playing golf this morning. I've got to get hold of Henry and make sure he doesn't say anything to him about finding the slide."

Kendall nodded, watching Williams as he waited with the phone to his ear.

"I'm sorry, who did you say this was? Timmy? . . . What? Slow down and say that again, please . . . . When did this happen? . . . Where did they take him? . . . Timmy, is my son Chad there? . . . When? . . . Okay, thanks, Timmy. I'll call the manager."

Bob Williams hung up and stared at the phone for several seconds. When he looked up there was now fear in his eyes. "Something happened to Henry. They took him out in an ambulance. They think he might have fainted and hit his head on the floor or a counter."

"That's what the paramedics said, or someone saw him fall?"

"I don't know. That's all Timmy knows right now. He's Henry's assistant."

Williams picked up the phone again and dialed. "Sarah, this is Dr. 'B.' Has Chad gotten in yet? . . . Okay, thanks. No, I don't have a phone with me . . . . Yes, please." Williams wrote down a phone number on Kendall's note pad. "Thanks. I'll be there shortly."

"He's not at the office," said Williams, dialing again. He waited, hung up, dialed again. "And he's not answering his cell phone."

Williams turned and looked at him. "I need to find Chad."

Kendall nodded. "Bob, I need to ask you something." Williams was still looking at him, but his mind seemed to be focused elsewhere. "Do you think it could have been Chad who tampered with the anesthetic machines at Fairfield?"

Williams didn't blink. "I suppose I understand the question, Ryan" he said, "but I would very seriously doubt that. Chad might be a liar, and maybe even a cheater, but . . . malice? No, I don't think so."

"I don't know, Bob. I know it's hard for you to hear it, but I think he might have tried to kill me."

Chad's father did not answer. He got up, took the slide off the microscope, put it back in his jacket pocket. "I'm sorry, Ryan," he said. "I need to find my son."

Seventeen

Ed Burke must have given Kendall's cell phone number to Detective Finotti, because the detective had called twice while Kendall was meeting with Bob Williams. He'd left a pleasant but pointed message with the second call: call him back, and soon.

"I've got to call this guy," said Kendall. He had not spoken with Colleen yet about the slide. They had walked from the office to the car in silence. When he got in the driver's side, she glared at him but didn't say anything.

"Well, did that help?" Colleen finally said when they were settled in the car. "Chad's father didn't look very happy coming in or going out."

"Yes and no. I'll tell you in a minute." Kendall sighed and looked out the window. Then he scrolled through his missed calls and dialed the detective's number.

"Hello, Detective Finotti? . . . I'm a little better, thanks. I'm still pretty hoarse, though, so it's hard to talk much . . . . Well, my schedule's a little up in the air. I'm actually at my office right now trying to put out some fires. I've got a surgical problem from last week and a couple of other sick people. Is it urgent? . . . I see . . . . Well, I can see how it's going and call you in a little bit . . . . Okay . . . . Yes, Dr. Burke mentioned that to me, and I've been thinking about it. We sometimes have the same problem with someone we fired or who quit and thought they were mistreated. And I always have a number of crazy patients so to speak, but they're generally pretty harmless. I'll think about it some more . . . . Okay. I'll call you. Thanks."

"Well, that certainly clarified everything," said Colleen. Her eyes narrowed and she stared at him.

"Bob needs to find him first," he said, starting the car, but staying in the lot.

"Excuse me. Fill me in, please."

His mind was racing, his thoughts outpacing the connections. There was a normal mole on the slide that Henry had found, but the slide that Chad had sent him, and the slides that Ammerman had received, had shown a Spitz Nevus.

"The slide showed a totally normal mole," said Kendall. "There was no Spitz Nevus in any of the cuts."

That obviously meant that the slides showing the Spitz Nevus were from someone else, thought Kendall. Chad had made up the whole Spitz Nevus story and then sent out slides that were from a lesion on a different patient to back it up.

"I don't understand," said Colleen. "Do you mean he made the wrong diagnosis? Is that he incompetent?"

"No, he's not. At least I don't think he is. He's very insecure, and he's probably not the best pathologist around, but I don't think he's actually incompetent. It's like I said on the way over here—he made up the whole story to make himself look good in some way. He actually sent out slides from a different patient who did have a Spitz Nevus. I think he thinks it makes him look conscientious, or it somehow makes him come off as a better pathologist. That's what Bob said, too—that's his modus operandi—it has been since he was a kid."

"Wow. You better not tell Donna that."

Kendall barely heard her, his mind working so fast that he could barely keep the thoughts in order. So, if the slides that were sent out to him and Ammerman were from a different person, then the question was—what about Lindsey Browning's tissue block? What if Donna Browning still couldn't sleep at night and she called Kendall to call Chevy Chase and tell Chad Williams that she wanted yet another opinion on Lindsey's lesion? What would Chad do then?

"Where did Bob find the slide?" Colleen was asking.

"Hidden Glen. Chad must have dropped it in his locker. That's another problem—Henry, the locker room attendant, left in an ambulance."

Colleen frowned.

Kendall's thoughts raced on. He would simply send out another set of Spitz Nevus slides! He had probably cut a whole series of them just in case of that event. But what if a slide were ever to be cut from the tissue block? What if someone like Ammerman had requested the slides *and* the tissue block?

Kendall picked up his phone and called Chevy Chase Pathology Associates. The elder Williams had not arrived yet. Kendall left a message for Dr. 'B' to call him as soon as he got to the office and gave the receptionist his cell phone number. Then he turned off the engine and opened the windows.

"They think Henry fell and hit his head. He might have had a heart attack or an episode of hypoglycemia. He does have pretty bad heart disease and diabetes."

"But?"

Silence, and Kendall shrugging.

"So now what?" Colleen asked.

"I don't know. That's what I'm trying to figure out. I need to speak to Bob again, and basically he needs to find Chad."

His phone rang.

"Bob, I've been sitting here going over all of this and I think you need to get Lindsey's tissue block . . . . Great. I thought you would have. How long will it take to process a slide? . . . That long?" Kendall looked at his watch—it was almost eleven now—it wouldn't be ready until mid afternoon. "Okay. Call me as soon as you look at it please. Is Chad there? . . . Any word from him? . . . What about Henry? . . . Okay. Let me know."

Kendall started the car again. "Okay, I don't want to go home. We need to pick up Matthew at three, right?"

She nodded.

He started to drive. He thought he had a pretty good grasp on most human emotions, either as a physician or an intellectual. If asked, even though he might not have experienced all of them, he also thought he could probably describe most of them pretty well. He would have been wrong about this one though, he thought. He would have never predicted the true effects of pure anxiety, of the sudden and almost overwhelming sensation of drowning even though there was air, of having no way out, no place to go, no place to hide, no place to disappear. Part of him wanted to jump out of the car and run, anywhere, just to somehow rid himself of the tingling and burning and pressure building in his chest and head. But he could not run, and there was nowhere to run to. He turned out onto Old Georgetown Road.

"Where are we going?"

"I don't know."

"Okay," said Colleen slowly.

His phone was ringing. It was Drew Garrett's office number. He let it go through to voice mail. He'd call him back as soon as they stopped. Wherever that was.

*   *   *

It turned out to be Great Falls Park on the Maryland side of the Potomac River. They parked and found a picnic table out of the way and in the shade near the old historic barge house. Colleen went to get two bottles of water and he called his voice mail. There was only one message, that being from Drew Garrett who had simply asked Kendall to return his call.

Garrett had called from his personal office line and picked up himself. "Thanks for calling me back," he said. "I realize you probably don't feel so hot yourself."

"I'm not too bad. It's a long story."

"They all seem to be these days. What happened to simple? Before I met you my life was simple. Hectic maybe, but in the big picture of things, simple."

"I know what you mean. I'm sorry."

"Hey, it's not your fault. You probably saved my life. Anyway, I was calling for two reasons. The first I've already pretty much worked through. I think I just panicked this morning. I didn't think I could wait until Monday for the surgery—the idea of possibly still having cancer cells in my body is driving me crazy."

"Your excision was clear," said Kendall. "I really think you're okay in that regard. And most likely the lymph node will be normal."

"I know, Doctor. I'm not talking about rational feelings here. Have you ever had cancer?"

"No."

"Well, don't start. So I called the surgeon to see if I could get it done today. I even called the hospital operating room to see if there was OR time. You're lucky I didn't call you."

Kendall smiled. He could see the scene, and he knew that Garret was smiling as well.

"Maybe you need some Valium or something to help you sleep before Monday."

"That's what my internist said. I called him, too. He called something in for me, but I don't think I'll need it. I feel a little better now."

"You need to get out of your office and go home. Go spend some time with your kids."

"That's exactly what I'm planning. I'm just cleaning up a few things here and then I'm leaving. You'll be back in your office on Monday?"

"Yes. I'll call you or Caroline after your surgery."

"Thanks. The other thing is, I've been following this Fairfield story in the news. Wasn't that the day you had your surgery?"

"It was the day I was supposed to have my surgery."

"That's what I was wondering. They probably shut down the whole place."

"Right."

"They said there were three rooms involved. Was one of them yours?"

Kendall didn't answer for a moment. No one else knew what had happened to him, and Ed Burke had asked him to keep everything to himself.

"You don't have to answer that," said Garrett, as if Kendall hadn't already. Then, he said: "Wow, that's something to think about. They think it's an ex-employee?"

"There was a note to that effect."

"Umm. Well, I guess it's like airplane crashes. Every hospital in the country will be checking everything for a while. It's probably a good time to have surgery."

"You're right about that."

"Okay, well, thank you again, Doctor. Wish me luck."

"It'll be fine, Drew. Dr. Uhle's very good."

Colleen was back with the water. Kendall stood and they headed out slowly to the overlook of the falls.

"Are you sure you're okay walking that far?" she said.

Kendall nodded. "We'll turn around if we need to."

"What's with you and this guy?" she asked as they walked. "I don't think I've ever seen you talk with a patient so much outside of the office."

Kendall thought about the question for a moment. "Self preservation for one," he said. "Initially the guy scared the shit out of me. Now I feel sorry for him. And he's kind of grown on me."

"Kind of like looking in the mirror?"

"Maybe," he said, smiling slightly. "I'm not sure if that's a compliment, though."

*　　*　　*

It was almost as if they were at the ocean, lying on their backs with the sun warm on their face and arms and the sounds of rushing water crashing all around them. The only difference was that the water crashing on the rocks below was a constant thunderous roar, and the rocks they were lying on were hard and unforgiving. He had actually fallen asleep and now woke with the yell of a kayaker several hundred feet below. Kendall sat up and watched him furiously dig his paddle into the water as he tried to maintain his position out in the current. When he reached the chute between a pile of huge sandstone rocks, he turned the nose of the kayak downstream and in seconds was whisked away by the river and shot down through the rocks. It was a tortuous run for about a hundred yards, and when he finally splashed into a calmer collecting pool he looked at a group of fellow kayakers standing along the Virginia shoreline and raised his arms in triumph.

"We need to go," said Colleen. "It's almost two."

Kendall stood and slowly flexed his knee. It was still swollen and stiff, but he had no idea now when he was going to have time to get it fixed. Peter Kane wanted to do it over the weekend, but he just didn't think he was up to it. And in some way he truly believed that Bob Williams needed him at the moment.

They were halfway back to the canal towpath when Bob Williams called.

Kendall stopped in the shade of a large sycamore tree.

"Chad called me," said Bob.

"Where is he?"

"With our minister. They've been talking for a while."

So all is forgiven, thought Kendall. You can't be serious. "So now what?" he said carefully.

"He wants to meet with me and talk. He's coming over to the office. I'm proud of him for that."

"Does anyone there know about the slide?"

"No."

"Does Sam know about any of this?"

"No. And for the time being, I'd like to leave it that way."

Kendall wondered if there was a slight edge in Williams' voice now, but he chose to leave it alone. "Is the new slide ready yet?"

"No. Probably another hour or so. The histo tech' is swamped because it's Friday and we have to get all of our regular specimens processed today. I'll call you later and tell you about everything."

"Okay. Thanks, Bob."

They were walking again, Kendall relaying the conversation to Colleen and moving as fast as his knee would take him.

"Meeting with his minister isn't a good thing?" asked Colleen.

"For whom?" He stopped and looked at her. "For me or for Bob?"

* * *

When they got home with Matthew, Kendall had an e-mail from Mancini waiting for him: I have a reception at River Club tonight at 5—meet me at 4:45?

Yes, typed Kendall. Meet you at Adirondack chairs next to putting green. See you then.

Matthew was going out with friends shortly, so Kendall cornered his son in the kitchen and talked with him about his day and week as much as a teenager was prone to do. Mixed in with the grunts and the "yeahs" and the "okays" were a few true smiles and anecdotes of hopeless tennis campers with overbearing parents, all thinking their child was the next tennis prodigy. Colleen left in running clothes as they sat at the kitchen table. She and Kendall had agreed on the way home that she could run at the high school track, but not alone through the neighborhoods. Matthew was picked up a few minutes later and, alone in the kitchen, Kendall dialed his daughter's cell phone. Kelley did not pick up, but her voice was animated and comforting. He left a message and went out on the deck with Mandy.

He did not have a good feeling about this meeting between Bob and Chad Williams. This father-son heart-to-heart that, by the sounds of it, was nothing new to them. If Bob did not stay firm it was going to be a difficult situation. Although Chad might not have broken any state or federal law with the slide transposition, he had broken the most basic tenets of the Hippocratic Oath and the standards of medical care. What had happened could not be ignored, even if he had been forgiven in the eyes of his minister or his God.

Kendall's phone rang—Detective Finotti. He let the call go to voice mail and looked around the back yard. Who knew? The detective could be calling him and watching him at the same time.

He decided he wasn't about to find out. He took his cell phone, locked the house, and got in his car. He'd get to The River Club a few minutes early and wait for Mancini, he figured. Even better, he could check on Colleen on the way. Though they'd agreed that she'd only run if there were other people on the track, he'd feel better setting eyes on her.

*   *   *

With the sun lower in the sky and the city's offices closing, the putting green was full of golfers. Kendall plopped down in a white Adirondack chair and shielded his eyes from the sun. Bret Hartman waved to him, then Martin Dranginis. He waved back and checked the large clock on a post next to the putting green. It was 4:48. Kendall scanned the driveway—Mancini was never late.

At 4:52 he sensed a figure behind him. Then a shadow passed over his face and Mancini was suddenly in the chair beside him. Still dressed in a coat and tie, his face was sweating and he looked drawn.

"Sorry, I'm late," he said. "I had to stop by Hidden Glen."

"How's Henry?" asked Kendall.

"You heard about him obviously. He died this afternoon."

"Oh, no. I'm sorry. Jesus, that's horrible. He was a great man."

"He was," said Mancini, his eyes watering. "His glucose was twenty in the emergency room. They think maybe he gave himself too much insulin and he had a hypoglycemic blackout. He probably hit his head on the way down. Apparently he had a big gash in his forehead."

"Have you talked with Bob Williams at all today?" said Kendall.

"No. I've been in court up until an hour ago. Why? Should I have?"

"Umm, I'm not sure. I know you two are pretty close."

"We are. I think Chad's the one who called 911, actually. I guess he was playing golf this morning. Kind of strange for a doctor, isn't it? I thought you guys played in the afternoon."

"He says he works late when he plays in the morning."

Mancini nodded, then looked at his watch. "Jesus, I've got to go in a minute. I'm introducing the guest of honor."

Kendall's phone was in vibrate mode and it started throbbing against his thigh. He took it out and cupped his hand around the display to see the number. Bob Williams, he mouthed to Mancini. Mancini stood and put his closed hand to his ear in a motion for Kendall to call him later. Kendall nodded and took the call.

"Hi, Bob. How'd it go?"

"It went very well, Ryan. Chad is obviously devastated and we had a real heart-to-heart talk. When you can give him some time, he'd like to also sit down with you and explain what happened."

"Bob, what happened is that he lied to me and sent phony slides up to a specialist. And that's not even touching what he did to the patient."

"I know what happened, Chad. But it wasn't with any malice intended. He was just trying to make himself look good in your eyes. He respects you. He thinks you're the best around, and he wanted you to respect him. He wanted you to think that he would do anything for you."

"Bob, if I didn't have any balls as Chad himself said, I would have cut off the tip of that poor girl's nose."

"That's why he used that slide that was clear at the base of the lesion. It was all very calculated, Ryan. He's not denying any of that."

"And how many more of my patients has he done this to? It's not the first time that he's sent slides out for a consult."

"I asked him that. Believe me. He said he's never done it with any other patients of yours. He did admit that he's done it with two other doctors because he thought we were losing business from them and he wanted to show them the personal attention we provided. But he specifically said he's never done it with you before this case."

"Jesus, Bob. I mean, what am I supposed to say? You want me to just forget it?"

"No. Nothing can be forgotten. I guess I'm hoping you might try to understand and at least meet with him, or with him and me if you'd prefer. Chad's not as confident as we are. He's been insecure since I can remember. It's hard for us to comprehend that."

"And what about the tissue block? What about the slide you were going to have cut?"

"It showed a Spitz Nevus like we thought it would."

"So he actually switched the block, too."

"He did. He admitted that on his own. He had the real block right in his desk drawer. He gave it to me in fact."

"Bob, do you know that Henry died?"

Silence. "No, I did not know that. I don't think Chad does either. He'll be heartbroken. He's known Henry since he was a kid. He was the one who found him and called 911. In fact, he helped them take him out."

Kendall closed his eyes. He wanted to scream at Williams, to reach through the phone and shake him.

"One more thing, Ryan," said the elder Williams. "I asked Chad point blank about Fairfield. He was truly hurt that you could even think such a thing. He respects you like no one else."

*   *   *

There were two news station vans sitting around the corner from his house. Kendall thought it odd that they would be parked there, unless they were planning on surprising him in the house as opposed to coming or going. When he got closer to his house he saw the reason. There was a gray sedan in the driveway with the unmistakable appearance of a government vehicle. He stopped in the street and started to call Colleen from his cell phone, but the driver's door to the sedan opened and a man got out and motioned him into the driveway.

Kendall pulled into the garage and walked out to the driveway with an exaggerated limp. Detective Finotti was not smiling.

"Dr. Kendall?" he said.

"Yes, how do you do?"

"I'd be better if you had called me today."

"I'm sorry—it's been very busy. I had—"

"Can we go inside please?"

"Sure," said Kendall. "Please come in."

EIGHTEEN

Saturday, June 16

They were more searches than dreams. It was as if he were at his computer typing in thoughts and names and watching the connections flash onto the monitor screen faster than anyone could have ever imagined. Faces of patients past appeared one after another, as if he were in his office watching them file through to the exam rooms. One after another they were culled from the depths of his memory, rolled around every which way in his mind that they would turn, and then stored again, either high in the cortex where they would be readily accessible, or deep into the discards. He was searching so hard that it was almost tiring, the mental energy output greater than what his resting body was supposed to be conserving. He turned fitfully in the bed, forcing himself to stay asleep, to keep the search engine running.

The computers in his office could answer many questions, but this was not one of them. This was purely his. Perhaps Sammie could help with the last year or two, but before that she had not been focused on the pathology reports. Chevy Chase Pathology Associates could no doubt help—they could generate a list of reports that had been issued to his office in the last five years. He could then take that list and pull every chart to find the two or three or four other Lindsey Brownings that he knew were there.

Not for one moment did he believe that Lindsey Browning was the only patient that Chad Williams had intellectually assaulted. And perhaps there was physical maiming as well. Who knew if there was a surgical procedure that had been done, or not done, based on phony slides and essentially a phony pathology report? Kendall knew they were there, their identities resting in the depths of his brain and the chart racks in his office. He just had to remember the faces and the names.

He was making progress. He had finally fallen asleep sometime after midnight and shortly thereafter he had resurrected several scenarios, each accompanied by a sudden start, a brief opening of his eyes, and then the plunge back down. Two or three years ago he had seen a young woman with a cystic basal cell carcinoma on her breast that had purportedly mimicked a ductal breast carcinoma for a few days. What was a potentially life-threatening tumor he had ended up treating in his office in about three minutes. Then there was the male college freshman with the blue nevus on his buttock that had looked under the microscope like a malignant blue nevus for about a week. Will Ammerman had eventually declared it to be a simple blue nevus that had actually been completely excised with the biopsy, but meanwhile the boy's parents had taken him out of school and had his life on hold while waiting for the final report. And then perhaps the case that bothered him the most—the young engineer with the questionable spindle cell sarcoma on his back that had ended up being a simple hypertrophic scar.

The scenarios in place, he was now recreating the faces and the times, both of which were slowly taking shape. It was an ordering and recall of his own life as much as theirs, for the months and years of the patients in his office were inexorably intertwined with his own. The faces and the phone calls and the worry and the stress were as much a part of his existence as the birthdays and anniversaries and graduations. He in fact remembered having to step out of Matthew's eighth grade graduation to speak with the mother of the college freshman. And indeed, as the night wore on, the faces became sharper, clearer, as alive as if they were lying on an exam table in front of him. Now it was only the names that he needed. The names so that he could pull the charts. The names so that he could get their reports. The names so that he could call Bob Williams and make him face his son.

The visages flew round and round, taunting him almost with their closeness. At 4:30 AM he opened his eyes. Megan. Megan had just graduated from Boston College. She had gone to high school in town. He could see her face, hear her voice. Megan Donan? He sat up. Megan Donavan.

He got out of bed and went down to his desk. He was taking no chances with his fifty-one-year-old brain. He wrote down her name, turned off the lights, and sat in the dark. The young man had been at Elon University when his parents kept him home from school. He'd just joined a fraternity; he was wearing the frat T-shirt; he'd had no idea what Kendall was talking about, as the possibility of cancer was not in the universe of a college freshman. His name would not come and Kendall moved on. The engineer. He'd been married—Kendall remembered his wife coming in when he had his sutures taken out. They had a baby; she had it with her; he worked for Bechtel.

Mandy came into the library and sat next to him, her head on his thigh. He stroked her head and listened to her deep throaty purr of content. The faces and names were so close, maddeningly close, just waiting to be pulled by some fragment of memory. For the moment, though, he could not find that fragment.

He climbed the stairs as quietly as he could and slipped on shorts, a golf shirt, sandals. In the kitchen, he wrote Colleen a note and left it on the granite island. Mandy stayed with him, wanting to follow him into the garage. He pushed her back into the house with his foot and quietly closed the door. It was 4:50—still night. The streets were quiet, empty. He headed out towards Democracy Boulevard and his office. He turned. There was a car behind him now. A single car, barely in his sight. He turned; it turned. He sped up and there it stayed, far enough away to be unobtrusive, yet close enough to see him.

Shrugging, he focused on the road ahead. Elon, frat boy. Baby, Bechtel.

The car stayed with him. As long as it stayed there, away from him, he could care less. He had nothing to hide in his office.

*   *   *

When he left his office with Megan Donavan's chart in hand, the first hint of light was showing in the eastern sky. He paused on the sidewalk outside of the building, breathing the cool, moist morning air deeply into his lungs. There'd been a heavy dew during the night and the bushes lining the sidewalks were laden with water. Even his car, which hadn't been in the lot more than a half-hour, had a new thin film of water on the hood and windshield. He saw no sign of Detective Finotti, or whoever had the unfortunate duty of watching him at this early hour. It was too early to go home and wake Colleen or to call Bob Williams. He headed to his car and then to Starbucks in the shopping center down the street.

Even Starbucks was quiet. He sat at a corner table and opened Megan Donavan's chart. Chad Williams had used a different consultant for her case—a breast cancer specialist at Johns Hopkins. Otherwise the pattern was the same. Triangular phone calls back and forth for days between Kendall, Megan, and Chad Williams. Each call was clearly documented in the chart. Then finally the good news, the happy ending.

Kendall closed the chart and made a list on a piece of scrap paper of everything he could remember from the other two cases. He was waiting for his second café-au-lait when Josh flashed through his mind. Josh . . . Josh Rickman. Back at his table, he wrote down Josh's name in big letters and circled it. Then somehow, as if the resurrection of Josh had somehow loosed a cache of memories, the engineer came quickly to life. He lived in Bethesda. Tim . . . Tim Slat . . . Slat . . . Tim Slattery. He wrote the name in even bigger letters, circled it, and headed for his car. With real light now in the sky he did not even look around for another car in the parking lot that he might recognize.

Colleen called. "What are you doing?" she said crossly. "I thought you were downstairs. I must not have heard the garage door go up."

"I've been to my office, I've been to Starbucks, and now I'm going back to my office. I remembered three different cases that I think he screwed me on."

"Okay," she said after a moment. "So now what?"

"I'm going to call Bob. I want the tissue blocks. I can get a hold of every one of these patients if I have to and get hair or saliva for DNA analysis. Then I can have a DNA match done between that and the tissue block. I'm presuming their slides have been switched, but I want to know if the tissue blocks were also switched."

"Why?"

"'*Why*? Because I want to know if the asshole's full of shit—that's why! I want to know if he's lying about never having done this to me before Lindsey, and I want to know if he switched the tissue blocks on all of these patients. If he switched slides and didn't switch the blocks, then the real lesion is still in the block if there was ever a future question. But if he switched the blocks, and it's now two years later, then he never had any intention of changing them back. What if he died? What if he moved? Who would ever know?"

"Right. I understand. By the way, I think the detective's gone."

"Someone followed me out. I presume it was him." Kendall looked in his rearview mirror. The road was full of cars now and it was hard to see more than several cars behind him, but he thought he saw the detective's sedan four or five cars back. "He's somewhere behind me I think. I don't care about him. Listen, I want to go pull these charts and call Bob. I'll call you in a little while."

In his office, he pushed the sliding chart rack down to expose the "R's," hoping that the charts had not been archived. Josh Rickman's chart was right where it was supposed to be, as was Tim Slattery's. He quickly scanned them. Rickman's consult was from Will Ammerman; Slattery's was from Sheila West, probably the world's expert on soft tissue tumors.

He sat down at Laurel's desk and wrote down on an index card the accession numbers from the pathology reports on all three patients. Then he looked at his watch. It was only 7:30 AM. He'd been planning on waiting until eight o'clock before calling Bob, mainly out of respect for his wife. But he was ready to go, his stomach churning, his heart slowly picking up its pace. He put his hand on the phone, then took it off, deciding to give the elder Williams a few more minutes.

He went to his desk and checked his e-mail—nothing. There was one message in his voice mail from Will Ammerman. He'd left it at 7:00 PM the night before.

Thanks for sending up the tissue block on Drew Garrett, Ammerman had said. He would definitely use some photomicrographs from the case in his new book. It was a classic spindle cell melanoma—they just didn't get any better. And it looked like someone else appreciated it too—the block was nearly half gone. There must have been several hundred slides cut from it, said Ammerman. Anyway, thanks again, and he hoped Mr. Garrett was doing well with his surgery. Let him know if he could help in any way. He'd mail the block back next week.

They must have cut it up at Duke, thought Kendall as he hung up. Chad also probably cut it up pretty good to get the slides he wanted.

He looked out the window—the sun was coming up. It was time to go. Bob had given him his cell phone number and he called it.

A woman answered on the fifth ring. She sounded half asleep. It took her a moment to digest who he was and what he wanted.

"Is everything okay?" she finally said.

"Umm, I suppose so. Is Bob there?" asked Kendall for the second time.

"He's here, but he must be down at the dock. I'm still inside. Can you hold on a moment?"

"Sure, thanks." Shit, he hadn't figured on Williams having gone back to their bay house. Shit. It was easily an hour away, maybe more.

"Good morning, Ryan." Bob Williams' voice was cool. "How can I help you?"

"I need to see you at your office, Bob. It's quarter of eight now. How about if we meet at nine?"

"How about if I see you on Monday? I'm down at the bay with my wife."

"That's not going to work, Bob. I need to see you today."

"Do you mind telling me why?"

"I'll tell you when I see you."

"I'll see you on Monday, Ryan. When would you like to meet?"

"You'll meet me at nine, Bob, or my next call is to the detective that I met with last night."

Williams was quiet for several seconds. Then, he said: "I'll meet you at nine. How long will it take?"

"I hope just five or ten minutes. And Bob?"

"Yes?"

"Don't tell anyone you're meeting me. Particularly anyone in your family. Meet me outside your office."

"I understand."

*   *   *

Even though Bob Williams had an hour-plus drive back to town, Kendall had no intention of letting him get to the office first. Still, he had at least a half-hour to kill. Hidden Glen Country Club was just a few minutes away from Chevy Chase Pathology Associates, so Kendall took a chance that Mancini might be playing tennis or hitting golf balls on the driving range. With Mancini out at his reception late and Kendall dozing until he had retired to his bedroom after eleven, they had not spoken the night before.

The guard at the gate knew him by name and waved him through. The driving range was on one side of the parking lot and he slowly drove down the entire length but did not see Mancini. He parked as close to the tennis facility as he could get and got out of the car. Although it was warming quickly and would soon be hot, at the moment it was still a beautiful temperate summer morning, perfect for anything outdoors. He took in a deep breath of air and exhaled slowly. He was going to have to clear his schedule again and get his knee fixed, he thought. As he'd been told innumerable times by his father, who'd learned his own sage advice too late in his own life, no one on their deathbed ever wished that they had worked more.

Mancini was on court four playing singles with Hunter Dolan. Kendall moved into a position where he was out of the way, but where Mancini might also still see him. For several points Mancini looked nowhere except from the ball to the court to Dolan. He ended a point with a cross-court backhand that skipped off the line and headed toward the bench. End of game and changeover. Kendall stepped out into the open and Mancini looked up. He put a hand to his face to shield his eyes, then motioned to Dolan that he'd be right back.

"Hey, Ryan, what's up? Sorry we missed each other last night. I got in late."

"I figured that. I'll call you later today. I have a few minutes to kill now and I thought I'd stop by. I'm meeting with Bob at nine."

"Sounds serious for a Saturday."

Kendall nodded. "It's not for fun."

"Call me later," said Mancini. "I need to get back." Then he stopped and turned for a moment. "By the way, I got a little more information from the hospital. It looks like Henry did give himself too much insulin. I don't know what the exact level was, but it was way high, and as I said before, his glucose was twenty. There was also some dirt in his head wound. And a piece of grass."

Dirt, grass, said Kendall to himself. Then aloud, "From the floor you mean?"

Mancini shrugged. "I suppose. He was big guy. He'd go down pretty hard. He's going to have a formal autopsy, so hopefully that'll help. Call me later—I need to go."

*   *   *

Kendall was out front of Chevy Chase Pathology Associates by 8:45. Bob Williams arrived at 9:10. He let them into the building with his security card, then turned left toward a hallway that looked like a back entrance to the office. Kendall glanced at the directory on the way in—Chevy Chase Pathology Associates occupied the entire first floor of the building.

Williams unlocked a door at the end of the hall and they stepped into an administrative area. He turned on the lights and looked at Kendall.

"How can I help you, Ryan?"

Kendall took the index card out of his pocket. "I need three tissue blocks, Bob."

Williams stared at him for a moment, started to object, then stopped. Looking at the card in Kendall's hand, he said: "You obviously have the numbers."

"I do."

Williams headed down another hall, through the processing lab, and into a wing of the building that was noticeably cooler. He stopped in front of a long bank of metal filing cabinets. "What year?"

"2005. 34617."

Williams scanned the cards on the front of the cabinets and pulled out a drawer. "What's the number again?"

"34617."

The blocks, some pink, some green, some blue, were stacked with the tapered end down and the flat end with the accession number up. Williams found the block and carefully pulled it out with his thumb and index finger. He held it up to the light, turned it over to check the accession number one more time, then handed it to Kendall.

"Two more," said Kendall. "Both 2006."

Williams quickly found both of them and handed them to Kendall. "Anything else?"

"That's it. Thanks."

Williams looked at him. "You don't believe that girl was the only case?"

"I'm not sure, Bob. But I need to be. I think you do, too."

"How will you know without asking him?"

"I know all of these people. It's easy to get DNA samples from them."

Williams nodded. "Be careful with the blocks, please. Remember the tissue's in paraffin wax. It's hot out—the paraffin will melt if it gets too warm."

Williams turned off the lights as they headed out. At the door, Kendall said: "Don't tell Chad about this, Bob. I've got at least one detective on my ass. They're not too impressed with the note that was found in the lounge at Fairfield."

"I'm going to pretend that I didn't hear that," said Williams. "And you better hope that none of this becomes public, or you better have a whole hell of a lot of insurance."

Kendall nodded. "Fair enough," he said.

Nineteen

Kendall had parked down the street from the Chevy Chase Pathology Associates office. It had been quiet then, still fairly early into the summer Saturday morning. With the stores now starting to open and the later risers exiting from their apartments, Wisconsin Avenue was coming alive with pedestrians and cars. He walked slowly towards his car, his mind on Bob and Chad Williams, his eyes searching for Detective Finotti or his cohort. The Saks parking lot had only a few cars in it, all luxury sedans. He scanned each side of the street, seeing nothing that seemed out of the ordinary.

In his car, he sat for a moment with the engine running. Even in his own mind, he still wasn't sure how much of what he'd just done was a bluff, and how far he really wanted to proceed. He suspected that both Megan Donovan and Tim Slattery were still in town working, and with a little explaining or hyperbole he could certainly get hair samples or saliva swabs from them. And Alice Chen, one of the dermatology research stars at the National Institutes of Health who specialized in gene rearrangement studies owed him a favor big-time. She could easily tissue type the DNA from those samples, and then from the tissue blocks with a PCR assay. He pulled out into the street. The question was, with what urgency? Although he would not hesitate to call her on a Saturday, he was inclined to wait until Monday, even though he presumed that Bob Williams would not be waiting to hear the results of his search. Despite Kendall's threat, Bob would most likely speak to Chad and somehow warn him. Hopefully Chad would just come clean. Still, there was no harm in speaking with Alice, he figured. Better to be prepared.

He stopped quickly in a grocery store across Wisconsin Avenue and bought a small soft cooler and several cold packs for the tissue blocks. Easing back out onto the main thoroughfare, he started watching his mirrors again.

He wasn't sure what caught his eye. Perhaps it was the sudden lane change, the sedan darting back into traffic behind him, now out of view again. Perhaps it was the sense that if someone were indeed following him, they were too close, too obvious. He slowed, one eye on the traffic ahead, one eye on the rearview mirror. The light changed. He sped up, passed a car, eased back in. A few seconds later a champagne-colored sedan pulled out, eased back in.

Kendall put on his phone earpiece and called home.

"Hi," he said. "I'll be home soon. They're still following me."

"Are you sure? When I went out a little while ago I thought I saw that car that was here last night down the street."

"Really. That's interesting." He checked his rearview mirror—the sedan was five cars back. Looking ahead, he moved out into the left lane. The Bradley Boulevard intersection was coming up and he eased into the left turn lane. A car moved in behind him, then another. The sedan had slowed as well. A dozen cars passed it before it slowly moved left. The light turned.

"Do me a favor, please," said Kendall. "Do you have running clothes on?" Colleen wore running clothes summer and winter unless there was a reason not to.

"Yes."

"Jog around the block and see if the detective's there."

"Okay," she said, drawing it out. "Do you mind telling me why?"

"I'm just curious if I rate two detectives." The sedan was behind him, barely in sight. "Can you go now, please?"

"I'm going, I'm going."

Kendall drove at the speed limit, staying in the right lane. At Arlington Boulevard he turned right. There were lights every quarter-mile on Arlington and he stopped at the first. The sedan turned onto Arlington and slowed. Kendall stayed in the right lane, the lights stopping him at almost every intersection. Approaching Old Georgetown Road, he moved left again.

Colleen called, her breaths quick and audible. "He's around the corner. I've never noticed it before, but there's a gap between Trish's house and Liz's house where you can see through to our driveway. Same car, same guy."

"Interesting. Thanks. I'll be home in a little while. I might stop by my office and clean up some paperwork."

"Do you really think that's a great idea? Can't it wait until Monday?"

"The building is open. A lot of people work on Saturdays, actually. It's pretty busy."

"Call me when you get there then."

"Okay."

Two detectives? he wondered. Or perhaps a nosy Chad Williams who'd been watching his father and had now turned his attention to him. Or maybe he'd been behind him all along. Maybe it was his car that had followed him out in the morning.

Kendall turned onto Old Georgetown Road and sped up, passing cars at every opportunity. The sedan stayed back, but kept pace with every move of Kendall's. When he got to Wildwood Shopping Center he pulled in and parked in the middle of the lot, as close to Starbucks as he could get. He limped in, not once looking behind him. In the store he headed for the back, passed the bathroom, and went out the rear service entrance. Moving as fast as he could, he turned right and headed down the back of the shopping center. He came to a walkway that cut through the stores and came out to the front, but decided it would come out too close to Starbuck's. He moved on, heading for the last store. At the end of the shopping center he turned right again and moved into a line of trees that separated the side entrance from the parking lot. Keeping the trees and shrubs between him and the parking lot, he moved slowly now, searching the lot. No sedan. He moved closer to Old Georgetown Road so as to see the farthest row of cars. There it was, backed into a space that was diagonal from Starbucks.

Kendall stayed low, moving between the trees. He circled around a stand-alone bank and came out onto the sidewalk fronting Old Georgetown Road. The sedan, either an Acura or an Infiniti, he thought, was twenty cars away. The windows had glare protection and he could not see into the car. He moved a few cars closer and crouched behind a SUV.

It was hot now, and he could feel the sweat running down his chest. His breaths were coming hard and fast, and his stomach felt as if there was an intruder in his house. He took out his phone and called Bob Williams—no answer. He called again—no answer. He dialed Paul Mancini.

"Hey, Ryan. Sorry I—"

"Paul, do you have Bob Williams' cell phone number."

"I don't think so."

Kendall had to stop and take a breath. "Let me give it to you. Call him right now please and tell him to call me immediately."

"Are you okay, Ryan? You sound horrible. What's the matter?"

"Call him, Paul. Now, please. Tell him to call me now or everything's off."

"Okay. Call me back then."

A couple passed him on the sidewalk, looking at him suspiciously. His knee was aching and he sat down on the curb to rest it and catch his breath. A minute later his phone rang.

"How can I help you, Ryan?" said Bob Williams, his voice neither cold nor warm.

"Do you know where your son is?"

"Which son?"

"Chad."

"I know exactly where Chad is. I just spoke with him. He's waiting outside of CVS for a prescription."

"I'm going to hang up, Bob, and I want you to call Chad right now." Kendall was starting to move, backing up slowly behind the cars. "Tell him to turn his headlights on for ten seconds and then turn them off. Do you understand?"

"Ryan, you're—"

"Call him, Bob!"

"Okay, Ryan. Have a good day."

Kendall kept moving, out from the behind the cars and into the trees again, all the while watching the headlights of the sedan. At the edge of the trees he stopped and waited. A minute went by, then another. A man got out of the sedan and walked out into the lot. It was Chad. Hands on his hips, he looked around and around. Kendall was almost on the ground now, the smell of dirt in his nose. He inched his head around a tree. Chad was moving towards Kendall's Lexus, a hand to his ear. Kendall's cell phone rang. He managed to get it out of his pocket—it was Chad. He shut off the ringer and put it on vibrate.

Chad reached Kendall's car. He looked in the Lexus' front passenger window and pulled on the door handle. Then he put his face right up to the window and cupped his hands around his eyes. Straightening, he looked around the parking lot, and then circled the car pulling on all of the door handles as he passed them. Facing the door to Starbucks, his hand went to his ear again. Kendall's phone vibrated, again and again. It stopped, then started again. Chad finally put his phone in his pocket and the vibrating stopped. He shook his head, looked around the parking lot again, and headed for Starbucks. At the door he stopped and turned around to scan the lot one more time. Then he turned and went in.

Kendall stood up and hobbled as fast as he could down the side entrance to the shopping center. He crossed the street and was into a neighborhood. At the first house he stopped behind a car. His breaths could not come fast enough. He bent over, trying to get enough air. Colleen was not an option—they might follow her. He took out his phone and called Mancini. Mancini answered on the first ring. He'd be there in ten minutes.

* * *

Mancini did not think it was a good idea for Kendall to go back to his house, particularly with a detective outside and a Maryland state judge bringing him home. He advised Kendall to call Colleen and tell her to lock the gates and the house and for her and Matthew to stay inside. Keep Mandy outside, he said. Dogs, particularly big ones, were the single biggest deterrent of unwanted visitors. They would go back to Mancini's house. On the way he listened to Kendall for ten minutes without saying a word.

When Kendall was done, he simply nodded. "A few things," he said. "Some are on the record and some are off. The first is, don't give up on Bob. This is his son, but it's like an alcoholic in crisis. And you don't know Pat, but she's as solid as a rock. She may be Chad's mother, but she's no fool. Second, I would consider calling your friend at NIH today, if nothing else to at least get the ball rolling. Depending on what she says, and depending on how comfortable you are with calling one of those patients, I'd consider getting this typing process started."

Kendall was leaning back in the seat, his head against the window. "Agree," he said. "I'll call Alice from your house."

"And then you have to resolve this detective issue," said Mancini. "There's a point at which you're withholding important information and you could get yourself in trouble."

Kendall didn't respond.

Mancini turned into his driveway and shut off the engine. "Plus," he said, turning his head to look at Kendall, "it's a little disturbing that Chad's following you. Particularly if he was the one who tampered with the hoses."

"Paul, I'm obviously very concerned about that, but I don't know that for sure. Nor does anyone else at this point. And you told Bob that I was to be trusted. That's the only reason he called me about Chad to begin with. Whether he's backing off now or not, he came to me, he confided in me. And the first thing he did when Henry gave him the slide was to call me. He didn't have to do that. He could have looked at it himself and never said a word except to Chad. I can't now just go and publicly accuse Chad of trying to kill me. What if I'm wrong? For Christ's sake, Bob just threatened to sue the shit out of me."

Mancini sighed and looked away. "I understand, Ryan. The last two things I said were off the record."

"And frankly," said Kendall, "I'm not too concerned about Chad trying to hurt me now. Maybe he would have before his father knew about my patient. But he'd be a complete idiot to do something to me now. I actually think he was following me more to try and talk, or to see if Bob and I were doing something behind his back."

Mancini nodded. "It is different now. Bob will only bend so much."

"I want to give Bob the weekend. If Chad screwed me on these other cases he knows the game is up. He's gotta come clean now, or he knows it's only going to get worse. I've got the tissue blocks, and I can get the patients. Speaking of the blocks, they're in a cooler in my car. I need to go back soon."

Mancini nodded and got out. "I'll take you back in a little while. Why don't you call your friend. You can sit in my library. I'm going to go out back and think about this Henry situation. I don't like the idea that Chad might have been angry with him."

* * *

Dr. Alice Chen loved two things in life—her family, and the genetic mysteries of DNA and RNA that she was determined to uncover. She had gone to medical school in Korea and come to the United States with her entire family, with whom she still lived in Alexandria, Virginia. Although she had passed her Foreign Medical School Graduate Exam with the highest score in the country, her spoken English had only been passable and had limited her ability to find training. When Kendall first met her she'd finally managed to get an internship in a local community hospital. She had severe eczema and saw him frequently in his office as a patient that year. He had helped her greatly with her skin, and with her internship as well. She'd had a seventy-seven-year-old training director who had served as a battalion surgeon in the Korean War and was doing everything he could to make her life miserable. Kendall had guided her through the year, not only with counsel, but with visible proof that she was welcome in this country as much for her intellect as the ease of immigration.

Perhaps because of her skin disease, perhaps because of Kendall, when she'd finally made it through the internship she'd applied to every dermatology residency program in the country. But with dermatology residencies being the most sought after training programs in the world, and with candidates from every top medical school in the country lining up for their shot at them, she had been on no one's short list. Eventually she'd come back to his office as an observer and spent a number of mornings and afternoons with him. He'd been so impressed with her clinical acumen and reasoning that he'd placed a personal call to Brent Coleman, the Chief of Dermatology at George Washington University. Coleman had agreed to interview her and she'd gone on to be the most accomplished resident and graduate in the history of the George Washington program.

Alice was delighted to hear from Kendall. In fact, with the heat and the pollens it sounded as if she was truly suffering with her dermatitis and she had wanted to call him anyway. She was happy to meet him at the National Institutes of Health that afternoon. Bring the blocks, she told him, and if she could find a histology tech to cut some sections she'd get started on them. Even if she couldn't find a tech', she said she could section them herself. The patients themselves were simple. If Kendall could get a hair or a saliva swab or some skin scrapings, she'd get that going as well. They took each other's cell phone numbers and agreed to meet at two o'clock.

His phone was ringing. It was Detective Finotti. He let it go.

Colleen called a minute later. "The detective wants to know where you are, what you're doing, and why a car registered to Chadwick Williams was following you," she said.

"Wow, they did have someone else following me. I never saw them."

"That's what they do for a living. What are you doing?"

"I've been talking with Alice Chen. Why don't you tell him I'm about to go over to NIH and do a consult on one of their ICU patients. It's going to take a while."

"Maybe you should call him. He sounded annoyed."

Kendall sighed. "All right. I'll call him in a little bit. Actually, I'm glad he's at the house. If you need anything just call him."

"Thanks," she said sarcastically. "Matthew's up. He needs to go out soon."

"Okay. Go ahead and take him where he needs to go. Just keep your cell phone with you."

"This better end soon, Ryan," she said. "It's getting old."

* * *

Kendall showered at Mancini's and borrowed some clean shorts and a shirt. Then they drove back to Wildwood

Shopping Center and stopped a block away for Kendall to get out. Mancini stayed there until Kendall reached his car and left the parking lot.

Kendall didn't bother to look for anyone behind him. He was going to NIH, just as he'd said, and good luck to anyone trying to follow him in. Since the 9/11 disaster NIH was a fortress, and he was meeting Alice outside one of the gates simply to facilitate himself getting in.

He was parked on Cedar Lane outside the west gate when Alice called at 1:45. The George Washington Parkway, which followed the Potomac River on the Virginia side from Alexandria to the Capitol Beltway, was at a standstill. She was also in between exits and had no option but to wait for traffic to clear. She had just turned the radio on to the local news, but hadn't heard a traffic report yet.

Kendall tuned the radio to WWDC and waited. A weather and traffic report came on every ten minutes. Hot and humid, said the announcer. Heat index approaching ninety-five degrees. Chance of thunderstorms thirty percent. Commercial. Announcer again. Avoid the GW parkway for the next several hours. The northbound lanes were completely blocked south of Chain Bridge Road and the backup now extended to Reagan National Airport. A car had gone through the guardrail, down the embankment, and into the rocks on the edge of the river. Emergency vehicles were on the scene, but it would most likely be hours before the lanes could be opened.

Kendall's first response to the news of a local accident was always the same—make sure his wife and children were not in it. Colleen, he knew was safe. He called Matthew's cell phone—he was at the pool with Colin. They talked for a minute and then he called Kelley. She was out on the beach, the wind whistling in her phone and making it difficult for him to hear her. He told her that he'd call her back later, that he just wanted to make sure she was safe.

Alice called. She'd heard the same report. Nothing to do but wait. She'd call him as soon as the traffic started moving.

Now what? He couldn't go back to Mancini's if there was a detective following him. He was just going to have to wait for a while. He'd told Finotti he was going to the NIH. He called Alice back. Maybe she could call the gate and get him into the compound at least. Then he could wait for her inside.

Twenty minutes later, the guard still on the phone with Dr. Alice Chen, he was given a visitor's pass and let inside the gate. He found the building that housed Alice's laboratory and parked. She had said there was a cafeteria that was open all weekend in the basement, and he was headed for the front door of Building 212 when his phone rang. It was Bob Williams. He moved into the shade of an oak tree and sat on a bench.

There was definitely something the matter with Bob Williams, but at first Kendall couldn't tell if he was angry or sad or some combination of the two.

"Bunny just called me," said Williams. "The police just called her. Chad's been in an accident. It's not good. They want her to meet them in the emergency room at Georgetown."

Kendall's chin dropped and his eyes closed. For a long moment the only sound he heard was the blood rushing through his head. "I'm sorry, Bob," he said. "I'm really sorry."

"I'm going to ask Pat and Sam to go to the hospital," said Bob. "Can you meet me at my office? Then I suspect we'll need to go to the house."

Kendall didn't know what to say.

"I think we have some work to do," said Bob. "I don't want to wait. How soon can you be there?"

"Ten minutes."

"I'll be waiting for you in the back parking lot."

TWENTY

Kendall was up off the bench and moving for his car almost before Williams finished speaking. He figured he probably only had a few more minutes to get out of the NIH campus before the detective managed to get himself in. He hobbled as fast as he could, got in his car, and sped around the corner of the building. The NIH campus was spread out over hundreds of acres, with streets and walkways crisscrossing it like the center of a small town. He turned at a stop sign, turned again, and cut through a parking lot. He could see Wisconsin Avenue to the left and knew there was an exit across from Bethesda Naval Hospital. Left, and left again. He just kept turning, heading left every time he could and finally found the road that led to the exit. The guard made him give up his pass, but he let him out without a question. He hit Wisconsin, turned right into traffic, and sped into the middle lane.

He called Alice Chen and told her to turn around when she could and he'd call her later. Colleen was calling him as he pressed the speed dial for his home.

"Are you still at NIH?" she asked. "The detective wants to know. I've got him on hold."

"Yes."

"He said to call him as soon as you're ready to leave."

Kendall had told Finotti not to call him while he was at NIH. Cell phones were not allowed in the ICU because they interfered with pacemakers and some of the monitoring equipment.

"Okay. Tell him I'll be a while. This patient's sick as hell."

"Right," said Colleen. "It's getting old, Ryan."

"The patient's going to die, if he hasn't already," said Kendall. "Do you understand?"

She didn't answer for a moment. "I think so," she said, her tone softer. "I'll tell him."

He was only a block from Williams' office. He passed a car, then another. Swerving abruptly into the right lane, he passed the building, turned onto the next side street, and circled back. He knew he would never know for sure, but he did not think that there was anyone behind him.

Bob Williams was waiting inside the parking lot by the back door. He was dressed neatly in slacks and a golf shirt, his face firm and otherwise expressionless.

"I want to go through his office first," he said, letting them into the building. "Let's start with his desk."

Kendall followed him down the hall, wanting to say something in condolence about Chad, but somehow also knowing that Bob didn't want to hear it at the moment. When they were inside, Kendall said, "I presume you told Chad about me this morning?"

They reached Chad's office, Williams flipping through keys on his keyring. "Of course I did. Did you think I was going to hear from you that my son's a liar?"

Williams turned on the light. They both paused, looking around at the desk, the microscope table, the cabinets, the closet.

"What did he say?"

"That you could do all the matching that you wanted, but he had nothing to hide." Williams was at his son's desk now, a smaller key in his hand. "When I ordered this furniture, I hoped I'd never need this key. But I also knew

"If he doesn't have anything to hide, then what are we looking for?" said Kendall.

"I don't know. Slides, notes. Anything to sort this out. You know he's lying. This lab is my life, it's Sam's life, and I'll be goddamned if he's going to take us down with him."

Notepads, empty slide cases, desk paraphernalia. They found nothing of interest in the side drawers. Williams opened the center drawer—more of the same.

"Obviously you're right about your other patients, and who knows how many more there are," said Williams, standing and looking around the room. "He's been playing this game for years probably. But as stupid as he was, he's not completely stupid. If he had to, he could have come up with the real blocks. They're somewhere, but they're probably not in here. It gets too warm on the weekends in the summer when they turn off the air in the building."

"Maybe they're at his house. Does he have a wine cellar or anything like that?"

"Not that I know of, but that's where we're going next. But we need to finish here."

Williams moved to the filing cabinet and started with the top drawer. Every drawer and file was filled with journal articles and case reports. He shut the last drawer and kicked it. His jaw clenched, he walked over to the closet and almost yanked the door off of its runners. They went through the top shelf—nothing. There was an old golf bag on the floor that Williams pulled out and pushed behind them. Several jackets and lab coats—nothing else. Williams stepped back, picked up the golf bag and flung it across the room. It rattled off the wall and fell onto Chad's desk chair with a thud. His face was flushed and there were small droplets of sweat on his forehead.

"That son-of-a-bitch didn't run his car through the parkway guardrail because of little Miss Browning. And I don't think it's those patients of yours either. He's lied his way through more trouble than that before. And even when he does get caught, he always manages to go on. With my help," he added. "Shit!" he yelled, looking around. "What are we missing? What the hell was he up to?"

Williams obviously wasn't expecting an answer. He took out his phone and dialed a stored number. "Hi, Janet. Did Sam go to the hospital? . . . Good . . . . I know we can't leave them there. Can you go over and pick them up? Probably best to take them back to your house . . . . Okay. I'll probably see you there. We'll be there in a few minutes."

Williams hung up and looked at Kendall. "Janet'll get the kids out of there."

For some reason, Kendall had never thought of Chad Williams as having children. "How many does he have?"

"Two. Fourteen and twelve. Boy and a girl."

"Jesus."

The elder Williams said nothing. He was staring out the office door, his hands on his hips. "I always thought him knowing how to cut and stain slides was a bad thing," he said. "He's pretty much of a control freak, and I just figured it was part of that."

"Of course you did," said Kendall. "So would I. I mean, what else would you think, Bob? This is not normal. You can't think like that."

"I know. That's what I'm standing here doing. I'm trying to think like him. Where would you hide blocks and slides and maybe even processing equipment?"

"If he had the tissue blocks, he could have had someone else cut the slides."

"Maybe. I don't know if that's Chad, though." He turned off the light and headed out. "Come on—let's go to the house."

Kendall followed Bob Williams through the side streets of Chevy Chase Village. The radio news updates now said that there was at least one fatality in the parkway accident, and that the police and Coast Guard were searching the river to make sure no one else had fallen out of the car. The identity of the victim was pending notification of relatives, but it appeared to be a local resident.

Williams pulled into the driveway of a white brick colonial and got out. He motioned to Kendall to park on the street and then walked over to Kendall's car. "I don't see Janet's car. Why don't you let me go in and talk to the kids until she comes."

Williams went into the house, and a few minutes later a maroon Volvo wagon pulled up in front. A woman around fifty got out and hurried up the walkway. Five minutes later she came out, one arm around a teenage boy and the other around a teenage girl, both of whom were obviously shaken. She ushered them to her car and sped away. Williams appeared in the door and waved him in.

The first thing Kendall noticed was how quiet the house was. Maybe it was just the specter of death and mourning that had already settled in, but it was eerily quiet. No radios, no television, no voices, no dog. Williams walked straight to the back of the house and into a library off of the family room. There was an entire wall of bookshelves and a desk facing a window that looked out to the back yard. On one side of the desk was a pile of journals; on the other was an antique microscope.

"He paid ten thousand dollars for that," said Bob Williams, nodding toward the brass microscope. "He wanted me to pay for it out of the office. My accountant told him to work harder."

Chad's father sat in his son's desk chair and folded his hands on top of the desk. "Okay," he said. "Where would I hide things if I were Chad Williams?" He looked to Kendall. "Be my guest," he said. "Everything's fair game."

Williams started in the desk drawers and Kendall started in the cabinets behind the desk. For a while they worked silently, Bob pulling out a few keys from the center drawer of the desk, then a few scraps of loose paper with notes on them. Otherwise the elder Williams found nothing in the drawers that caught his eye. Kendall had worked through several cabinets of old computer equipment and office supplies when he got to a drawer of files. They were labeled and in alphabetical order, starting with "Autos" and ending with "Washington U." Kendall went to the beginning and flipped through them. Computers, electronics, schools. There were two that caught his eye and he went back to them.

The first was labeled "Hidden Glen." He took out the folder, set it on the side of the desk, and opened it: Chad's letter of acceptance to the junior membership program, a promissory note, a letter from the Green Committee Chairman thanking him for his help in a recent member-guest tournament. He put it back and took out the second file that was labeled "Office." The folder was full of equipment brochures: processors for dehydrating specimens, microtomes, embedding stations, slides, staining supplies. Some were opened and folded to certain pages, but there was no writing or notes or anything that pointed to a specific piece of equipment or company.

"You need to see this," said Kendall. Williams was examining the keys he had found in the drawer, all of which were single and unlabeled.

"I saw it. Any notes or anything?"

"No."

Williams lined the keys up on Chad's leather blotter. "I think these are all old luggage keys, or maybe even house keys. They're not our office keys—I know that. We'll hold onto them, but I don't think they're going to help us." He spun around in the chair. "Let's look in their bedroom, and then the basement. If there's nothing there, then I have to speak to Bunny."

"Uh, maybe you should do that, Bob. I don't think I'd feel quite right up there at the moment."

Williams shrugged. "Okay. Stay here and look around some more. Or if you want you can go ahead and go downstairs."

Kendall's phone rang—Detective Finotti. He let it go and started leafing through the "Office" file again. His phone rang again—Colleen.

"Are you still at NIH?" she said.

"Depends who's asking?"

"I'm asking. Have you seen or heard the news?"

"You mean the car accident?"

"Right. You know then?"

"I'm in his house with his father."

Holding onto the phone with one hand, Kendall closed the file and put it away with the others.

"Say that again."

He had moved into the family room, then into the entry hall towards the stairs to the second floor. He could hear Williams opening and closing drawers above him.

"You need to tell Finotti that I'm still at NIH." Kendall was at the bottom of the stairs now, looking out the glass panes on either side of the front door. "Bob!" he yelled. There was a new car in the driveway behind Williams' Mercedes, and an older woman was coming up the walkway with her arm around a middle-aged woman who was shaking. "Bob!" he yelled again. "Gotta go," he said to Colleen and hung up.

Kendall backed up reflexively, facing the door. He heard a key go in the lock. The door opened and Bunny Williams almost fell through the doorway, her mother-in-law holding onto her tightly. They both saw him at the same time and stopped short.

"And you are?" said the older woman.

"Dr. Kendall," said Bob Williams from the upstairs landing. "He's a client of our laboratory."

Both women looked from Williams to Kendall and back to Williams.

"Where have you been?" sobbed Bunny, looking at her father-in-law who was coming down the stairs. "Your son just died and you can't even come to the fucking hospital!" Pat took Bunny's face in her hands and whispered something to her, but Bunny broke free and lunged for Williams as he got to the bottom of the stairs. She started pounding on his chest with her fists and sobbed even louder. "You hated him! You always have! All he wanted was to be like you and Sam and you hated him! Both of you hated him!"

Williams took her in his arms and she collapsed into him, her body shaking against his. Then looking at his wife over Bunny's shoulder, he motioned for her and Sam, who had just come through the door, to go into the kitchen. Kendall looked at him, but he motioned for Kendall to stay. Then he moved backwards until he could sit on the stairs and pulled Bunny down next to him. One arm around her shoulder, he pulled her tight to him and let her sob.

Bunny's crying only worsened in the next minute and Kendall mouthed to Williams whether he should go. Williams shook his head no and lifted Bunny's chin with a finger. Bunny quieted somewhat and her father-in-law wiped her eyes with his hand. "Bunny," he said, "I helped Chad in every way I could. So did his mother and his brother. But sometimes Chad didn't want to be helped. He had his own ideas about things. You have to understand that."

She quieted some more, but said nothing.

"I need your help now, Bunny. Chad was not being honest with us before he died. He intentionally misled Dr. Kendall with several of his patients for his own gain."

Halfway through Williams' sentences, Bunny had started shaking her head no.

"Yes, Bunny, he did. And we all need your help now. I do, Dr. Kendall does, and your family does. There are very significant legal issues here, and if you don't help me, everything you have might be lost. Everything all of us have might be lost. You have to think about Carter and Kristin now."

Bunny's head quieted against Williams' chest, but her shoulders were still heaving involuntarily. "All you care about is your fucking money," she sobbed. "I don't care about your fucking money! Don't you get that!"

"It's not that at all, Bunny. It's about honor and respect and fairness."

Bunny was silent and Williams went on: "Chad must have a place in the house or somewhere else where he could store slides and tissue blocks and maybe even lab equipment. Do you know where that might be? Does he have a wine cellar that I don't know about, or a special place in the basement or somewhere else in the house?"

She didn't answer. She balled up her fists and pressed them against her chest.

"You have to help us, Bunny. If you don't, Dr. Kendall is going to tell the police everything he knows."

"Oh, you can't be serious," she said with disgust, pulling away from him. "It's just like he said—you'd never understand."

Kendall watched Williams look at her, the older man obviously trying his best to stay calm.

"What do you mean, Bunny?"

"He was better than any of you," she said, sobbing again. "He wanted to do something, to be something, and he knew you'd never let him."

"I don't understand, Bunny."

"He wanted to publish a book!" she almost screamed at him. "All he was doing was collecting slides and waiting for you to die so he could publish his book without being laughed at. He knew none of you ever took him seriously," she yelled. "And you told him once that no one was going to profit off of your patients. He had no choice!" She buried her head in his chest again, her body heaving uncontrollably. "Oh, God," she sobbed. "He told me to never ever tell you that."

"Where does he keep his slides, Bunny? In the house?"

She shook her head no.

"Where then?"

"I don't know," she said softly. "Some storage facility so you'd never find them."

"Do you know where it is?"

"No."

"Do you have a bill or anything that would have a name on it?"

She nodded.

"Will you get it for me?"

Yes, she nodded.

"Do you have a key?"

She shook her head no.

"Do you have any idea where a key might be?"

Bunny straightened, wiped her eyes, and stood. "Yeah, Bob," she said, looking down at him. "In the fucking river with the rest of him. Why don't you climb down there and get your fucking key. Then you can say good-bye to your son, too." She pushed past him and ran up the stairs.

Williams looked at Kendall. "We need to get his car keys," he said. A door slammed upstairs, then another. He moved his gaze up to the master bedroom. "And she's going to have to help us."

TWENTY-ONE

A drawer banged in an upstairs room. It jarred Kendall's ears and he reflexively closed his eyes for a moment. When he opened them, he said: "Bob, maybe this can wait until tomorrow."

Williams, still sitting on the stairs, looked at him and shook his head no.

Bunny Williams was crying again, her sobs audible through the open bedroom doors.

"Maybe you should go home for a little while, though," said Williams. "I can go get the keys with Bunny. I'm going to need her with me, I think."

"Is the car still down there?"

Williams shrugged. "I don't know. But I will climb down there if I have to."

Pat Williams walked out from the kitchen and looked at the two of them, but was quiet.

"What happened, Pat?" said Bob. "Do they know?"

"He went off the Parkway near one of the overlooks. They think he just missed the curve."

Bob Williams looked at her and said nothing.

"When we left the hospital the car was still down there," she said. "And so was Chad. They had thought they could get him out and bring him to the hospital so Bunny could see him, but . . . everything's too crumpled I think." Tears welled up in her eyes. "He was pronounced dead in the car and they called us at the hospital."

Williams nodded. "I need two things from Bunny, Pat. Maybe you can help. First I need Chad's car keys. She's going to have to go over to the Parkway with me and see if the car's still there. Did the police give you a contact number?"

She nodded. "I have one of the officer's card with several numbers."

"I also need the bill or statement or whatever Bunny has for Chad's slide collection. I think she's up there looking for it now."

Pat frowned.

"Chad was apparently collecting slides so he could write a book," said Williams, looking at her in a way that said much more. A way forged over forty-plus years of marriage.

Kendall watched Pat's face harden. She wiped her eyes and looked upstairs. "Give her another minute and then I'll go up," she said.

"Why don't you go home," said Williams, looking to Kendall. "I'll call you in a while."

Kendall had put his phone on vibrate when they had entered the house and he could now feel it going off in his pocket. Wanting to say something to the both of them, he let the call go unanswered, looking from Bob to Pat.

Bob Williams spoke first. "I'm sorry, Ryan," he said. "I'm sorry you have to go through this."

Pat moved to the steps and sat next to her husband, a hand on his thigh.

"Bob," said Kendall, "I'm—"

Williams put up a hand and stopped him. "There's nothing to say, Ryan. Not until this is done."

* * *

The call was from home. "Colleen?"

"Detective Finotti's here, Ryan. He would like to speak with you."

"Where are you, Dr. Kendall?" said the detective.

"I'm in my car."

"I asked you to call me if you left NIH."

Kendall turned on the engine and pulled away from the curb. His face was warming and he told himself to calm down. "Detective Finotti, let me ask you something," he said.

"I'm listening."

"Are you in my house?"

"I am."

"Are you in my house alone with my wife?"

"I, uh, yes. There's an investigation going on, Dr. Kendall."

"Do you have authorization to be in my house? Do you have authorization to be alone with my wife in my house without my permission?"

Finotti didn't answer.

Kendall turned onto Wisconsin Avenue and headed towards River Road. "Detective Finotti, let me tell you a few things. First of all, I told you everything I know last night. I don't know anyone who would want to kill me. That hasn't changed. I am out conducting personal and medical business and I don't appreciate being followed, which at this point I construe not only to be harassment, but as you believing that I've lied to you."

"I never—"

"Let me finish please." Kendall sped up, his face flushed now. "Now what really bothers me is that you are in my house alone with my wife. I am on my way home and I expect to hear from my wife in about one minute that you are no longer in my house. Do you understand that?"

"I understand that you—"

Kendall took a deep breath. Mancini was not going to be happy.

"Detective Finotti, do you know Judge Paul Mancini?"

"Yes," he answered after a moment.

"Are you in my kitchen?"

"Yes."

"Then walk over to the bulletin board by the door and look at the photographs. Go ahead—right now." Kendall paused long enough for him to walk a few steps. "Do you see Judge Mancini there with his arm around me?"

"Yes."

"Good. Well, if I don't get a call from my wife in one minute that you're gone, my next call is to Judge Mancini."

"All we want is some help, Doctor. You need to remember that you and someone else almost died the other day."

"I understand that, Detective. And if there's some way I can help you, I will. I have your number. Now I'm going to hang up and wait for my wife to call."

Kendall hung up and banged the steering wheel in anger. He was on River Road now, ten miles over the speed limit and with an eye on the rearview mirror.

Colleen called thirty seconds later. "He left," she said. "I don't know what you said to him, but he wasn't very happy."

"I told him to tell it to the Judge," said Kendall, smiling to himself.

*   *   *

Colleen grilled sea bass outside and they ate dinner on the deck. Kendall had not shaved since Friday, and she was looking at him with disapproval.

"You need a shave and some sleep," she said. "You look like someone a detective would be following."

"He'll be back," said Kendall. "If nothing else just on the principle of it."

"You mean the macho principle?"

Kendall nodded. "Plus, he's right, and he knows it."

"You're going to end up getting yourself in trouble."

Kendall didn't answer. He sat back and looked up into the oak tree. The first fireflies were lighting up in tiny neon green flashes interspersed between the dark branches.

"Chad's dead. What difference does it make?"

"It makes a difference to the hospital, and it might make a difference to that man in the ICU."

"I don't know that it was Chad. What if it wasn't?"

Colleen looked at him. "I'm not the detective, Ryan."

Kendall picked up his fork. "It's not that easy, Colleen," he said. "First of all, I don't know that it was Chad. And secondly, it affects Bob and Sam and their families, too. It's just not that easy. Besides the fact that Bob will sue the living shit out of me if that gets public and it isn't true."

He could hear his phone ringing inside the kitchen. Colleen got up and brought it to him. He frowned. The call was from Drew Garrett's home number.

"I'm sorry to bother you," said Garrett. "Is this a bad time?"

Kendall stood and limped over to a bench on the side of the deck. "No. Are you alright?"

"Yeah. A little antsy, but I'm okay. This Parkway incident hasn't helped me any. I suppose you've heard about what happened today?"

"Yes. It's a tragedy."

Garrett was silent for a moment. "I'm not going to beat around the bush, Doctor. It doesn't sound like an accident."

"Maybe not," said Kendall. "I've actually been with the family today. They're not sure."

"You're friends with them?"

"I know Bob, Chad's father."

"I see."

"So why did you say that what happened today hasn't helped you?"

Garrett was quiet again. Then he said: "If I were your attorney, Doctor, and I killed myself, what would you think?"

"I see," said Kendall.

"It makes one think, that's all. Life has to be pretty shitty to drive off the GW Parkway at ninety miles-per-hour."

"I understand. If it's any consolation, he's not the only one who signed off on your case so to speak."

"I realize that. It's just not the news I needed ahead of surgery Monday morning."

Kendall was quite for a moment, then said: "When you were in my office you said you knew who Chad was. Did you know him at Somerset?"

"What else have you learned about me, Doctor?"

"What do you mean, Drew?"

"Well, you've obviously been researching me on the Internet or through friends."

"Your wife told my wife that you and Joel Lieberman went to school together. I thought she said Somerset. I'm sorry. Did I get that wrong?"

"No," said Garrett, his voice softer. "Williams was three years behind me. I didn't really know him."

Kendall waited for Garrett to go on, but the attorney said nothing. After the silence between them had gone on long enough that Kendall found it uncomfortable, he said:

"Maybe you should take what your doctor gave you tonight so you can sleep. You sound a little anxious to me."

"Maybe I will," he said. "I've got a lot on my mind."

*   *   *

Bob Williams called at nine o'clock. He had Chad's keys and the code to get through the gate of the storage facility. The storage facility was in Rockville. He said he'd pick up Kendall on his way out.

"It's getting late, Bob. We've all had a long day. Why don't we go in the morning?"

"I'm going tonight, Ryan. I understand if you don't want to come."

Kendall looked at Colleen. She was shaking her head and mouthing that he needed to get some sleep.

"I don't think it's a good idea to pick me up," said Kendall. "There's probably a detective watching the house." He thought for a moment. "Why don't you do this. There's a back entrance to The River Club off MacArthur Boulevard. Do you know where it is?"

"I know exactly where it is."

"I'm going to drive into the Club and park and go into the clubhouse. Then I'll go out the back and meet you there."

"Nine-thirty?"

"See you then."

"You can come if you want," said Kendall to Colleen.

She wasn't listening. She turned for the kitchen, went to the refrigerator, and poured herself a large glass of wine.

*   *   *

Bob Williams stood in front of storage space 114 and looked at the sliding metal door. "It's perfect," he said. "It's climate controlled."

With Bunny's help, the elder Williams had narrowed the key possibilities to three. The first wasn't even close. The second key went into the lock. Williams put some pressure on it and the key turned with a metal click. He took hold of the door handle, took a deep breath, and lifted the door.

There really weren't many surprises. Perhaps the extent of the laboratory equipment and the neatness of it all. Solid wood workbenches lined the left and rear walls of the garage-sized space with tissue processing equipment lined up sequentially along the benches. The last piece of equipment on the far wall was a labeling machine. Next to it was a pencil holder with several marking pencils protruding from the top. The right wall was lined with filing cabinets. One set looked to Kendall like the cabinets that Williams had retrieved the tissue blocks from earlier that morning. The other set had much smaller drawers that he deduced were for glass microscope slides.

Kendall looked to Williams. Williams wiped his eyes and walked closer to the benches. "Everything's a duplicate of what we have in the office," he said. "Right down to the labeling machine." He picked up a marking pencil and turned it over in his hand. "Some labs like us still use these Tissue Tek pencils, but some are going to automated labeling. We had a presentation on it, but Chad was adamant that it wasn't cost effective with the reimbursements going down." He shook his head and jammed the pencil back into the holder.

Williams turned and faced the cabinets. "I'm almost afraid to look," he said. "Blocks are to the left and slides to the right." He stepped to the cabinets of blocks and pulled open one of the drawers. Tissue blocks of different colors were lined up front to back with accession numbers on them just as they normally would be in their office. Williams started looking through them, shaking his head as he went along.

Kendall turned and looked to the benches on the left wall, then the back. There were drawers spaced along the width of each bench, six in all. He went to the first, then the second and third—they all had supplies and order forms. He found what he was looking for in the first drawer in the back bench—a school binder with laminated pages inside of it. He opened it and flipped through the pages—it was a list of pathology diagnoses in alphabetical order.

He turned towards Williams. "Eccrine spiradenoma," he said. "54689. 1981."

Williams turned. He looked from Kendall to the notebook to the cabinets. He closed the drawer and opened another, then another. "They're filed by year," said Williams. He carefully extricated a tissue block from the cabinet and held it up to the light—this one's from the AFIP—they use a special government contractor for all of their supplies. He put it back, flipped through some more, and pulled out a tissue block with the number that Kendall had just read to him.

"So how did he change the numbers on the blocks that he switched?" asked Kendall.

Williams snorted. "That's actually a special type of pencil that's made primarily for labs," he said, motioning with his head towards the cup on the back bench. "It's supposed to be permanent, so theoretically once it's on the plastic it won't come off with normal wear and tear." Williams was staring at the tissue block in his hand. "It'll come off, though, if you really want it off. We actually have special erasers in case someone makes a mistake labeling one. I'm sure there's a whole box of them in one those drawers."

"Got it. Check the slides now," said Kendall. "They're probably filed in the same order."

Williams opened a drawer, closed it, opened another. He found the drawer with the 1981 slides, then 54689-81. There were three slides. Eccrine spiradenomas were tumors of the sweat glands that were large solid masses and characteristically stained deep blue. "Big blue ball in the dermis," one of Kendall's histology professors used to say. Williams held one of the slides up to the light. From five feet away Kendall could see the mass of blue cells on the slide.

"Atypical fibroxanthoma, metastatic carcinoma, Spitz Nevus," read Kendall. "There's pretty much everything here. And two or three of some diagnoses. I guess they're all 'classic' cases."

Williams pursed his lips, then said: "Some of them are from the AFIP, some are ours, and some are probably from Boston and Washington University."

"Did Bunny ever see this?" asked Kendall.

Williams shook his head no, but he was obviously thinking about something else. "There's something we're missing," he said. "Somehow he had to keep track of the cases from our office that he switched. The original real blocks have to be here. Probably the slides, too." He looked at the far left set of drawers that he'd been looking through. "But they won't be in there, because those are his library so to speak. Those are the ones that he collected and stored for his reference specimens. The diagnoses on the cases that he switched from our office are nothing special—they'll probably just be filed by number, or some other way that he could keep track of them."

"If they're filed by year," said Kendall, "then they'll only be since he joined you out of residency. And they'll all be the type of blocks that you use in your office."

Williams started opening drawers. When he got to the bottom two drawers of the last of the larger cabinets, he stopped, took the flashlight he had brought, and shined it right up on the backs of the blocks. "These are newer," he said. "I think these are them. It makes sense, too, because there aren't that many of them." He looked up. "Check the bottom right drawer of the last slide cabinet."

Kendall pulled open the last drawer.

"Give me the accession number of the last slide."

"17569-10."

Williams nodded. "Now give me the number just before that."

"08764-10."

"That's them." Williams closed the drawer and straightened. "There's a dolly in the hall. Let's just take these bottom drawers for now. They're the most important ones. We can come back for the rest later."

"You can access the reports by the accession number can't you?" said Kendall.

Williams, kneeling, his head bent, nodded yes. When he looked up his eyes were glazed with a film of tears. "The other day when I couldn't find him. After he left Hidden Glen."

Kendall nodded, the tragedy of Hidden Glen still an unspoken presence between them.

"He came over here," said Williams. "He came over here and got that girl's block before he went to our church and met with the minister and me."

"Did you believe him then?" asked Kendall.

"I wanted to believe him," he said. "I wanted to believe him with all my heart."

TWENTY-TWO

Sunday, June 17

Kendall woke with bright sunshine coming through their bedroom window. Jesus, he said to himself. He'd overslept. He was supposed to meet Bob Williams at nine o'clock. He lifted his head and looked at the clock beside the bed—it was only eight. He gently shook Colleen and headed for the shower.

They were ready to leave by eight-thirty. There'd been a strange SUV on his block with a lone figure in it when he'd returned home the night before, and they assumed it would be no different this morning. Kendall was dressed in a coat and tie, and Colleen was dressed in church attire as well. She had a purse slung over her shoulder, and a cloth bag he did not recognize slung over the purse. He started to question her, then stopped. Though she'd been more than happy to help him this morning, her patience was wearing even thinner.

They took separate cars and headed out. There was only one way out of their street, and then one way up to any egress out of their neighborhood. A gray Jeep Cherokee parked around the corner eased out well behind Kendall and kept its distance.

Our Lady of Lourdes was less than two miles away. Kendall pulled into the lot and Colleen drove on. The Jeep slowed, then pulled off to the side of the road in front of the church. Kendall got out and went in the front door of the church. He walked through to the sanctuary and then out a back door that opened onto a path that led to the rectory. Behind the rectory was a patch of woods, and then a street of houses, most of whose owners were parishioners at the church. There was a path from the rectory that led through the trees and then into another path in one of the house's back yards. Colleen had parked on the street fronting the houses and walked through a side yard to the path. They met in the stretch of trees, where they exchanged car keys, kissed, and moved on. Two minutes later, Kendall was in her car and headed for River Road.

Bob Williams was waiting in the back parking lot of his office. Neither of them had had the energy to do anything else but go home the night before. Williams had moved the drawers with the blocks into his basement for the night so that the paraffin wax wouldn't melt. Now they were in the trunk of his Mercedes with the slides.

Williams got out a small dolly from the back seat. Although the drawers were not particularly large, they were solidly constructed out of steel and were heavy, especially the ones that were full of slides. Together they carefully moved them onto the dolly and headed into the office, Kendall walking beside the dolly and holding onto the drawers.

"Let's go into my office," said Bob, steering the dolly down a hallway of the lab proper. The door to his office was open and he backed in with the dolly, angling it as close as he could to his desk. He was sweating and his breaths were short and fast. He wiped his brow and sat down at his desk. "It'll take me a minute to get the system up."

Kendall moved a chair around the desk so that he could sit next to him and see the monitor.

"Okay," said Williams. "Let's check the cases you asked for yesterday first. Do you still have that index card?"

Kendall handed him the card.

"I'll read off the accession numbers and you check and see if the blocks are in that first drawer."

Williams read off a number and Kendall, his index finger running down the plastic casings, stopped near the front. "It's here."

Williams was already typing the number into the computer. "Megan Donavan," he said. He scrolled down the pathology report that had come up onto the screen. "Cystic basal cell carcinoma." He scrolled down some more. "Sent out to Johns Hopkins for a consult because of a question of adenocarcinoma. Final diagnosis—basal cell carcinoma." He looked at Kendall.

"That's right," said Kendall. "Next."

Williams read off a number, Kendall nodded yes, and Williams typed it in. "Joshua Rickman. Cellular blue nevus. Sent to Will Ammerman in New York to rule out malignant cellular blue nevus."

Williams read out the last number on the card and pulled up Tim Slattery's report.

"So he lied to me about you," said Bob. "As I expected, I guess. And he would have lied to you, too."

Kendall said nothing. There were sixteen blocks from Chevy Chase Pathology left—he dreaded knowing how many more of them were his patients.

"Let's check the rest," said Williams, "but I think we should start with the most recent ones."

Kendall agreed and bent over the cabinet. There were three cassettes with accession numbers from 2010. The numbers were in the order that they had come into the lab, so the highest was the most recent. He took out the cassette labeled 26859-10 and read off the number to Williams.

Williams typed it in. "Drew Garrett," he said. "Spindle cell melanoma. Breslow level—"

Kendall's head had jerked up toward Williams. He thought he was going to vomit, and he must have looked the same.

Williams stopped, looked at him, and looked back to the report that was on the monitor. "It's yours," he said. "The biopsy was done on June 2."

Kendall was looking through him, his heart pounding. You son-of-a-bitch! he wanted to scream. You fucking son-of-a-bitch!

Chad's father looked back to the screen, read some more of the report, and frowned. "Is that the case where there was all that commotion with the lawyers?"

Kendall nodded.

"Shit!" said Williams, scrolling down the rest of the report. He quickly went back to the top, then down again. He frowned and shook his head. "It doesn't make sense, though. It's not what Chad did. He was in the business of giving out good news, not bad news."

Kendall closed his eyes and once again took himself back to his office the week before. Once again he envisioned Drew Garret sitting in front of him, asking him about Chad Williams. "I know who he is," he'd said. Not, sure, we went to the same school for a while. Not, sure, he was a few years behind me and I didn't know him very well, as had finally come out last night. Just, "I know who he is." And the call itself. It had been awkward, uncomfortable. But why? Because Garrett had been waiting for Kendall to say something about Chad Williams. He'd been looking for something. Two days before his surgery, Garrett was wondering if Kendall knew something about Chad that he wasn't telling him.

"I need to speak with him," said Kendall, wiping his brow. He'd taken off his jacket and tie, but he still had on a long-sleeve shirt. "He's having surgery tomorrow."

Williams closed his eyes. When he opened them, he said: "A node dissection and the whole bit?"

"Yep. And the node's in his chest. Paraortic. A thoracic surgeon is scrubbing with the general surgeon who's doing the case."

"Fuck."

"We need to know what's in that block," said Kendall, looking to the drawer. "We need to know that before tomorrow."

"It's going to be tough to get slides cut on Sunday," said Williams. "Can't he put off the surgery for a day or two?"

Kendall was shaking his head. "He's going to flip out. If you have any chance of saving your lab, you need to get slides cut from that block today."

"He's a lawyer?" asked Williams.

Kendall looked hard at him. "He's the toughest fucking lawyer you ever want to meet."

Williams was quiet then, thinking.

"He's going to want us to somehow prove which block is really his," he finally said. "I mean, we know what Chad was doing, and we assume that that block"—he nodded toward the drawer—"is the real one." He paused again then, his head cocked in thought. "But," he went on, "this is not a matter of a simple basal cell carcinoma. We're talking about a potentially fatal melanoma. If I have any sense of this guy, he's going to want to know unequivocally which one is his, especially if that block shows something different."

"I can do that," said Kendall. "I can DNA type both blocks and him, but I need the block that was sent out from here. And it's in New York."

"We have slides here. Can you DNA type a slide once it's been mounted?"

"You can, but it's harder with the Xylene. Plus, you might not have any slides here. I think Garrett checked them all out."

Williams shrugged. "Then someone's going to have to go to New York and get the block. Sam or Pat will go. Where is it?"

"Will Ammerman has it."

"Well, if you can call him and tell me where to send someone, I'll get it back here. They can take a train or the air shuttle and be back by six or seven tonight."

Kendall nodded, his mind on Drew and Caroline Garrett.

"Then I'll call Robyn," Williams went on, "and have her call all of our tech's and we'll see who we can get in here to cut slides. I wish I could help, but I have no idea how to do it."

Kendall leaned down and took out the plastic cassette with Drew Garrett's accession number on it. Then he turned for the door, still feeling like he was going to vomit. "Keep your phone on," he said.

*   *   *

Drew Garrett did not answer his home phone or his cell phone. He tried Caroline—no answer. Garret's home number was unlisted, so the information operator was of no help in getting his address. Kendall knew they lived in Chevy Chase, but he didn't know where. He headed for his office to get Garrett's chart.

He called home on the way—no answer. Colleen was apparently still out, and Matthew apparently was still asleep. Next he dialed Will Ammerman's office, but as expected, Ammerman was not there on Sunday morning. He called information again and got transferred to the main number for New York Hospital for Special. The operator would never give out Dr. Ammerman's home number, Kendall knew, but he or she would call him at home and give him a message. The woman who answered was pleasant and helpful. Kendall gave her his cell phone number and asked her to tell Dr. Ammerman that it was an emergency.

He called Alice Chen next. Alice said she could be at the NIH within the hour and would start getting the assays ready. He asked her how long it might take. At least twelve hours, she said. Probably closer to fifteen or sixteen, depending on the tissue block assay. Although she could certainly do it, the assay on formalin-fixed, paraffin-embedded tissue was more complicated than on unadulterated samples.

Which meant he was screwed with the block from New York, he thought, pulling into the parking lot of his building. His only hope was that the tissue block bearing Garrett's accession number that they'd found in storage would match to DNA in whatever specimen he would shortly obtain from Garrett.

Garrett's chart was still on his desk. Kendall typed his address into his phone, pulled up a map, and jotted down some notes. Alice Chen had asked for hair and saliva swabs. He found a sterile specimen cup for the hair and took a number of sterile cotton swabs from one of the exam rooms.

His phone rang—it was a number with a New York area code. Will Ammerman did not seem overly surprised to hear from him on a Sunday morning. Kendall simply told him that Garrett's specimen had possibly been interchanged with another patient's in Chevy Chase's lab. They needed the tissue block that Kendall had sent up there for DNA typing—Garrett's surgery was scheduled for tomorrow. Was there any way that Ammerman could get the block and leave it at the hospital's front desk or some other place that was convenient for him? Someone from Chevy Chase Pathology was on their way to the airport and would be on the next shuttle to LaGuardia.

Ammerman was gracious. He didn't ask any questions about the mix-up, and he said he'd been planning on making the trip into the city anyway and he'd be happy to get the block. He'd already cut all the slides that he needed. It was getting a little thin, he remarked again. And the paraffin was degrading, almost like it was old wax. Ammerman even volunteered to drive the block out to the airport.

Kendall thanked him profusely again, seemingly the tenth time he'd done so in the last two weeks, and wished him well. He thanked him for his offer but said Chevy Chase's courier would be happy to pick up the block at the hospital. Then he called Bob Williams. Williams said Sam was on his way to the airport. He had a seat on the 11:30 shuttle.

Colleen was still not home. He didn't want to call her on her cell since she might still be in church, but she stayed in his mind as he drove to Drew Garrett's home.

Garrett lived less than a mile from Chad Williams, on the other side of Connecticut Avenue. It was a similar neighborhood of old stately colonials on small but comfortable lots. Kendall parked on the street and went to the door. No one answered.

He heard a car behind him and turned on the stoop to see a new silver BMW sedan pull into the driveway. It stopped and three boys in coats and ties hopped out and ran down the driveway towards the back of the house. Then it pulled up closer and stopped again. Caroline got out, then Drew. Garrett was also wearing a coat and tie; Caroline had on a cream-colored summer dress. Church, thought Kendall. With special prayers for the morning.

"Good morning, Doctor," said Drew Garrett. The attorney and his wife both stopped short of the front stoop. "I'm presuming you don't have good news for me."

Caroline Garrett could barely look at him. Her lower lip was trembling and she rolled it into her mouth.

"I have news for you. I don't know yet if it's good or bad."

Garrett nodded. "Why don't you come in. Can I get you something to drink?"

"No, thank you."

"Caroline?"

She shook her head no.

Garrett went into the living room and motioned for Kendall to have a seat in an armchair. He sat on a sofa across from Kendall with his wife, his hands interlocked and resting on his thighs.

"Did they find something on one of my scans?" asked Garrett.

"No, it's nothing like that." Kendall took a deep breath. "It's possible that Dr. Williams was less than forthright with some of his pathology work," he said.

Garrett's eyes immediately hardened and he leaned forward. Caroline frowned and straightened on the couch.

"This has all come to light since his death, so I'm telling you what I know." They did not respond so Kendall went on. "Over the years it seems that he wanted to make himself look good or conscientious with certain cases or doctors, and he made more out of these cases than there really was. He would actually switch the original slides with someone else's slides. Slides that showed whatever it was that he wanted a consulting pathologist to see. He would actually switch the tissue blocks also, so if the pathologist asked for the block to cut more slides he or she would get more of the same slides that he'd sent in the first place. In the instances that we know about, it all turned out to be fine in the long run, and he probably did make himself look good in the process." Kendall paused to let them digest what he'd said.

"And I presume you're here because you think he did this with my slides?" said Garrett.

"Yes. Chad's father and I found a tissue block with your accession number on it. There's another tissue block in New York with your accession number on it." He looked at Caroline. "The one you gave me the other day. The one that was checked out from the Chevy Chase lab."

Garrett stood and moved to a bay window that looked out into the back yard. His boys were there, their coats off now but their ties still on. The oldest one was pitching a wiffle ball to the younger two.

"I'm sorry, but I don't understand," said Caroline. "You said he did this to make himself look good."

Kendall nodded. "In every case we know about, that's correct."

"But how—"

"It doesn't, Caroline," said Garrett, still looking out the window. He turned, his face flushed. He looked to Kendall. "So basically you're saying that you're not sure if I have a melanoma, or if I have something else that's in this tissue block that you just found. Is that correct?"

"That's correct."

Garrett turned back to the window for a moment, then slammed the wall next to the window with his fist. A framed photograph on a table next to him crashed to the hardwood floor, the sound sharp and penetrating off the polished wood. For several more seconds he stayed there, hands on his hips, staring out the window.

"Drew?" said Caroline, looking both afraid and hurt. As if she knew that somehow he had deceived her. "Drew, what is it?"

He turned back, his hands still on his hips. "And you want to know why Dr. Chadwick Williams would do that to me. Is that what you want to know, Doctor?"

Burn, tighten. The wood pressing hard against his back, the lights bright and warm on his face.

"I just want to help you, Drew."

Garrett stepped closer to Kendall, just a few feet away. His face was as hard as Kendall could ever imagine, anger turning to fury and then to hate. "Because I kicked his cheating ass out of school—that's why!" Garrett was almost hissing the words now. "I was the President of the Somerset Honor Council, and I kicked the little scum bag out of school because he cheated on an English exam. It was a five to four vote, and guess who won."

"Oh my God, Drew." Caroline stood and moved toward him.

Garrett put up a hand and stopped her several feet away. "And I didn't realize the little fuck had his name on my pathology report until it was too late. Now does that help you, Doctor?"

"Why didn't you say something before?" cried Caroline. "How could you keep that to yourself?"

Garrett cocked his head and looked at her for a long moment. "Because it's an honor code, Caroline. What happens in an honor council is a private matter. It's what trust is all about. Can you understand that?"

"I understand that you could die from a surgery you might not need," she almost yelled at him.

"But we don't know that," said Garrett, turning to face Kendall. "Do we, Doctor?"

"No, but hopefully we will very soon." Kendall took a breath. "We might want to push back your surgery a day or so."

Garrett's angry eyes fixed on him. "I'm having my surgery, Doctor. Do you see those boys out there?"

Kendall did not need to look out the window.

"Drew, maybe—"

Garrett put up a hand and stopped his wife again. "Dr. Kendall, I'll ask you the same question that I asked you the other day. What if you're wrong? What if it is a melanoma? Can you tell me that every day I wait to have it definitively removed that it is not another day that it might spread? Can you tell me that the nodes they saw on the CT scan have really been that way for years? Can you tell me that they're not full of cancer? Can you tell me all of those things, *Doctor?*"

Kendall just looked at him. All he could see was Sammie pointing at Garrett's chart and telling him that the specimen had to go to American Labs, the lab that was contracted with Garrett's insurance. He had chosen not to do that. He had sent the specimen to Chevy Chase Pathology Associates and to Chad Williams on his own. Without Garrett's knowledge, or his consent.

TWENTY-THREE

Colleen was breathing hard, her breaths short and quick.

His stomach, already unsettled, turned over again. "Where are you?" he said.

"On the tow path. South of Great Falls."

He let out a breath. The extra bag slung over her shoulder had been for her running clothes. He wondered where she'd changed, then decided maybe he really didn't want to know. "Running, I presume," he said.

"Jogging." She paused to catch her breath. "I needed to get out and I figured this would mess him up if he's following me."

"That's one way to get rid of him. Jogging on the towpath in June probably isn't in his top ten list of things to do."

"No, probably not."

"Do you think that Jeep followed you?"

"I think so, but I'm not positive. There was an SUV behind me but it was a ways back."

"Call me in a while," he said. "I need to meet Alice over at NIH."

"How'd it go?"

"Bad. Chad messed with Drew Garrett's slides."

She didn't answer for a moment, her breaths whistling through the phone. "That's not good," she finally said.

"No, it's not. Call me later."

*　　*　　*

Bob Williams answered on the second ring. He was still in his office. He'd managed to speak with Robyn, but she was having trouble reaching the histology technicians.

"So where are we?" said Kendall.

"We have calls into all of their home phones and cell phones. It's an old phone list though," he said, clearly irritated. "We're not sure about some of the numbers."

"Do you have addresses?"

"Yes. Through our payroll records. I'm writing them down right now."

"What about Fairfield? Are they processing tissue today?"

"I already called them. They're only open for emergency surgery. There are no histo' tech's there today."

"Are there any other hospitals where you work or is there anyone else who you know that might be able to do it?"

"Not for that. Try and be a little patient, Ryan—everyone's just out right now. I'm sure I can get the slides cut today. I just don't know if it's going to be at three in the afternoon, or three in the morning."

Kendall sighed. "Call me," he said. "I'm going over to NIH to give my friend Alice the block, and soon as she cuts what she needs I'll get it back to you."

*　　*　　*

Alice Chen was in her lab when he called. She walked out to the NIH guardhouse to meet him and get him a day guest pass. He hadn't seen her in a while and she gave him a hug through the open car window. The lots were empty

251

and she directed him over to a spot in the shade near her building.

The building that housed her lab was quiet, the hallways dim except for the lights in her wing. He paused at the door to read the brass plaque that bore her name: *Alice Chen, M.D., Ph.D., Director of Cutaneous Clinical Immunology and Immunogenetics*. Watching her unlock the door of her own laboratory, he smiled. Having your own lab at NIH was one of the pinnacles of success that few achieved.

Kendall handed her two bags. One was from his office and contained the specimen cup with Garrett's hair and three sterile swabs in plastic sheaths that were coated with his saliva. Hair and spit. Forensic investigators often needed to rely upon blood or semen or fingernail scrapings, but ordinary hair and saliva were the mainstays of routine DNA testing.

The second bag was the small soft cooler that he'd bought the day before. Garrett's tissue block was wrapped in a paper towel and covered by one of the cold packs. Alice had explained to him again on the way in that the DNA assay on the tissue block would be harder since the tissue had been fixed in formalin, dehydrated, and packed into paraffin wax. She would need to use a DNA PCR assay, a polymerase chain reaction process that amplified the DNA in the sections that she would cut so that it could be measured. Then the DNA sequences or markers could be matched with an accuracy as close to one hundred percent as science could get. Genes and DNA sequences—the very fabric of life—did not lie. They did not rearrange themselves at the whim of their owners.

Alice took the block and turned it over in her hand. "I've got the histo' lab open," she said. "I want to section this and get it started. You're welcome to stay if you want, but it's pretty boring from here."

"I need to take the block back over to the pathology lab after you've got what you need," he said.

"Okay. Give me fifteen minutes or so. Do you want to wait in my office?"

Kendall looked at his watch. She was obviously going to be here all day and probably halfway through the night. "I'm sorry to get you involved in this, Alice. I can't tell you—"

"Shhh," said Alice, putting a finger to her lips, and looking as if she were about to cry. "Fifteen minutes," she said.

*   *   *

It was two o'clock when he left NIH. He dropped the tissue block from the storage facility off with Bob Williams and spoke with him briefly. Williams had no new news for him, and he was getting harried as he simultaneously tried to deal with the realities of Chad's death at home, and the realities of Chad's death at his office. Kendall got back in his car and left. He did not want to go home and risk an encounter with Finotti, so he drove aimlessly for a while. Matthew was up and he talked with him for a few minutes. He felt as if he hadn't seen his son in weeks and made plans in his head for several family dinners that week. Kelley he felt as if he hadn't seen in a year. Though he took pride in her independence, and knew it was borne at least partially from the firm base that she knew she had at home, he still missed her. She'd be graduating from college before he knew it, and he felt his eyes suddenly getting moist. It seemed that it was only yesterday that he himself had sat in the heat and listened to Jimmy Carter's Chief of Staff, whose name he did not even remember, deliver a commencement address of which he could not recall a single seminal word. He'd been too busy thinking ahead already. Of medical school and Colleen and what would become of them.

Colleen, who was probably still out jogging in the now sweltering heat. Colleen, who—his phone was ringing—was now calling him. "Ryan," she said, her voice steady. "Detective Finotti is here. He wants to speak with you."

"Hello, Dr. Kendall."

"Hello, Detective Finotti. You're not bothering my wife again, are you?"

"No, sir. I just happened to see her here. I was actually looking for you. I have warrants to search your house and your office. Where would you like to start?"

Kendall fought the urge to lash out at him. Instead, he worked the time and the different scenarios in his head. He did not want to finish with Finotti at his home and then have to try and ditch him again. He figured if he finished at his office, one way or another, he'd have a better chance of heading off again alone.

"I'll meet you at my house in twenty minutes," he said. "Now would you please put my wife back on the phone . . . . Are you okay?"

"I'm fine. Are you coming home?"

"I'll see you there in twenty minutes."

*   *   *

Kendall poured iced tea for Colleen and himself and they sat in the shade on the deck.

"You don't care what he's doing?" she said.

"I have nothing to hide."

"What about the letter?"

"I shredded it."

"'You shredded it.'"

He nodded. "All gone."

"What about on your computer? What about e-mails? When I walked by the library he was sitting at your desk."

Kendall thought for a long moment, then shook his head. "I don't think there's anything on my computer that he'd care about."

The door from the kitchen to the deck opened a few minutes later and Finotti stepped out. "I'd like to go upstairs," he said.

"Go ahead," said Kendall, looking out toward the Brownings' house.

Finotti paused, then shrugged and went back in.

"Do you think my underwear's safe," said Colleen, smiling.

"Probably not."

"Maybe I should search him on the way out."

Finotti returned ten minutes later.

"All done?" said Kendall.

"Yes, sir."

"I'll see you later," Kendall said to Colleen. "After the detective finishes in my office I may need to go see that patient over at NIH."

Colleen nodded. "I hope he's better," she said.

He called Bob Williams from the car. Sam had picked up the tissue block from Ammerman and was on his way back to the airport. Bob had also gotten hold of Brad, one of the histology technicians. The good news was that he was coming into the lab; the bad news was that he was at Deep Creek Lake and wouldn't be getting home until nine or so. Robyn was still working on Nina and Emily. They had apparently gotten new cell phones and numbers since the last employee list had been printed.

Kendall put his phone on vibrate and led Finotti inside his office building. They did not speak as they rode the elevator and Kendall unlocked the rear door. Inside, the detective was visibly uneasy, and between his nervousness and the air warm and stuffy without the air conditioning, Finotti was sweating within minutes. Kendall let him flounder, watching him search through drawers of supplies and forms and instruments. The detective slowly made his way toward Kendall's office where he took much more time, particularly at Kendall's desk, where he looked through every drawer and paper.

"I'm sorry, Doctor," he said, "but I need to look at your computer."

Kendall shrugged and sat in a chair behind him. Whatever uneasiness the detective had shown with the medical aspects of the office was now gone. The detective's fingers zipped around the keyboard, looking through Internet searches and data files that Kendall didn't even know existed. Kendall saw his search on Drew Garrett come up on the screen, then another on spindle cell melanomas. Intermittently Finotti would stop to write in a small notebook. Then he would start tapping again, his fingers moving around the keyboard as fast as Kendall had ever seen anyone type.

Kendall's phone was vibrating. He stared straight ahead, trying to sit still, the vibrations every three seconds feeling like an electric shock through his leg.

Finotti stopped typing. Without turning around, he said: "Aren't you going to answer your phone, Doctor?"

Kendall took out his phone—it was Drew Garrett. "Hello," he said.

"I'm checking in," said Garrett.

Finotti was facing the monitor, his hands resting on the keyboard.

"I don't know anything yet," said Kendall.

"I'll plan on being at the hospital then," said Garrett.

Kendall paused, formulating an answer.

Garrett hung up.

"May I ask who that was?" said Finotti.

"A patient of mine who has cancer. He's having surgery tomorrow morning and we're going over his biopsies again. He has a significant chance of dying during the surgery. Have you ever had cancer, Detective?"

"No, I haven't." He turned all the way to face Kendall. "When you say you're going over his biopsies again, is that what you were doing at the pathology lab yesterday?"

Kendall stared at him. "Yes."

"May I see your phone please?"

Kendall's face flushed instantaneously as he yelled at himself to stay calm. Instead of handing the phone to the detective, part of him wanted to call Mancini, but the detective already knew that they were close friends. The detective was baiting him, he figured. Finotti knew that Kendall probably didn't know shit about the laws pertaining to search warrants and cell phones.

He shrugged again and handed him the phone. Finotti scrolled through his ingoing and outgoing calls, then gave it back to him without taking down any of the names or numbers. He was bluffing, thought Kendall. Any of the numbers could have easily been Judge Mancini's.

"Thanks," said Finotti, taking out his notepad. "I think I'm done. Before I leave though, would you mind telling me the name of your patient over at NIH?"

Finotti was looking straight at him. Kendall held his gaze, thinking that the detective probably knew as much about medical privacy as he himself did about warrants and phone searches.

"I'm sorry, Detective, but you know I can't tell you that. That's a straight-out HIPPA violation. I could be sanctioned."

Finotti kept looking at him. "You're not making this easy, Doctor."

"It's not my rule, Detective. It's our government's."

"And that's what I don't understand," said Finotti, staring at him. "Why are you being so difficult? Why do you go to such great lengths to avoid us? The other guy doesn't do that."

"What other guy?"

"The other lucky guy from the operating room who's not in the ICU. The lawyer."

"Maybe he's used to it," said Kendall. Then after a pause: "If you want to know the truth, Detective, I don't know what you want from me, and it's really starting to piss me off. You've been through my house and now you've been through my office. I have real work to do today, and it's time for you to leave me alone."

"All I want, Doctor, is to find who put Mr. Keefer into the intensive care unit, and who might have tried to kill you and the lucky lawyer." Finotti was staring at him, watching every flick of his eyes. "We think the note's bullshit. And if we're right, that means whoever cut those hoses probably wanted one of you dead. I'm guessing it wasn't Mr. Keefer.

That leaves you and the lawyer. Fifty-fifty," he said, standing, "and I'm feeling lucky."

*   *   *

When Kendall left his office, the parking lot and adjoining side street were clear of vehicles. He did not see the gray Jeep nor the sedan that had been at their house the day before. All of this probably meant nothing, he surmised, but it at least made him wonder if perhaps the detective had gone home for the night. Hopefully the specters of Mancini, and a patient with cancer facing surgery in the morning, were not battles he wanted to fight.

He sat in the car with the engine and air conditioning running. Drew Garrett did not answer his home phone or his cell. He tried Caroline's cell—no answer. He called their house again and left a message explaining why he couldn't talk when Garret had called and asked Garrett to call him when he could.

He called Bob Williams. Nine hours after they'd met in the Chevy Chase Pathology Associates office that morning, he was still there. Williams told him that Sam had gotten on a shuttle back to Reagan National and would land in a half-hour. Kendall arranged to meet Sam in the lobby of Roosevelt Hospital, which was only a short drive from NIH. It also was the hospital where Garrett was to have his surgery in the morning. Robyn had still not been able to reach Nina or Emily, both of whom Williams was thinking might be away for the weekend. If either Robyn or he couldn't reach them in the next few minutes, he was going to go to their houses. However, Williams also said, the worst-case scenario was that Brad could manage the entire process. It might take a little longer, but Brad had worked in the lab for a few years and he could cut the slides as well as stain them and fix them with Xylene.

He did not want to bother Alice. She would of course immediately call him if there was anything to say. And as he worked the time and the different scenarios in his head, he was thinking he might just end up staying with her most of the night anyway. Post 9/11, NIH was a formidable place even to him, and it was probably downright scary to lay visitors such as Detective Finotti or his cohorts.

Putting his head back on the headrest, Kendall then thought about his own Monday morning. When he'd been in his office with Finotti, he'd realized that he had a whole day of patients scheduled. The original plan with Peter Kane was that he'd be back to work tomorrow. While Finotti had searched through the lab area he'd checked his morning schedule on the computer. It was packed with both his regularly scheduled patients and patients from the week before who had been rescheduled. His first patient was scheduled at 8:30. Although it sounded as if the new slides that would be prepared from Garrett's tissue block would probably be ready before Garrett's surgery, he was not confident that Alice would have any answers for them by then. 8:30 was not looking good.

He called both Laurel and Sammie at home and left messages asking them if they could get to the office a little early and start rescheduling his 8:30 patients and work down the schedule. Put them in at lunch, at the end of the day, wherever they could. Thanks, and he'd call them in the office again in the morning.

He glanced at himself in the rearview mirror. He looked tired and almost dirty with dried sweat on his face and neck. His shirt and pants were no better. He needed a shower and a shave.

Colleen answered his next call. "One more favor," he said.

"Are you sure?"

"Pretty sure."

"Yes?"

"Would you please put some casual clothes and some office clothes in a bag for me and drop them off at The River Club's front desk."

"You're not coming home tonight?"

"Probably not. I can't leave Alice up all night alone, and I may need to go to the hospital early. Garrett's the first case."

"Okay," she said. "I'll leave in a few minutes. If you talk to Caroline, tell her she's in my prayers."

TWENTY-FOUR

Monday, June 18

The couch in Alice's office was short and narrow and his legs hung off the end. He turned on it fitfully, each little shift causing a different place on his pants and shirt to stick to the old, tacky imitation leather. Sleep was out the question, and he didn't as much try to doze as simply rest for a few minutes before opening his eyes to once again check his watch and phone. He had stayed up with Alice for a while when he'd gotten back from meeting Sam, talking about her family and work. He'd sensed that he was distracting her, though, and at her suggestion he'd retired to her office and the couch well after midnight. Several times since then he'd also gotten up to look in on her. Each time it was the same, him marveling over her concentration and skills. She moved from counter to counter like a master chef, pausing only momentarily to stop and survey her domain, to ensure that nothing had changed, that everything was as it should be. On each of these forays to her lab he'd also called Bob Williams. Brad had been delayed getting back to town with the interstate traffic and it had been well past midnight before he'd gotten started preparing the slides. The parting message from Williams was always the same—he would call Kendall as soon as the slides were ready.

Now, on the couch in the dark, his thoughts ran once again to Drew Garrett. Garrett, he was certain, wasn't

262

sleeping any more soundly than he was. And the afternoon's conversation, which on one level was surely hopeful, had probably roiled all of his emotions to the breaking point. The attorney had never returned Kendall's call, and he was now just a couple of hours from his preoperative check-in time.

Then, as had been the case whenever his mind was distracted from the matter at hand for even the slightest moment, it circled once again around the new issues that were just as disturbing as Garrett. Henry. Henry and his fall. Henry and his hypoglycemic episode. Henry and his head wound and the dirt and grass. Henry, who may have given his life for simply being Henry. And Mr. Keefer, whom he did not know, but who had simply wanted his hernia fixed.

The image of Henry was large in his mind when his phone rang. The slides were ready, said Bob Williams. Williams also said that he had called Sam and asked him to come into the office as well. Sam used to read all of the skin slides before Chad joined the practice, and even though he was not board-certified in dermatopathology, he was quite proficient in signing out skin pathology. Williams said he'd wait for Kendall to get there before either he or Sam looked at any of the slides.

Kendall turned on the light in the office, ran a hand through his hair, and grabbed his bag. He found Alice hunched over a tray with a thin glass micropipette.

"The hair and saliva markers are done," she said when he came in. "They came out great."

"How much longer do you think the tissue block assay will take?" he asked. Alice was starting to look tired. She was wearing glasses now and her forehead was furrowed. "At least another hour or two. Are you leaving?"

"I need to go to the path lab, and then I'll probably go to the hospital."

"I'll call you," she said.

He hugged her again. "You're the best."

*   *   *

Bob let him in the back door and led him to a conference room with a multi-headed microscope. Sam was there, his face grim. On the table were a single gray cardboard slide case and a pad of paper with three pens.

Bob sat at the head of the table with the microscope controls. He opened the slide case—there were four slides inside of it, all labeled with the same accession number. "Brad is cutting more slides, but I think we can get started with these," he said. He looked to Kendall. "We haven't looked at the slides. What I would suggest is that we all look at them and write down a diagnosis independently."

Kendall nodded. "Fair enough."

Bob picked up the first slide and held it up to the ceiling light. There were three pieces of tissue on the slide. Each was a cross-section of a dome-shaped lesion and, even from three feet away, Kendall could see that the lesion was some type of a dermal tumor. He could also see that in the center of the tissue was an area that had picked up the blue stain and was darker.

Bob Williams put the slide under the microscope and Kendall felt his heart speed up, its muscular contractions rocking his sternum and spine as if it were a live animal trying desperately to get out. Williams bent his head and focused under low power. Kendall adjusted his own lenses and then, with just one glance through the microscope, his breaths were lighter, easier. There was no melanoma here.

Though he wasn't a pathologist, he had looked at thousands of skin lesions under a microscope, and this was categorically no spindle cell melanoma. In fact, it wasn't even a mole.

Williams moved to the next piece, and then the next piece under low power. He focused up and down, his fingers deftly moving back and forth from the focus to the slide control. "Ready to go down?" he asked.

Sam and Kendall said yes.

Bob swung in a high power lens and focused again.

Kendall smiled to himself. As he had thought at first glance, both now and in his exam room, this lesion was benign. Certainly there were some areas of spindle-shaped cells in the dermis around it, but they looked like scar tissue, which would also make sense since he thought the lesion was something they termed a dermatofibroma. Dermatofibromas were a response in the skin to injury, often insect bites or similar inflammatory lesions. They were scars in a sense—benign proliferations that the body concocted to trauma, some odd evolutionary response of unknown significance. Cancer they were not.

Bob took the slide off the microscope stage and put on the next one. He repeated the same sequence with the same results in Kendall's mind. The only difference was that in several of the sections there was also some pigment that accounted for the slight brown hue that Kendall had seen in his office. Williams then repeated the process with the next two slides, the entire time without saying a word. When he'd finished with the fourth slide he took the notepad, tore off three pieces of paper, and handed one to Kendall and Sam.

Dermatofibroma with associated scar, wrote Kendall. He folded the paper and handed it to Bob. Bob folded his and handed both of them to Sam. Sam looked to his father.

"Go ahead, Sam. Read them aloud."

"Dermatofibroma with associated scar," read Sam and put the first paper aside. "Benign cellular dermatofibroma and scar tissue," he read from the next. He opened the last. "Histiocytoma," he said. "No evidence of malignancy."

Bob looked to Kendall. "Are you okay with that? Do you want to see more cuts?"

Kendall shook his head no. Histiocytoma was an old name for dermatofibroma, a term Bob would have used to sign out a report. He stood and thanked the both of them. "I need to go to the hospital," he said.

Bob walked out with him. At Kendall's car, he put an arm on Kendall, turned him, and held his gaze. "I can't take back anything that Chad has done," he said. "I can only do everything in my power to fix it. For the patients, for his family, for Sam, and for anyone else he might have harmed."

Kendall said nothing, his mind on Drew and Caroline Garrett, who were either awake in their home by now, or already on their way to Roosevelt Hospital. Knowing Garrett, he might even already be there, waiting for them to open.

Williams was still talking. "I've been through all of the reports from the blocks we found. I'll also have slides cut from all of them and we'll go through every case. You can do it with me if you want. Honestly though, from what I've seen, I think the others will all be okay. I really think he was just trying to make himself look good. Why he would do this to this man, I don't know."

Kendall looked at the elder Williams, part of him wanting to help the man understand, part of him wondering how much even he knew about his son's honor trial. Maybe Chad had lied to him about that. Maybe the school had given Chad the option of leaving on his own before they kicked him out. Garrett's words, now imprinted in his mind, easily solved the dilemma. "It's what trust is all about," he had said.

"I don't know, Bob," said Kendall, "but I need to go see him. I'll call you later."

*　　*　　*

Drew and Caroline Garrett were sitting in the preoperative suite. Drew was staring straight ahead; Caroline was staring at her hands folded in her lap. They both looked up as he approached them. Garrett's grim face didn't change; Caroline studied Kendall hopefully, searching his face for answers. When she saw none, she reached into her purse.

"I found a photograph I think you should see," she said.

There were only two other people in the room and they were still at the check-in desk. Kendall pulled up a chair in front of them and took the photograph. Garrett was probably sixteen or seventeen, he guessed, shirtless with beach sand in the background. It was a close-up of his face and upper torso, with his back to the camera and his head turned and making a face at the photographer. Even with the age of the photograph, a small reddish bump was visible on his right upper shoulder.

Kendall nodded and gave her back the photograph. "I just looked at slides that were cut from the tissue block we found yesterday. The block that we believe is yours," he said, looking at Garrett. "They show a benign lesion. Something called a dermatofibroma. Just like that photograph."

Caroline closed her eyes and bowed her head.

"How certain are you?" said Garrett.

"Certain enough that I think you should postpone your surgery. The DNA assay from that same tissue block will be ready this morning. Maybe even in an hour. She's already got the DNA bands from your hair and saliva."

Garrett stared at him. "You took it off of me. What do you think?"

"I think it's a benign dermatofibroma."

Garrett looked away. "So you think he saw my name and he . . ."

"I'm afraid so."

"Drew," said Caroline, "you have—"

Garrett put up a hand. "I'll wait, Caroline."

Kendall stood. "Let me speak with Dr. Uhle. He'll understand. Is that okay?"

Garrett nodded. Caroline took her husband's hand and squeezed it.

The receptionist put Kendall through to the hospital operator who paged Dr. Uhle to Kendall's cell phone. Kendall stepped outside and waited.

Five minutes later Dr. Uhle called.

"Thanks for getting back to me, Ted," said Kendall. "We have a problem with Drew Garrett, and I'm thinking you might want to push his surgery back a few hours. Here's what happened. I had a temporary medical assistant the day I did his biopsy and it was busy and she didn't label the bottle in the room. You know how it goes. Anyway, she got two specimens mixed up and we're in the process of sorting everything out. We had to get DNA assays done on the two tissue blocks so we could match them up to the patients. Garrett's will be ready in an hour or so. But I'm pretty sure that's not his melanoma."

"That's fine with me," said Uhle. "Believe me, I don't want to go into that guy's chest. I've got a car accident I'm up to my eyeballs in anyway. Let me know. Wow—bummer for the other guy."

"Yeah, that's the next call I don't want to make. Thanks, Ted."

Kendall hung up, told the receptionist to let the OR nurses know that Mr. Garrett's surgery would be postponed for at least several hours, and called Alice.

"I was just about to call you," she said. "The tissue block is an unequivocal match with both the hair and the saliva. I matched nine satellite markers."

"How accurate is that? He's going to ask me."

"One in four billion."

Kendall closed his eyes and smiled. "I can't thank you enough, Alice."

"The assay from the other block will be ready later this morning. I'll call you, but it's not going to match. It can't."

*   *   *

There was a black Mercedes parked next to Kendall's car. When Kendall drew near, Bob Williams got out of the Mercedes and waited for him.

"Is everything okay?" said Williams.

"The block that we found matched with Garrett's hair and saliva. The tests on the block from New York will be ready later this morning, but it's really just a confirmatory assay. They canceled the surgery."

"Thank God," said Williams, his face as old and sad as Kendall had seen it. Then, "Ryan, I can't tell you how sorry I am that you had to go through this. I looked at all the reports again while I was waiting, and I still don't see any other ones like this." He shook his head and looked away. "I'm sorry."

Kendall watched him, wondering why he had come. "Is there something you need to tell me, Bob?"

Williams looked at the cell phone he was holding in his right hand.

"The police and the insurance company have finished with Chad's car. Someone from the lot where they towed it just called me. Bunny's not really capable of making any decisions right now. The car's going out to wherever today. Junk yard, I guess. There's a golf club wedged in the trunk. They want to make sure we don't want it before the car goes out." Williams paused and then looked directly at Kendall. "I wanted to ask you before I said anything."

Kendall nodded, his lips pursed, his mind racing. Henry was dead. Irrevocably. Nevertheless, Henry had also been irrevocably wronged. Himself he really didn't care about at this point—Chad, too, was irrevocably dead. The lawyer, as Detective Finotti had said, was simply lucky.

"What about Henry's family?" said Kendall. "What's going to happen to them?"

"I will take care of Henry's family in any way that they need."

Kendall was quiet. He looked away, looked back. "Do you want it?" he finally said.

"No. And I don't want his kids to have it either. I'd like for them to have the chance to remember their father as their father. They're young. They're innocent."

Kendall held the elder Williams' gaze for a long moment. Without him, he knew, Drew Garrett would be getting ready to have his chest cracked open and who knew what else. The morning that Henry had found Lindsey Browning's slide, Bob Williams could have just as easily waited and shown it to his son as to Kendall. Innately, Williams had surely known that there was nothing good about the slide that had fallen in Chad's locker. The slide without a name label. The slide that had come from the lab he founded, and that no matter what it showed under the microscope, had already been changed, violated.

"Well, Chad certainly doesn't need it," said Kendall, getting in his car. He drove off slowly, watching Williams in his rearview mirror. Watching him open his phone, dial, hang up. Watching him bow his head and begin to shake, his shoulders rocking up and down, up and down.

TWENTY-FIVE

Detective Finotti was sitting in Kendall's waiting room. Kendall ducked through the reception area and turned for his office. Judge Paul Mancini was sitting in a chair across from Kendall's desk looking out the window.

"I start a little later today," said Mancini, swiveling in the chair to face him. "Thought I'd stop by and see you. Colleen told me Russell was looking for you, too."

"Thanks," said Kendall, rubbing his eyes and then brushing his hair back with his hands. "First thing you can do is get that bulldog in the waiting room off my ass."

"I saw him. Try not to mind him. He's a good cop."

"Great,"

"Long week, huh?"

"I've had better."

"Me, too. I found out this morning that Henry had a will and he named me executor of his estate. He doesn't have any immediate family, which makes it a little easier. His wife died years ago, and their only son had bad diabetes. He died when he was twenty or so." Mancini paused and looked out the window wistfully as if he were thinking about Henry. "Bob Williams is going to help out, too. I spoke with him on the way over here. He's going to start a scholarship in Henry's name. In fact, he already wrote a check for the first year. For one of Henry's nephews." Mancini looked back to Kendall. "Salt of the earth," he said. "Not a bad bone in him."

Kendall nodded his agreement, but was quiet. Finally he said, "What about Henry's autopsy? Did it show anything else?"

"Not really. They don't know if it was the low glucose or the fall that got him."

"What about the dirt and the grass in his wound."

Mancini offered a slight shrug. "They didn't want to make much of it. It's a locker room. Henry cleaned dirt and grass off of golf shoes all day."

Kendall picked up a pen off his desk and rolled it in his fingers.

"So was I right about Drew Garrett?" asked Mancini.

"In what way?"

"Straight-shooter. Tough, but fair."

Kendall thought about it for a moment. "That pretty much sums it up."

"That's what people say about you, you know."

Kendall rolled his eyes, stood, and put on his white coat.

"Do you want to take care of the detective now?" said Mancini. "While I'm still here."

Kendall looked hard at the judge. "I don't know. Do you want me to take of the detective, Paul? You're the one who grew up with Henry. And Bob, I guess," he added after a moment.

Mancini sighed and looked away. "Henry's dead, Ryan. I don't know how he died or really why he died." The judge was quiet then, thinking, deliberating. "I've been in this business a long time now, though," he went on, "and I do know that God makes good people and, for whatever reason, God also makes bad people. Bob and Sam are good people, and I don't have any reason to believe that Chad's family are not good people as well. Bob loved Henry as much as I did.

Henry and his legacy will be cared for." Mancini turned back to him. "I can't tell you anything else."

Kendall held his gaze, then called out to Laurel on the intercom and asked her to bring Mr. Finotti back to the office. "Please help me get this douche-bag out of my office."

Mancini gave him his best attempt at a wry smile, then faced the door.

Detective Finotti came through, saw Mancini, and stopped.

"Good morning, Russell," said Mancini, standing to shake his hand. He motioned to another chair a few feet away. "Have a seat. Dr. Kendall and I were just catching up on a few things."

"I can come back."

"No, please have a seat," said Mancini, motioning again to the chair. "We're all busy. Particularly Dr. Kendall here."

Finotti sat down and looked at Mancini as if the judge were about to reprimand him.

"Did you want to ask the doctor something, Russell?"

Finotti shifted in his chair, then looked at Kendall. "Just if he'd thought of anything else since we'd last talked."

Mancini looked to Kendall. "Is there anything you want to say to Detective Finotti, Dr. Kendall?"

Kendall, still standing, finished buttoning his white coat. "I'm afraid I don't have anything new to tell you, Detective," he said, putting his hands in the side pockets. "I'll call you if I do."

Finotti nodded, stood, and handed him a card. "All of my numbers are on there," he said. "And I'll let you know if we hear anything."

Sammie stuck her head in the door as the detective left. "I've got Mrs. Harrington in a room, Dr. Kendall."

"Thanks, Sammie. I'll be right there."

He looked to Mancini when Finotti was gone. "Do you mind if I ask you something?"

"Not at all."

"Who wrote the reference letter?"

Mancini looked into Kendall's eyes for what seemed like an eternity. "I can't tell you that, Ryan. Does it matter?"

Kendall held his gaze just as long. "No," he finally said, slipping a set of magnifying glasses on a loop over his head. He took out a cloth and studiously cleaned the lenses. When he looked up, he said, "Game time."

Mancini stood and patted his arm. "Call Peter this week," he said, turning for the door. "I need you back out on the court."

He should have been a priest, thought Kendall as he watched him walk away. Forgiveness was always within one's realm, within God's realm.

Mancini was almost out the door when he stopped and turned. His face screwed up as if he were trying hard to remember something. "Did I ever tell you about the junior best-ball tournament we used to have at Hidden Glen?"

"I don't believe so."

"Geez, this was thirty years or so ago now. I was playing with Peter's brother, Jim. Chad was playing with Sam. Chad was a little young to be playing. Maybe a little too young, but he was good enough. Anyway, Chad hit a ball in the woods. He played a provisional ball, but when they went up to look for it Chad found his original one. It was sitting up in the rough in pretty good shape. Must have hit a tree and kicked out." Mancini paused. "Only problem was, the group after them found a ball out-of-bounds with his mark on it. They ended up beating us by a stroke." He shook his head ruefully. "That was the last year we had that tournament. The pro canceled it." Mancini turned once more for the door. "See you, Ryan," he said. "Make sure you call Peter."

THE END